HARDCASTLE'S MANDARIN

HARDCASTLE'S MANDARIN

A Hardcastle and Marriott Historical Mystery

Graham Ison

This first world edition published 2009
in Great Britain and in the USA by
SEVERN HOUSE PUBLISHERS LTD of
9–15 High Street, Sutton, Surrey, England, SM1 1DF.
Trade paperback edition published
in Great Britain and the USA 2009 by
SEVERN HOUSE PUBLISHERS LTD

British Library Cataloguing in Publication Data

Ison, Graham
  Hardcastle's mandarin
  1. Hardcastle, Detective Inspector (Fictitious character) -
  Fiction 2. Police - England - London - Fiction 3. Murder -
  Investigation - Fiction 4. World War, 1914-1918 - Secret
  service - Germany - Fiction 5. Great Britain - History -
  George V, 1910-1936 - Fiction 6. Detective and mystery
  stories
  I. Title
  823.9'14[F]

ISBN-13: 978-0-7278-6733-9   (cased)
ISBN-13: 978-1-84751-112-6   (trade paper)

Typeset by Palimpsest Book Production Ltd.,
Grangemouth, Stirlingshire, Scotland.
Printed and bound in Great Britain by
MPG Books Ltd., Bodmin, Cornwall.

X ooo ooo o33 6559

GLOSSARY

ALL MY EYE AND BETTY MARTIN: nonsense.
ANDREW, The: seamen's slang for the Royal Navy.
APM: assistant provost marshal (a lieutenant colonel of the military police).

BAILEY, the: Central Criminal Court, Old Bailey, London.
BEF: British Expeditionary Force in France and Flanders.
BLIGHTY ONE: a wound suffered in battle that necessitated repatriation to the United Kingdom.
BOOZER: a public house.
BRADBURY: a pound note. From Sir John Bradbury, Secretary to the Treasury, who introduced pound notes in 1914 to replace gold sovereigns.
BREWSTER SESSIONS: magistrates' sessions for the issue of licences to permit trade in alcoholic liquors.

CB: Companion of the Most Honourable Order of the Bath.
CLOBBER: clothing.
COPPER: a policeman.
CUTPURSE: a thief or street robber. Originally one who, literally, cut a purse to steal the money therein.

DARTMOOR: a remote prison on Dartmoor in Devon.
DDI: Divisional Detective Inspector.
DIGS or DIGGINGS: rented lodgings, usually short term.
DOG'S DINNER, a: a mess.

EIGHT O'CLOCK WALK, to take the: to be hanged.

FEEL THE COLLAR, to: to make an arrest.
FORM: previous convictions.
FOURPENNY CANNON, a: a steak and kidney pie.
FRONT, The: theatre of WW1 operations in France and Flanders.

GLIM: a look (a foreshortening of 'glimpse').

HALF A CROWN *or* HALF A DOLLAR: two shillings and sixpence (12½p).
HAVE IT UP, to: to engage in sexual intercourse.
HOSPITAL BLUES: A blue uniform, with white shirt and red tie, issued to wounded soldiers who were convalescing.

IRONCLAD: a battleship.

JILDI: quickly (*ex* Hindi).

KATE CARNEY: army (rhyming slang: from Kate Carney, a music hall comedienne of the late 19th /early 20th century).
KATE short for KATE CARNEY: see above.
KNOCKING SHOP: a brothel.

LINEN DRAPERS: newspapers (rhyming slang).
LONG BOW, to draw the: to exaggerate *or* to tell unbelievable stories.

MI5: counter-espionage service of the United Kingdom.
MINCES: eyes (rhyming slang: mince pies).
MONS, to make a: to make a mess of things, as in the disastrous Battle of Mons in 1914.

NICK: a police station *or* prison *or* to arrest *or* to steal.
NICKED: arrested *or* stolen
NOOKIE: sexual intercourse.

OLD BAILEY: Central Criminal Court, in Old Bailey, London.

PICCADILLY WINDOW: a monocle.
PIMP: a prostitute's 'minder'.
PLANTING, a: a burial.
PLONK, the: the mud of no-man's-land.
PUSSER'S RUM: Royal Navy issue rum, stronger than that normally available to the public. 'Pusser' being a contraction of 'Purser'.

QUID: £1 sterling.

RECORD: record of previous convictions.
REDCAPS: members of the Corps of Military Police.
ROZZER: a policeman.

SCRIMSHANKER: one who evades duty or work.
SECTION 66: that section of the Metropolitan Police Act 1839 that gave police the power to stop, search, and detain suspected persons.
SHILLING: now 5p.
SINE DIE: (Latin) at a day to be appointed; adjourned indefinitely.
SITTER, a: an arrest handed to another officer.
SKIP *or* SKIPPER: an informal police alternative to station-sergeant, clerk-sergeant and sergeant.

THREE SHEETS TO THE WIND: drunk.
TOM: a prostitute.
TOMMING: pursuing a life of prostitution.
TOPPED: murdered or hanged.
TOPPING: a murder or hanging.
TRICK, a: a prostitute's client.
TRICK, to turn a: to engage in sexual intercourse.
TUMBLE, a: sexual intercourse.
TUPPENNY-HA'PENNY: a contraction of twopence-halfpenny, indicating something or someone of little worth.
TWO-AND-EIGHT, in a: in a state (rhyming slang).

VAD: Voluntary Aid Detachment: wartime nursing auxiliaries.

WIPERS: Army slang for Ypres in Belgium, scene of several fierce Great War battles.

ONE

The milkman was somewhat of a dandy. His navy-blue apron covered the top of his gaiters, which in turn covered the top of his boots. But he wore a waistcoat – an albert strung between the pockets – and a bowler hat. And he was whistling.

It was Tuesday, the fifteenth of May 1917, and the Great War, as it became known, had been dragging on for two years and nine months. The optimists who had forecast that it would be over by Christmas 1914 had been proved disastrously wrong.

'Morning, guv'nor,' said the milkman cheerfully, as he limped across Kennington Road, Lambeth, a small churn of milk in his hand. The limp was a legacy of the Battle of the Somme, a battle that had marked the end of his brief military career.

'That for twenty-seven?' asked the policeman.

'That's right, guv. It's that Scotland Yard detective who lives there, so they say.' In fact, the occupant was a divisional officer, but his police station was immediately opposite the Yard, hence the milkman's belief.

'Give us it here, then,' growled the policeman in reply. It was just past six in the morning, and he should have been off duty ten minutes ago. He was not, therefore, in the best of moods. With some trepidation, he banged loudly on the door of number twenty-seven, a house not far from where the legendary Charlie Chaplin had been born.

It was some time, and several knocks, later, that the door was opened by a stocky man, some five foot ten in height. His greying hair was tousled, and he wore an old jacket over a nightshirt.

'DDI Hardcastle, sir?' queried the policeman.

'Yes, and what the hell do you want at this hour of the morning?' Hardcastle glanced at the milk churn in the policeman's hand. 'You taken to delivering milk in your spare time, lad? That's against the regulations, you know.'

'No, sir, I was just doing the milkman a favour.'

'Well, you're not doing me any. What d'you want?' Hardcastle asked again.

The policeman placed the milk churn on the doorstep, and fumbled in one of his tunic pockets, eventually producing a message flimsy. 'It's from Detective Inspector Rhodes at Cannon Row, sir. There's been a murder in Whitehall.' The PC handed over the message form. 'He requests your immediate attendance.'

'Well, at least this one's on my own patch.' Ernest Hardcastle, the divisional detective inspector of the A or Whitehall Division of the Metropolitan Police, had had a surfeit of out-of-town enquiries recently. He tugged at his Kitchener-style moustache as he glanced through the hand-written message. He grunted and looked at the PC. 'Are the bus drivers still on strike, lad?'

'Yes, sir, and the trams are crowded fit to bust.'

'In that case you can find me a cab while I get dressed.' And with that, Hardcastle slammed the door leaving the policeman, and the milk churn, on the doorstep.

It took the DDI less than ten minutes to shave, attire himself in his customary blue serge suit, and don his bowler hat. Seizing his umbrella, he shouted to Alice, his wife, to tell her where he was going, and walked out to the street.

'Where to, guv?' ask the cab driver.

'Ministry of Munitions in Whitehall, and be quick about it,' said Hardcastle.

An A Division policeman stood at the entrance to the building bearing a brass plate proclaiming it to be the offices not only of the Ministry of Munitions, but of the Ministries of Food and Health also. He saluted as Hardcastle approached him. 'All correct, sir.'

'Matter of opinion,' muttered Hardcastle, as ever irritated by the requirement that junior ranks should make such a report, whether things were all correct or not. 'Where is it?'

'Top of the stairs, sir. It's the big door facing you. There's a PC outside.'

Hardcastle produced his warrant card to the custodian, and mounted the broad, stone-flagged staircase. As the policeman at the front door had said, there was another policeman stationed outside a large oaken door. He too saluted and reported that all was correct before opening the door for Hardcastle.

Detective Inspector Rhodes stepped across as Hardcastle entered the room. 'Good morning, sir.'

'Good morning, Mr Rhodes.' Hardcastle gazed around the well-ordered office. There was a large desk, and a high-backed chair. To one side stood a large bookcase, and his eye lighted on a copy of the *Army List 1917*; he wondered briefly why the office's occupant should have such a volume.

'I'm sorry to have called you out, sir,' Rhodes continued, 'but this murder could have repercussions.'

'Repercussions, Mr Rhodes? Who is it, then?'

'Sir Nigel Strang, sir. He's permanent under-secretary at the Ministry of Munitions.'

Although Hardcastle was surprised at the murder of so senior a civil servant, he showed no signs of that surprise. 'D'you know that for sure, Mr Rhodes?'

'None of the officials have arrived yet, sir, but the night-duty custodian, a man called Bowles, has positively identified him.'

'Cause of death?' Hardcastle walked across the room to where a body was lying on the floor between the large desk and a window that gave a view of Whitehall. The victim's waistcoat was stained red with blood.

'Looks like a single stab wound to the heart, sir,' suggested Rhodes. 'It was either a lucky hit, or he knew what he was doing.'

'Find any weapon, did you?' asked Hardcastle, as he knelt to examine the body more closely.

'No, sir.'

'Well, that rules out suicide, I suppose,' muttered Hardcastle, somewhat jocularly, as he stood up again. 'Who found him, Mr Rhodes?'

'A charwoman, sir. There's four or five of 'em come in at about half past five each morning to clean the offices.'

'How did they get in?'

'The night-duty custodian let them in, sir.'

'Where's he?'

'In the next room, sir, along with the charwoman. DS Marriott's taking statements.' Rhodes pointed at a door on the far side of the office.

Hardcastle entered the smaller office that, he later learned, was normally occupied by Sir Nigel Strang's secretary. Detective Sergeant Charles Marriott sat behind the desk, writing. An elderly man in a blue uniform with crowns on the collar was sitting in front of Marriott. Seated next to the custodian was a young woman, probably no older than twenty-five, whose tear-stained face was still drained of colour, doubtless with the shock of having discovered Strang's body.

'Morning, Marriott.'

'Good morning, sir.' Marriott rose to his feet.

'I'll have a word with these two before you carry on,' said Hardcastle. He switched his gaze to the custodian. 'What's your name?'

'Bowles, sir. Henry Bowles.'

'When did you start duty here?'

'Last night, sir, at ten o'clock. I'm supposed to be off at six. Me relief's downstairs already.'

'Yes, and I wasn't supposed to start until nine o'clock,' Hardcastle said, with no show of sympathy, although he was often to be found in his office at eight. 'But there's a war on. Tell me what your duties are, Bowles.' He sat down and began to fill his pipe.

'To be stationed at the main entrance, sir, but once each tour of duty, I has a walk round the offices to make sure that no lights has been left on, nor no safes left unlocked. They're very tight on security here.'

'So tight that the permanent secretary got himself murdered,' said Hardcastle drily. 'When did you last visit Sir Nigel's office?'

'Must've been about eleven o'clock last night, sir. Like I said, I checked that the lights was out, and that Sir Nigel's safe was locked.'

'Does that mean that you didn't know that Sir Nigel was in the building?'

'That's right, sir. But the bosses has their own key and can come and go as they like.'

'Their own key to where?'

'There's a private entrance at the back of the building, sir, and a flight of stairs what leads up to the floor where their offices is. That's this floor.'

'Oh, very secure,' said Hardcastle sarcastically. 'And do these important people always use that entrance?'

'Not always, sir. Like as not they comes and goes through the front door.'

'And how d'you get to this secret entrance, Bowles?'

'You goes through archway off of King Charles Street, sir, into the quadrangle and the door's on the left.'

Hardcastle glanced at his sergeant. 'People coming and going without so much as a by-your-leave. You wouldn't think there was a war on, would you, Marriott?'

'No, sir.' Sensing that his chief was on the point of launching into one of his usual diatribes about lack of wartime security, Marriott confined himself to monosyllabic words of agreement.

'Seems odd having the Food, Health and Munitions Ministries all together,' commented Hardcastle.

'Oh, they don't have nothing to do with each other, sir,' said Bowles. 'They just shares the same building, if you takes my drift. They're all separate.'

'D'you always do night duty, Bowles?'

'No, sir, we does lates, earlies and nights, week and week about.'

'Did anyone leave the building or, in fact, arrive here during your tour of duty?'

'No, sir, nobody. Apart from the cleaning ladies, and they gets here about half past five of a morning.'

'And what about you, miss?' Hardcastle directed his gaze at the young woman sitting next to Bowles. 'What's your name?'

'Daisy Johnson, sir. Mrs Daisy Johnson.'

'And how long have you been a cleaner here?'

'About a year and a half, sir, ever since my Gerald was called up,' said Daisy. 'He's a lance-sergeant in the Grenadier Guards,' she added proudly, 'but even so, the marriage allowance don't add up to much, not when there's two bairns to feed and clothe.'

'Who looks after them while you're working?' asked Hardcastle, as ever a stickler for gathering inconsequential pieces of information.

'Me mother, sir.'

'Live near you, does she?'

'Yes, sir. She lives with me in Peabody Buildings, off Wild Street. It's not far from Bow Street.'

'Do you always clean Sir Nigel's office, Daisy?'

'Yes, sir. And it's the first one I does each morning.'

'Have you ever found Sir Nigel in his office that early in the morning before?'

Daisy Johnson put a hand to her mouth, but Hardcastle noticed that she hesitated. 'No, sir, never. And I never saw him this morning till I went round behind the desk. Give me the shock of me life, I can tell you, sir, seeing him lying there.'

'What time was that?' asked Hardcastle.

'Twenty to six,' said Daisy promptly.

'How can you be so sure?'

'There's a clock on the wall in his office, sir, and I noticed that's what the time was.'

'What did you do then?'

'I ran downstairs and told Mr Bowles what had happened.'

Hardcastle turned to Bowles. 'Is that correct?'

'Yes, sir. Just coming up to a quarter of the hour it was.'

'And you called the police immediately, I presume.'

'Not straight off, sir. First I went up to check what Daisy had said. To see if Sir Nigel really was dead, having done a bit of first aid like. Then I ran out to the street because I knows there's a copper – er, sorry, constable – on a fixed point right outside. He come on up and had a look at the body, and then asked if he could use the telephone.'

'Who was this PC, Marriott?' asked Hardcastle.

'PC 527A Vaughan, sir.' Marriott had worked with Hardcastle long enough to know that the DDI expected his sergeant to know the answer to any question put to him. 'DS Wood's taken a statement from him.'

'I should hope so,' muttered Hardcastle. 'Tell me, Bowles: when do the officials arrive at this terribly important ministry of yours?'

'Usually about nine o'clock, sir, although Sir Nigel's often a bit later than that, 'specially if he's had to go to an early meeting at Downing Street. And there's been a few of them lately, what with the strike and that.'

'What, the bus drivers' strike?'

'No, sir, the munitions workers.'

'There's been nothing in the newspapers about that,' said Hardcastle.

'No, there wouldn't have been, sir,' said Bowles. 'It's the press censors what keeps it out of the linen drapers, but between you and me, there's more than a hundred thousand out. Lancashire, Sheffield, Coventry and Derby. And some of 'em down here at Woolwich, an' all. But they was at pains to keep it dark. Sir Nigel was vexed something cruel about it, to say nothing of Dr Addison.'

'Who's Dr Addison?' queried Hardcastle.

'He's the minister hisself, sir. Dr Christopher Addison, he is.'

'How d'you know all this?' demanded Hardcastle, somewhat piqued that a ministry doorman should know more about such a crippling strike than he did.

Bowles permitted himself a brief chuckle. 'You'd be surprised what I hears, just being in the front hall, sir.'

'Well, you shouldn't go bandying it about in time of war, Bowles. You never know who's listening.' Having, in his view, redressed the balance, Hardcastle returned to the matter in hand. 'Who's the next most important official after Sir Nigel.'

'That'd be Mr Cresswell, sir. Mr James Cresswell, CB, sir.'

'What's he?'

'Deputy secretary, sir.'

'And where's his office when he deigns to turn up?'

'Right next door to Sir Nigel's, sir,' said Bowles. 'It's the other door that leads out of his office,' he added.

'Carry on, Marriott,' said Hardcastle, having recognized a booming voice coming from Strang's office. 'Sounds as though Dr Spilsbury's here.'

'Ah, Hardcastle, a very good morning to you,' said Spilsbury, as Hardcastle returned to Strang's office.

'Good morning, Dr Spilsbury.'

Bernard Spilsbury was the foremost forensic pathologist in the country, if not the world. His skill at determining the cause of death was legion, and defending counsel always dreaded the sight of his tall, stocky figure ascending the witness box to give evidence for the Crown. His greatest forensic triumph was probably securing the conviction of George Joseph Smith, the infamous brides-in-the-bath murderer, two years previously.

'I see the quality of your victims is getting better all the time.'

'It would seem so, Doctor.'

'Got a mandarin this time, by Jove.'

'A what, sir?' Hardcastle had not the faintest idea what Spilsbury was talking about.

'Officials like this fellow are called mandarins, Hardcastle.' Spilsbury gestured at the body of Sir Nigel Strang. 'The original mandarins were high-ranking officials of the Chinese Empire, and our senior civil servants seem to have assumed the term to describe themselves, or at least their subordinates have.'

'Well, I'll go to the foot of our stairs,' muttered Hardcastle. The only mandarins he knew about were the small oranges that Mrs Hardcastle occasionally bought from the green-grocer at the end of Kennington Road. Not that any had been available since the start of the war.

Spilsbury knelt down and began to examine the body, occasionally asking questions. But at last he finished his preliminary examination, although to Hardcastle it appeared that the pathologist had not done very much. 'Have the cadaver taken to St Mary's, Paddington, Hardcastle, there's a good fellow. I'll let you have my report as soon as possible.' He stood up, packed his few instruments into his Gladstone bag, and left.

'Well, you heard what the doctor said, Mr Rhodes. Get a police van down here to take the body up to Paddington.'

'Very good, sir. I'll get someone to do it.' Rhodes immediately left the room to instruct the constable outside to do what Hardcastle had ordered.

'What about the charwoman and the custodian, sir?' asked Marriott, appearing from the next office.

'Got the full statements?'

'Yes, sir.'

'And home addresses?'

'Yes, sir.'

'Right, you can send them home.' Hardcastle pulled out his chromium hunter, looked at it, briefly wound it, and dropped it back into his waistcoat pocket. 'I don't know about you, Marriott, but I'm starving. We'll take a turn down to that cafe near Craig's Court and have a bite of breakfast. Then we can get back here in time to welcome these civil servants that come in half way through the day.' He paused as Inspector Rhodes returned to the office. 'Better send a message for DI Collins, too, Mr Rhodes. Ask him to have the office examined for fingerprints.'

'Very good, sir.'

Hardcastle, like so many officers of his age and service, had still to accustom himself to the comparatively new science of fingerprint identification. It was only as recently as 1909 that it had been accepted in evidence. Detective Inspector Charles Stockley Collins was the leading expert in the field and had been head of the Yard's Fingerprint Department since 1908.

'And if any of these civil servants arrive before I get back, don't let any of 'em in here. I shall need to talk to 'em before they start their important war work, but don't tell 'em why.'

'Of course not, sir,' said Rhodes, slightly offended at being told something that to any detective was second nature. 'I'll arrange with the security people for an office where they can all be assembled.'

'Good idea,' said Hardcastle, and seized his bowler hat and umbrella. 'Come, Marriott.'

On his return, at just after nine o'clock, Hardcastle walked into a storm of protest. Detective Inspector Rhodes had corralled the arriving staff in a conference room on the first floor of the Ministry.

'Are you in charge?' demanded a tall man attired in black jacket, pinstriped trousers, and a grey cravat held in place by a pearl tiepin.

'Who are you?' asked Hardcastle.

'James Cresswell, the deputy secretary.'

'Yes, I'm in charge. Divisional Detective Inspector Hardcastle of the Whitehall Division.'

'Are you indeed? Well, Inspector, I want to know the meaning of this. The moment we arrived, that fellow told us all to come in here, but gave us no reason at all.' Cresswell extended a languid hand towards DI Rhodes. 'I'll have you know that the Ministry of Munitions is conducting important business vital to the war effort. Sir Nigel Strang will be extremely annoyed when he hears of this.'

Hardcastle drew the deputy secretary away from the others in the room. 'Sir Nigel won't be hearing of it, Mr Cresswell,' he said quietly. 'He's dead. Someone murdered him. In his office.'

'Good God!' exclaimed Cresswell. 'When did this happen?'

'I'll be better placed to answer that when the pathologist sends me his report,' said Hardcastle mildly. 'And now, I suggest that your people get to work. Apart from you, that is. I want a word with you. Perhaps you'd show me to your office.'

A shaken Cresswell led the way along a corridor and ushered Hardcastle and Marriott into his well-appointed office.

'This has come as a terrible shock, Inspector.'

'I daresay it has,' said Hardcastle, as he and Marriott sat down.

Cresswell seated himself at his desk. 'Are you able to tell me what happened, Inspector?'

Hardcastle outlined the sequence of events as related to him by Bowles, the custodian, and Daisy Johnson, the cleaning woman.

'And now, Mr Cresswell, you know nearly as much as me.'

'Do you think that there is some sinister motive behind this tragedy, Inspector?' Cresswell had, by now, recovered his customary aplomb.

Hardcastle shrugged. 'I've no idea,' he said. 'Are you suggesting that Sir Nigel was assassinated by some foreign agent?'

'Well, I have to admit it crossed my mind.'

'Has Sir Nigel ever stayed here the night, to the best of your knowledge?'

'No, Inspector. There could be no reason. He usually leaves here about six or seven, unless something arises to demand his attention. But he's usually at home in Dulwich during the evening.' A sudden thought occurred to Cresswell. 'My God, someone will have to tell Lady Strang, *and* his two sons who are serving with the Grenadier Guards at the Front.'

'Leave that to me, Mr Cresswell. Perhaps you'd let my sergeant here have a note of the address.'

'Certainly.' From memory, Cresswell reeled off an address in Dulwich Village.

'Now then,' continued Hardcastle, 'I've been hearing stories about a secret entrance that allows people like Sir Nigel to come and go as they please.'

'That's correct, Inspector.'

'And how many people have a key to this entrance?'

Cresswell gave that some thought. 'About half a dozen, I should think,' he said eventually.

'*About* half a dozen? Isn't there a list somewhere?'

'Very likely, but I imagine the security staff keep it.'

'When you say half a dozen, who would they be?'

'Well, obviously Dr Addison – he's the Minister – Sir Nigel, the assistant secretary and me. I'm not sure who else holds one.'

'Do you usually use that entrance, Mr Cresswell?'

'Not that often. But if I've been to a meeting at Downing Street, or the Cabinet Office, I tend to walk through the Foreign Office quadrangle, and come in that way.'

'Well, I don't know,' said Hardcastle. 'It all seems a bit slapdash to me, given that there's a war on.'

'We're all very conscious of the need for security, Inspector,' said Cresswell defensively. 'I can assure you that should a key be lost, then the locks would be changed immediately.'

'If you gave me your key, Mr Cresswell, I could go across to the locksmith in Palmer Street, and be back here in half an hour with six copies of it. Has there ever been a report of a lost key?'

'Not to my knowledge, no,' said Cresswell.

'Finally, have you any idea who might've wanted to murder Sir Nigel?'

'No idea at all, Inspector.' Cresswell paused. 'I suppose it's all right to inform the Minister?'

'Yes, but perhaps you'd warn him that I might need to speak to him at some time.'

TWO

Hardcastle walked through the door between James Cresswell's office and that of Sir Nigel Strang.

'Morning, Charles.'

'Morning, Ernie.' DI Charles Stockley Collins looked up from examining the windowsill. 'There are fingerprints all over the place here, Ernie,' he said, putting his magnifying glass on Sir Nigel's desk. 'I doubt that we'll get anything useful, because, by the time we're through, they'll likely all belong to people who've legitimate access. But I'll let you know if I find a print that isn't accounted for.' And with that, he carried on dusting the windowsill with fingerprint powder.

'I'll leave you to it, then,' said Hardcastle, and turned to DI Rhodes. 'Marriott and I are going to Dulwich to break the news to Lady Strang, Mr Rhodes. Perhaps you'd be so good as to finish up here.'

'Very good, sir,' said Rhodes.

Hardcastle paused, his gloved hand on the doorknob. 'Would you also arrange with DI Collins to have fingerprints taken of all those who had access to Sir Nigel's office.'

'Yes, sir.'

'That should upset 'em,' Hardcastle added with a chuckle.

It was nearing ten o'clock when Hardcastle and Marriott arrived at The Lodge. It was an imposing Georgian house on the east side of a road with the curious name of Dulwich Village.

'Well, pay the cabby, Marriott,' said Hardcastle impatiently, and waited while his sergeant ferreted about in his pocket for the fare. 'And don't forget to get the plate number.'

It was one of the requirements of a parsimonious police force to demand that a cab's plate number be submitted with any claim for taxi expenses. It had been known in the past for checks to be made, just in case some officers, intent upon defrauding the police fund, had fabricated a claim. But most cabbies, fearing retribution, would always confirm that they had carried a police passenger at the date and time queried, whether they had or not. The police had the power to deprive a cab driver of his licence, and, therefore, his livelihood.

'Good morning, sir.' A butler opened the door and examined the two men on his doorstep.

'Is Lady Strang at home?' asked Hardcastle.

'Who may I say it is?'

'The police.'

'If you care to step inside, sir, I shall enquire if her ladyship is at home.' The butler's expression remained impassive, as though the arrival of the police at The Lodge was an everyday occurrence. 'I shan't keep you a moment, sir.'

'These here civil servants seem to do all right for themselves, Marriott,' said Hardcastle, looking round the large entrance hall while the two of them were waiting. 'What was it Dr Spilsbury called 'em: mandarins?'

'Her ladyship will see you now, sir,' said the butler, reappearing from a door on the left.

Lady Strang was seated by the fireplace; a walnut fire screen with an embroidered centrepiece stood in the empty grate. She wore a grey taffeta day dress that matched her grey hair. She clearly despised prevailing fashion, for the dress was long enough not to afford even a glimpse of ankle. Hardcastle reckoned her to be about forty-eight years of age. But she was no beauty.

'Hobson tells me you're from the police.'

'That's correct, Lady Strang. I'm Divisional Detective Inspector Hardcastle of the Whitehall Division. And this here is Detective Sergeant Marriott.'

'Whitehall?' Rosalind Strang inclined her head. 'If it's Sir Nigel you want, I'm—'

'It's about Sir Nigel that I've come, ma'am.'

'Oh? What about him?'

This was the part of police work that Hardcastle disliked most. Ever since being sworn in as a constable twenty-six years ago, he had delivered quite a few death messages, but had never seemed able to find the most suitable form of words.

'I'm sorry to have to tell you that Sir Nigel is dead, ma'am.'

To Hardcastle's surprise there was hardly a flicker of reaction to this momentous news: just a tightening of the jaw muscles, and a slight lift of the eyebrows.

'How did it happen, Inspector? Was it a heart attack?' It was clear that Lady Strang was unfamiliar with police procedure. Had Sir Nigel Strang suffered a heart attack, or a stroke had caused his death, or he had been the victim of a traffic accident, a constable would most likely have brought the news. Certainly not a divisional detective inspector.

'I regret to say he was murdered, Lady Strang.'

'Oh! Where did this happen? On the way to his club perhaps? He sometimes walked from the office to the Athenaeum. Just to get a breath of fresh air, he would say. He works terribly hard, you know. Was he set upon by some cutpurse?'

Hardcastle smiled at the old term for a street robber. 'No, ma'am. He was found dead in his office at the ministry. At twenty to six this morning. A young cleaning woman found him.'

'Oh, the poor girl. What a terrible shock for her.' Expressing no surprise that her husband had been at work at that unearthly hour, Lady Strang rose to her feet, and crossed to the tasselled velvet bell-pull. 'Thank you for coming to tell me, Inspector,' she said.

'I do have one or two questions.' Hardcastle was amazed at the woman's composure, and surmised that she was of a class of person who would not display grief in the presence of strangers.

'Oh, very well.' Rosalind Strang resumed her seat.

'At the moment we have no idea why Sir Nigel should have been murdered. Are you aware, Lady Strang, of any threats that might have been made against your husband? Did he mention any concerns of that sort that he might have had?' Hardcastle tried to make his questions sound professional, hoping that Sir Nigel's widow would not take him for a bumbling, incompetent fool.

'My husband never suggested that he was in fear of his life, Inspector. You know, of course, that he was engaged in work of the highest importance.'

'Yes, ma'am.'

'Had it, therefore, occurred to you that some German agent might have been responsible for his death?'

'It is something that the police will look into, Lady Strang,' said Hardcastle, although he was none too sure how he would go about it. He did not, however, have to wait too long to find out.

'When did you last see Sir Nigel, ma'am?'

'At about half past eight yesterday morning, when he left to go to the office.'

'Were you aware that he was going to remain there all night?'

'No, although he was sometimes obliged to attend meetings quite late into the evening. In those cases he would usually stay at his club, rather than coming in late and disturbing me.'

'Did he say that he was going to do that yesterday, ma'am?'

'No, he didn't. But very often he didn't know in advance. I can assure you, Inspector, that when the minister – or even the prime minister – sent for my husband, he went.'

'Did he not telephone you, ma'am?' Hardcastle paused. 'I suppose you are connected.'

'Of course.' Lady Strang's imperious response implied that her household could not possibly survive without such an instrument.

'There is one other thing, Lady Strang. Do you have a photograph of Sir Nigel that we could have? It would assist us in our investigation.'

'I daresay there's one about the place somewhere, Inspector. Speak to Hobson on your way out. He'll find one for you.'

'Thank you for your assistance, Lady Strang,' said Hardcastle, as he and Marriott stood up, 'and I'm sorry to be the bearer of bad news.'

Rosalind Strang merely nodded as they left the room.

In the hall, Hobson the butler appeared as if by some secret awareness of their departure, and handed the two detectives their hats and umbrellas.

'You might as well know, Hobson,' said Hardcastle, 'that we've just told Lady Strang that her husband has been murdered.'

'I see, sir,' said Hobson, as grave-faced as ever. 'I'm obliged to you for telling me.'

'Lady Strang told us that Sir Nigel left here at about eight-thirty yesterday morning, Mr Hobson,' said Marriott.

'That is my recollection, sir.'

'And were there any telephone calls from him, or maybe his secretary, to say that he wouldn't be returning home last night?'

'Not that I'm aware of, sir. And I would know. The instrument is in the servants' quarters, and I'm obliged to ring up to the drawing room if there's a call for her ladyship, and put the call through. And to my knowledge there was only a single call yesterday evening.'

'Who was that from?' asked Hardcastle.

'One of her ladyship's friends, sir.'

'A female friend?' asked Hardcastle.

Hobson lifted his chin slightly. 'Naturally, sir.'

'Thank you, Hobson.'

'Are you aware of when Sir Nigel's body will be released for burial, sir? Doubtless her ladyship will require me to make the arrangements.'

'Not at the moment, no, but I'll let you know as soon as I can.' Hardcastle paused. 'You know that there'll have to be an inquest, of course.'

'Of course, sir,' murmured Hobson.

'Lady Strang said that you could lay your hands on a photograph of Sir Nigel that we might have.'

'Certainly, sir. Bear with me for one moment.'

Five minutes later, Hobson returned with a framed print of Sir Nigel Strang.

'Well, if that don't beat cockfighting, Marriott.' Hardcastle peered up and down the street searching for a cab. 'Never in all my service – and I've told a few people that their nearest and dearest have snuffed it – have I come across a reaction like Lady Strang's to the murder of her husband. Or for that matter, that high and mighty butler. She's as cold as charity, and it's a bloody mystery that she ever allowed Sir Nigel to sire two sons by her.'

'It's almost as if she was expecting to hear of his death,

sir.' Marriott paused. 'D'you think she might have had some-thing to do with it?'

Hardcastle turned to face his sergeant. 'You mean she might have popped up to Whitehall in the middle of the night, stabbed her old man, and then calmly went home to bed.'

'Not exactly, sir, but she might have known that someone was going to do him in.'

'Yes, and Kaiser Bill's my uncle,' retorted Hardcastle dismissively.

It was almost lunchtime when Hardcastle and Marriott returned to Westminster. But despite the pressing urgency of their murder enquiry, they made time to call in at the Red Lion in Derby Gate for a couple of pints of best bitter, and a mutton pie.

'If this is *best* bitter, Marriott, Lord knows what the rest is like.'

'It's probably all the same, sir,' said Marriott, forbearing to mention that, as usual, neither he nor Hardcastle had paid for their beer, and that they should be grateful for that.

'Well, Marriott, I suppose we'd better go and get on with this murder of ours. It's a right bloody dog's dinner.'

'Indeed, sir.' Marriott reflected briefly that to Hardcastle, every investigation was a dog's dinner, although occasionally his chief would opt for 'a dog's breakfast' as a variation.

Leaving the pub, the two detectives walked through the broad gateway of New Scotland Yard, and into Cannon Row police station on the right. Constructed to Sir Norman Shaw's plans, both were awesome buildings built from granite hewn by Dartmoor convicts.

But no sooner had Hardcastle placed his bowler hat and umbrella on the hatstand, than there was a knock on his office door.

'Good afternoon, sir.'

Hardcastle gazed at the smartly dressed young man standing in the doorway. 'Well, well, if it isn't Detective Sergeant Drew of Special Branch. I didn't think it'd be too long before you turned up on the scene. And what do Special Branch want?'

'Superintendent Quinn sends his compliments, sir, and he'd like to see you as soon as it's convenient.'

Hardcastle sighed, and took his hat and umbrella from the hatstand. Even though Quinn's office was only across the road between New Scotland Yard and his police station, Hardcastle never went outside without those two essential items.

Only last year, Hardcastle had been involved in the unsuccessful investigation into the murder of a German secret agent, and his dealings with Special Branch – the political branch of the Metropolitan Police – had left an impression of deviousness. DS Aubrey Drew had been the liaison officer on that occasion, and had been under orders to steer Hardcastle away from the true murderer.

'Come in, Mr Hardcastle, and take a seat.'

Superintendent Patrick Quinn, the head of Special Branch for the past fourteen years, was a native of County Mayo in Ireland. He was a tall man, possessed of a grey goatee beard, an aquiline nose, and bushy eyebrows. And Hardcastle did not like him for the very good reason that Quinn was a man of obsessive secrecy. His years in Special Branch had made him cautious of telling anyone about anything, even other policemen. He was secure in the knowledge that he had reached the zenith of his profession, and even Basil Thomson, the Assistant Commissioner, would send for him in vain. Thomson would eventually yield and call on Quinn, who was to become the only superintendent in the Metropolitan Police ever to be knighted, receiving the accolade in 1919.

Quinn signed his name on a file, and placed it on the corner of his desk.

'Well now, Mr Hardcastle, I believe you're dealing with the murder of Sir Nigel Strang.'

'Yes, sir.' Hardcastle was surprised that Quinn – busy with affairs of state and espionage – should know of a murder to which police had been called less than eight hours ago. But Quinn, like a spider, sat at the centre of his intelligence web, and was aware of the slightest tremor.

'Colonel Kell, the head of MI5, whom you've met, of course, is very interested to know how you're getting on. But to save you the trouble of reporting to me daily, I have assigned Detective Sergeant Drew to act as your liaison.'

'Do you think that there might be some foreign involvement in Strang's murder, then, sir?' Hardcastle was unhappy at having a Special Branch officer imposed on his investigation. A wintry smile crossed Quinn's face. 'That's for you to find out, Mr Hardcastle, but I can tell you that it was nothing to do with Mrs MacLeod.' He waved a hand of dismissal. 'I'll not delay you any longer, you must have much to do.' 'Very good, sir.'

'Well, Drew,' said Hardcastle, when he had returned to his own office, 'are you going to solve this little problem for me?' He waved at a couple of hardback chairs. 'And take the weight off of your plates. You look untidy standing there. You too, Marriott.'

'I'm afraid I don't know anything about it, sir,' said Drew, once he had seated himself. He liked Hardcastle, and having worked with him previously had some knowledge of his ways and foibles.

'Better tell you what's what, then.' Hardcastle settled himself behind his desk and began to fill his pipe with his favourite St Bruno tobacco. For the next few minutes he outlined what was known of the death of Sir Nigel Strang. 'There's one thing you might be able to explain, Drew, seeing as how you're one of these clever Special Branch men.'

'I will if I can, sir.'

'Mr Quinn said something about a Mrs MacLeod having nothing to do with this here murder. Now I know you chaps always talk in riddles over there, Drew, but can you explain what he was going on about?'

'Yes, sir. Margaretha Gertrude MacLeod, née Zelle. She's a Dutch national, sir, an exotic dancer who uses the stage name of Mata Hari. She was arrested in Paris in February, and charged with being a German agent. The story is that she seduced senior army officers, and obtained information from them that she then passed on to the Germans. As a matter of fact she was in this country last year, and was interviewed by Mr Thomson himself, but was then allowed to go to Spain.'

'How did she come by the name MacLeod, then?'

'She was married to a Dutch army officer at one time, sir. Captain John MacLeod.'

'A Dutch army officer called MacLeod? Are you having me on, Drew?'

'No, sir, not at all. He was Dutch of Scottish descent.'

'What's this Mata Hari business then? Why's she call herself that?'

'It's Hindi for "eye of the morning", sir,' replied Drew flatly.

'Well, fancy that, Marriott,' said Hardcastle, relighting his pipe. 'I always knew they were clever buggers in Special Branch. And our friend Drew here's only a sergeant. Just think how smart their inspectors must be.'

'Yes, sir,' said Marriott.

'Well, as you're so bright, Drew, tell me how to solve this here murder.'

'I'm not that clever, sir,' said Drew, risking a grin.

'No, I thought as much. But did Mr Quinn tell you what he wanted you to do when you was sent here to get under my feet?'

'To act as liaison between you and Special Branch, sir. I understand that Colonel Kell is taking a special interest in this murder.'

'Yes, so am I, Drew, and I don't want any of them MI5 experts trampling all over my investigation. I had enough of them buggers last year.'

'I don't think there's any chance of that, sir.'

'There certainly won't be if we go out early in the morning or late at night, and that's a fact.'

Hardcastle spent the next few minutes reading through the statements that had been taken from Bowles, the custodian, Mrs Daisy Johnson, and PC 527A Vaughan, who had been on duty at the main door of the munitions ministry.

'Well, there's not much there to whet the appetite, Marriott.'

'I wonder how many other people had keys to the back door to the ministry's offices, sir,' said Marriott.

'When I spoke to that Cresswell toff, he didn't seem to have any idea, Marriott, but it might be a good thing for you to have a word with the head security man, and see if he knows. Seems a damned funny way to carry on.' Hardcastle shook his head, and then turned to the Special Branch sergeant. 'And while you've got nothing to do, Drew, pop next door to Mr Rhodes and ask him when Dr Spilsbury proposes to do the post-mortem.'

'I spoke to him while you were across the road talking to Mr Quinn, sir. He said it'll be tomorrow morning first thing.' Like Marriott, Drew had learned, somewhat belatedly, that it was a good idea to have answers to Hardcastle's questions.

'You're coming on a treat, Drew,' said Hardcastle. 'We'll make a proper detective of you yet.'

The following morning, Hardcastle, Marriott and Drew attended St Mary's Hospital at Paddington.

'I've just finished, Hardcastle,' said Dr Spilsbury, laying down a scalpel. 'The cause of death was a stab wound to the heart. It was a single blow made with some force, and penetrated the left ventricle. Death would have been almost instantaneous. As to the time of death, I would calculate it at sometime between three-thirty a.m., and when he was found at five-forty.'

'That means that someone gained access to Sir Nigel's office sometime after eleven o'clock when Bowles, the custodian, did his rounds,' mused Hardcastle.

Spilsbury smiled. 'I've done my bit, Hardcastle,' he said. 'The rest is up to you.'

'Indeed, sir. I'm obliged. You say that the blow was made with some force. D'you think it possible that a woman murdered Sir Nigel.'

Spilsbury pondered the question for a moment or two before replying. 'It's possible, I suppose,' he said eventually. 'Particularly if the woman concerned was a manual worker. And since the war started there are quite a few of them, I imagine. But she'd have to be fairly strong. If it's of any assistance, I'd say that Sir Nigel's killer was right-handed.'

'I suppose it's possible that the murderer was already in the building before Bowles started his tour of duty at ten o'clock the previous night, and somehow hid himself so that Bowles didn't see him,' ventured DS Drew.

Hardcastle gazed at the Special Branch sergeant with a sour expression. 'Yes, thank you, Drew.'

THREE

'I think it's time we had another word with that charwoman, Marriott. What's her name?'

'Johnson, sir. Mrs Daisy Johnson.'

'That's her. Where does she live?'

'Peabody Buildings, Wild Street, sir,' said Marriott, 'just behind Bow Street police court.'

'So she does. I should have remembered that,' said Hardcastle, but he had remembered it; it was one of his foibles to give the impression of absent-mindedness at times.

'I doubt that she's got much to add to the statement she made, sir.' Marriott was concerned that his chief was about to go off on another wild-goose chase. He had done it before – many times – but the irony was that the DDI was often proved to have been justified in so doing.

'Shan't know until we ask her,' said Hardcastle.

The woman who answered the door was probably about fifty years of age, but looked older.

'Yes? What is it?' The woman regarded the two detectives with a suspicious glance. 'If you're selling something, we ain't got no money.'

'We're police officers, madam,' said Hardcastle, raising his hat. 'I wanted to speak to Mrs Johnson, Mrs Daisy Johnson.'

'Is it about the murder? Daisy told me all about it.'

'Yes, madam.'

'You'd better come in, then.' The woman opened the door wide, and ushered the two policemen into a sparsely furnished sitting room. On the mantelpiece was a framed photograph of a young man in Grenadier Guards uniform, presumably Daisy's husband. From another room came the sound of children playing. 'I'll just get Daisy for you, mister.'

'Are you Daisy's mother?'

'Yes, I am. I'm Mrs Harding.'

A few moments later, Daisy Johnson entered the room. 'I

told you all I know yesterday,' she said. She was wearing a white ninon blouse and a black skirt, a good eight inches clear of the ground, and her hair was piled high on her head. Out of her working clothes, it was apparent that she was a very attractive woman, albeit a little coarse. In short, she was the sort of woman that Mrs Hardcastle would have described as having made the best of poor beginnings. But to Hardcastle's eye, her apparel seemed rather expensive for a charwoman.

'I'm sure you did, Daisy, but I'd just like you to go through it again in case there was anything you forgot.'

'Well, like I said,' Daisy began as she settled herself in one of the worn armchairs, 'I went in Sir Nigel's office, like I always do of a morning, and there he was lying dead on the floor. Then I ran downstairs and told Mr Bowles. He come back up with me and felt Sir Nigel's pulse. Then he said, "Yes, Daisy love, he's a goner all right". And then he went downstairs and told the rozzer on the door.'

'Remind me of the time again.' Hardcastle knew exactly what Daisy Johnson had told him before, but he liked to compare a witness's first account with their second. Just in case there were any discrepancies that would cause him to be suspicious.

'Well, I got to the offices about my usual time.' Daisy Johnson was clearly apprehensive at having the police talking to her again, and Hardcastle wondered why.

'Which is when?'

'Half past five. And like I told you, I always does Sir Nigel's office first. It must've took me about five minutes getting my stuff from the cupboard in the corridor—'

'What cupboard's this?'

'It's where we keep all our brooms and brushes, and the dusters and polish, and that.'

'Yes, go on.'

'I always start with the bookcase just inside the door of Sir Nigel's office, then I moves across to the desk and starts on that. But when I went round behind the desk, there he was, just lying there with blood all over his waistcoat. Fair give me a turn that did.'

'Yes, I suppose it would have done,' said Hardcastle. 'Now,

Daisy, I want you to think very carefully about this. Did you
see anyone else, anyone at all, between the time you arrived
and when you found Sir Nigel?'

'Only Mr Bowles.'

'You're absolutely sure?'

'Yeah, cross me heart and hope to die.'

'And this was at twenty minutes to six, when you discovered Sir Nigel's body.'

'That's right.'

'What happened then?'

'The copper come up and had a look, and he felt Sir N's
pulse an' all. Then he told Mr Bowles to lock the door, and
he took the key. The copper I mean.'

'What did you do then?'

'Mr Bowles suggested that I ought to make a start on some
of the other offices, but I was so shook up that he said not
to bother, and he made me a cup of tea. Then a couple of
detectives turned up, and I had to make a statement to him.'
Daisy pointed at Marriott.

'Have you heard from your husband lately?' Hardcastle
nodded towards the photograph on the mantelpiece. 'That's
him, is it?'

'Yes, that's my Gerald. Handsome, ain't he?' Daisy looked
at the photograph and smiled. 'He writes as often as he can,
but the letters seem to come in fits and starts. Sometimes I
don't hear for weeks, then six or seven letters will arrive all
at once.'

'In France, is he?'

'No, Belgium. Last time he come home on leave, he said
he was at some place called Wipers.'

'That'll be the Ypres Salient,' put in Marriott, whose
brother-in-law was serving there, but forbore from saying
that it was one of the most vulnerable and dangerous places
on the Western Front.

'Possibly,' said Daisy doubtfully, 'but I don't know if he's
still there. He was saying that they get moved about all over
the place.'

Back in Wild Street, Hardcastle hailed a cab with his
umbrella. 'Scotland Yard, cabbie,' he said, once he and

Marriott were seated. And then, in an aside to his sergeant, added, 'Tell 'em Cannon Row, Marriott, and half the time you'll finish up at Cannon Street in the City.'

'Yes, sir,' said Marriott flatly. He had received this advice on almost every occasion that he and the DDI shared a cab back to the police station.

But once at their destination, Hardcastle led the way into the Red Lion public house. 'I think better when I've had a pint, Marriott,' he said.

'What's next, sir?' asked Marriott, once the two of them were settled at one end of the bar.

'I think we'll have a go at Henry Bowles. His story don't hang together in my book. He was a bit too confident for my liking. Dr Spilsbury says the earliest that Strang was murdered was three-thirty, two hours and ten minutes before Daisy Johnson found his body. Bowles also says that he didn't let anyone in, and he didn't let anyone out, and he didn't see anybody. So how did our killer get in? Or he was in already and had hidden himself? Like Drew suggested,' Hardcastle added, somewhat reluctantly.

'There's always the back entrance, sir,' said Marriott.

'Yes, and that's something that'll have to be looked into. Did you find out from the security chief how many keys had been issued?'

'Not yet, sir.'

'No, I suppose you've not really had the time,' admitted Hardcastle. 'Better make that a priority.' He paused. 'On second thoughts, I'll give that little job to Drew. He should know his way round government departments, being a Special Branch man.'

'When d'you want to see Bowles, sir?'

'Where's he live?'

'Tachbrook Street, sir.'

'We'll call in at the nick first, and I'll tell Drew what I want, and then we'll see Bowles.'

Hardcastle put his head round the door of the detectives' office, and crooked a finger in DS Drew's direction.

'I've got a couple of jobs for you, Drew, seeing as how you're well qualified for these particular enquiries. First off,

find the head of security at the Ministry of Munitions, and find
out how many keys have been issued for the back entrance.
Then, when you've done that, have a stroll along to the
Athenaeum and find out if Sir Nigel Strang was in there any
time after, say, six o'clock on Monday, the fourteenth of May.'

'Very good, sir.' Drew was unsure whether making
enquiries on Hardcastle's behalf constituted acting as a liaison
officer between the DDI and Special Branch, but in truth he
was pleased to have something to do.

'Come along, Marriott. It's a pleasant day, so we'll take
a walk across the division to Tachbrook Street, and beard
Mr Bowles in his den.'

'Are you Mrs Bowles?' Hardcastle raised his hat to the woman
who answered the door to Henry Bowles's flat in Tachbrook
Street.

'Yes. What's wrong?'

'Nothing's wrong, Mrs Bowles. We're police officers, and
we'd like to talk to your husband.'

'You'd better come in, then. It'll be about the shocking
murder, I suppose. I've just made a cup of tea if you're interested.'

'Thank you, that'd be most welcome.'

Mrs Bowles showed the two policemen into the sitting
room, and disappeared to the kitchen to fetch the tea.

'Inspector!' Henry Bowles leaped up from his armchair,
and folded a copy of the *Daily Mirror* that he had been
reading. 'Have a seat, sir, and you too, Mr Marriott. Is my
Gwen getting you some tea?'

'Yes, she is,' said Hardcastle.

Mrs Bowles came into the room with a tray of tea, and
some biscuits.

'Ah, ginger snaps, my favourite,' exclaimed Hardcastle.

'I'll leave you to have a chat, then,' said Gwen Bowles,
and left the room, closing the door behind her.

Bowles handed round the cups of tea, and sat back in his
chair. 'So what can I do for you, Inspector?'

'You haven't been quite straight with me, have you,
Bowles?' said Hardcastle.

Marriott was astonished at the DDI's line of questioning,

but Hardcastle had years of experience of interviewing witnesses, and he had an innate sense that told him when they were lying.

'I don't know what you mean, sir.'

'I'll explain. You're the custodian who was responsible for the ministry building from ten o'clock last Monday evening until six o'clock the following morning. Is that correct?'

'Yes, sir.'

'Tell me, is the main door locked?'

'No, sir. You see we often have messengers arriving at all hours with urgent mail, and we have next day's newspapers delivered round about midnight.'

'Now then, about you doing your rounds. You said you checked the offices at about eleven o'clock.'

'That's right, sir.'

'And how long does that take you?'

'About twenty minutes.'

'And then it's back to the front door, is it?'

'Yes, that's right, sir.' Bowles was beginning to look a little worried, and had started fidgeting.

'So, as the front door is left unlocked while you're doing your rounds, anyone could walk in.'

'There's a policeman stationed outside, sir. He always checks who's coming in.'

'Not much point in your being there, then, is there, Bowles?' Hardcastle finished his tea, and put the cup and saucer on the tray. 'But the truth of the matter is that you spent most of the night playing cards with a couple of the other custodians. One from the Ministry of Health and the other from the Ministry of Food.' It was pure guesswork on the DDI's part, but he had been stationed on A Division long enough to familiarise himself with the habits of the army of custodians who were, supposedly, ensuring the security of the offices to which they were assigned.

'Er, well, I did have a hand or two of brag round about two o'clock, sir.'

'I thought so. And did the policeman on the front door join in by any chance?'

'Oh no, sir.' Bowles hesitated. 'I hope you won't mention it to my boss, sir.'

Hardcastle laughed. 'Someone entered the building for which you were responsible and murdered the permanent secretary, Bowles. I can't think of any worse dereliction of duty for a custodian than to allow that to happen. To be honest, I think you'll be very lucky to hang on to your job.' He stood up. 'Thank your good lady for the tea. Very nice. Come, Marriott, we've work to do.'

'How on earth did you know Bowles had been playing cards, sir?' asked Marriott, as they strode back towards Cannon Row police station.

'I didn't, Marriott, I guessed,' said Hardcastle. 'The next thing I want done is for you to find the PC who was on night duty last Monday night, and I want to see him in my office without delay.'

It had taken Marriott a matter of minutes to examine the duty slate, and locate the PC who had been on duty at the Ministry of Munitions' protection post when Strang's murder had occurred. He then sent an urgent message to the police section house in Ambrosden Avenue directing the officer to report to the DDI immediately.

'This is 602A Lewis, sir,' said Marriott, as he entered Hardcastle's office accompanied by a uniformed constable.

'All correct, sir,' said Lewis.

Hardcastle peered thoughtfully at the PC, now standing rigidly to attention in front of his desk, his helmet in the crook of his arm. The DDI spent a moment or two filling his pipe, and then lighting it.

'What service have you got, lad?'

'Two years and six months, sir.'

'You were assigned to night duty on the protection post at the Ministry of Munitions on the night of Monday the fourteenth of May. Correct?'

'Yes, sir.'

'Who was the early turn who relieved you?'

'PC 527A Vaughan, sir,' said Lewis promptly.

'At what time?'

Lewis paused momentarily. 'Er, ten minutes to six, sir.'

'Ten minutes early, eh? Why did he do that?'

'He gets dismissed off the parade to draw a firearm, sir.

He relieves me early so's I can hand in my firearm to the station officer, and still be in time to parade off duty.'

'When you came on did you relieve the late turn man early?'

'Yes, sir. At ten minutes to ten, sir.' Lewis began to look worried; he did not care for the way this interview was progressing.

'What are your duties?'

'To prevent unauthorised access to the premises, sir.'

'Well, Lewis, someone got in during your tour of duty, and murdered the permanent secretary. What d'you say to that, eh?'

'I don't know anything about it, sir.' Lewis, a fit young man some twenty-three years of age, had visions of his dismissal followed by conscription under Lord Derby's scheme. And if that happened, he would be in the trenches in a matter of weeks.

'I see.' Hardcastle struck a match and applied it to his pipe. Waving away the smoke, he asked, 'Did anything untoward happen during your tour of duty?'

'No, sir, nothing as how I can recall.'

'What time were you relieved for grub?'

'I was early grub, sir. Five minutes to two o'clock.'

'And who relieved you?'

'PC 144A Marshall, sir. He was the man on two beat.'

'And you returned at what time?'

'Five and twenty to three, sir.'

'Were you visited by the patrolling officer?'

'Yes, sir. At about eleven o'clock, and by the section sergeant at twenty past four.'

'D'you smoke, Lewis?'

'Yes, sir.'

'Much?'

'About ten a day, sir.' Lewis was mystified by the DDI's question.

'And did you have a quick spit and a draw while you was on duty?'

'Er, well, I—'

Hardcastle smote the top of his desk, causing both Lewis and Sergeant Marriott to start in alarm. 'Don't play games with me, lad. I'm investigating the murder of a senior civil servant. One who's so important that even Mr Lloyd George is taking an interest in my catching the man who did it.' That was exaggerating a little, but the DDI thought it not far from the truth.

'Well, I did nip round the corner, out of sight like, once or twice, yes, sir.' Lewis was aghast that the prime minister might get to hear of his neglect of duty. And if that happened, the Commissioner would learn of it very soon afterwards. 'But I could still see the door, sir.'

'Is that a fact?' For some moments, Hardcastle surveyed the young constable in silence. 'You do know, I suppose, that the main door is left unlocked?'

'Yes, sir,' said the miserable Lewis.

'And it's left unlocked because there's supposed to be an armed policeman outside, and a custodian inside. But the custodian went off to play cards, and you buggered off to have a quick smoke. Well, it's not bloody good enough, Lewis.' Hardcastle turned to Marriott. 'Place this officer on the report, Sergeant,' he said, and waved a hand of dismissal.

'DS Drew's waiting to see you, sir,' said Marriott, as he escorted the luckless Lewis from the DDI's office.

'Send him in. And I want to see Marshall.'

Drew entered the office still clutching his straw boater. 'I've been to the Athenaeum, sir.'

'What did you find out?'

'They'd never heard of Sir Nigel Strang, sir. I spoke to the doorkeeper and he said that Sir Nigel's not a member of the Athenaeum.'

'Is that a fact?' Hardcastle leaned back in his chair as he digested this latest twist in the hunt for Strang's killer. 'But Lady Strang said that it was his club, didn't she, Marriott?'

'Yes, sir.'

'Well, he didn't go home, so he must have had dinner somewhere, and he must've slept somewhere. I don't see a distinguished—' Hardcastle broke off. 'What was it Dr Spilsbury called him?'

'A mandarin, sir.'

'Yes, well I don't see one of them mandarins kipping down in his office,' said Hardcastle. 'So, assuming he *did* have dinner somewhere, I wonder what the hell he was doing between then and finishing up in his office, dead.'

'As far as the keys to the private entrance are concerned, sir,' said Drew, 'there have only been nine issued.'

'Nine?' echoed Hardcastle. 'Who has 'em, did you find that out?'

'Yes, sir,' said Drew. 'The permanent secretaries of the three ministries that share the building, along with their deputy and assistant secretaries. Oh, and there's a tenth which is held by the chief of security.'

'Any reports of keys being lost at any time?'

'No, sir.'

Hardcastle thought about that while he scraped out the bowl of his pipe. 'Of course, Drew, any one of 'em could have popped round to that place in Palmer Street, and had a copy made.'

'That's true, sir, but why would they want to do that?'

'Yes, why indeed.' Hardcastle had been wondering whether he should have enquiries made at the locksmith in Palmer Street, but at once realised that it would be a wasted journey. 'If there's a PC Marshall hanging around outside my office, send him in, Drew.'

'Very good, sir.'

Marriott had anticipated that Hardcastle would want to see the officer who had relieved PC Lewis for refreshments, and had him standing by.

'PC 144A, sir.' Marshall was about forty years of age, well turned out, and, as Lewis had done, held his helmet in the crook of his left arm.

'You were night duty Monday night. Is that right?'

'Yes, sir. Two beat.' Marshall had been given no opportunity to talk to PC Lewis, and had no idea why he had been sent for. But with his age and service, he was safe in assuming that he was not about to be asked to join the Criminal Investigation Department.

'At what time did you relieve Lewis for grub on the Ministry of Munitions protection post?'

Marshall thought only briefly about that. 'Must've been just before two o'clock, sir.'

'And Lewis returned at what time?'

'About two thirty-five, sir.'

'Did anything untoward occur during the time you were on that post? You know why I'm asking, of course.'

'Yes, sir.' In common with everyone else in the station, Marshall had heard of the murder of Sir Nigel Strang. 'But nothing untoward occurred.'

'Visited, were you?'

'Yes, sir. The patrolling officer and section sergeant at two-fifteen.'

'All right, Marshall, you can go.'

'By the way, sir,' said Marriott, once Marshall had departed, 'I had a look in *Who's Who* to see what it had to say about Sir Nigel.'

'Didn't tell you who topped him, did it?' asked Hardcastle drily.

'No, sir,' replied Marriott, keeping a perfectly straight face.

'Was there anything useful in it?'

'Not really, sir. He seems to have had a fairly straightforward career for a senior civil servant. Educated at Eton and Oxford, and married Rosalind Lucas in 1893. She was the daughter of Sir Rodney and Lady Lucas of London and Wilton in Wiltshire. They have two sons. There was no reference to a club in his entry, sir.'

'Well, that don't tell us much, Marriott.'

FOUR

'Good morning, Mr Hardcastle.' The Westminster coroner allowed his monocle to drop from his eye, and nodded in the direction of the DDI.

'Good morning, sir.'

The coroner's gaze travelled around his courtroom surveying the one or two disinterested members of the public seated at the rear of the court, and the reporters in the press box. 'As you are doubtless aware,' he said, addressing the court at large, 'I am obliged by law to convene a jury in cases of violent death. However, I am informed by the police,' he continued, nodding again in Hardcastle's direction, 'that they are unable to furnish full details at this stage. In the circumstances, a jury will be empanelled at the next hearing. Do you have a date in mind, Mr Hardcastle?'

'Difficult to say, sir,' said Hardcastle, rising to his feet.

'Shall we say two weeks, then?'

'That would be suitable, sir, although I can't guarantee that I will—'

The coroner held up his hand. 'Quite understood, Mr Hardcastle.' He fixed his gaze on a solicitor who, the DDI presumed, represented the Strang family's interests. 'Do you have an application?' he enquired.

'I do, sir. May the deceased's body be released for interment?'

'Is there any objection from the police, Mr Hardcastle? Is there any need of further pathological examination?'

'No, sir. Dr Spilsbury is satisfied as to the cause of death, and will, of course, be giving evidence at the full hearing.'

'Very well. This hearing is now adjourned until . . .' The coroner replaced his monocle, and turned a few pages in his ledger. 'Thursday the thirty-first of May.'

Leaving the coroner's court, Hardcastle led the way across the road to the Barley Mow Public House in Horseferry Road.

'I think we'll have a pint before we get on with this topping of ours, Marriott,' he said, pushing open the door of the pub.

'Hello, Inspector. Been across the road, have you?'

'All in a day's work, Albert. Two pints of your best, please.'

'Coming up.' The landlord drew the beer, and pushed Marriott's money away.

A man wearing a straw boater sidled up to Hardcastle. 'What's happening with this murder of yours, Mr Hardcastle?'

'Who the hell are you?' demanded Hardcastle, well knowing the reporter of old.

'Charlie Simpson, *London Daily Chronicle*, guv'nor.'

'Well, Charlie Simpson of the *London Daily Chronicle*, I never discuss cases in a pub. It makes my beer go flat. And you can pass that message on to all the other hacks in Fleet Street.' Hardcastle took a draught of his beer. 'Bloody press,' he muttered, as the abashed Simpson moved away.

To Marriott's dismay, Hardcastle decided to walk back to Cannon Row police station from the pub. But he often said that he liked to walk round the division, just to make sure that things were as they ought to be.

'Telephone Lady Strang, Marriott,' said Hardcastle, once he was back in his office, 'and tell her that Sir Nigel's body has been released for burial.'

'Very good, sir.'

'And then have a word with that butler fellow. What's his name?'

'Hobson, sir.'

'Yes, that's the chap. As he's taken it on himself to make the arrangements, ask him to let us know when and where the funeral is to take place.'

'Right, sir.'

Hardcastle took off his spats and shoes, and began to massage his feet.

On Thursday afternoon, Detective Inspector Collins of the Fingerprint Bureau visited Hardcastle in his office.

'Well, Charlie, got good news for me?' asked the DDI.

'Yes and no, Ernie,' said Collins. 'Quite a few people had legitimate access to Sir Nigel's office.'

'Thought that might be the case,' muttered Hardcastle.

'I've eliminated Cresswell, the deputy secretary, and the rest of them, including a pompous little upstart called Rawlings.'

'Who's he?'

'Sidney Rawlings is – or was – Sir Nigel's personal secretary. He occupies the room next to Strang. The assistant secretary, and one or two others that I won't bother you with had all left their fingerprints in various places. That said, there's one set that can't be accounted for, and that was on the brass fingerplate on the inside of the door that leads straight off the corridor to Sir Nigel's office.'

'So much for Mrs Johnson's cleaning abilities, but the one on the doorplate must be recent, because she's bound to clean that. But I doubt she did so on Tuesday morning. And I don't suppose I'd be lucky enough for you to tell me that these fingerprints you found are in your collection, would I?'

'You suppose right, Ernie. But I wasn't expecting to find them there. My collection consists mainly of burglars, robbers and the occasional murderer. And as all the murderers in my collection have been hanged, I doubt it'll be one of them.' Collins emitted a short cynical laugh. 'And I don't somehow think that whoever topped Strang was caught in the act of burgling the place.'

Hardcastle did not have long to wait to hear when Sir Nigel Strang's funeral was to take place. On Friday morning, he received a telephone call.

'Inspector Hardcastle?'

'Yes.'

'It's Hobson, sir, Lady Strang's butler.'

'What can I do for you, Hobson?' asked Hardcastle, noting that Hobson had amended his employment in the Strang household to that of butler to Lady Strang.

'It's about the funeral, sir. I have instructed Messrs Harrods to undertake the arrangements. The interment is to take place at two thirty on Monday afternoon.'

'Where, Hobson?'

'At West Norwood cemetery, sir. The entrance is in Norwood High Street.'

'Thank you, Hobson.'

'Am I to advise her ladyship that you'll be attending?'

'Yes,' said Hardcastle. 'I'll be there, but whether you advise her ladyship of that fact is a matter for you.' The DDI replaced the receiver, satisfied that he had scored a point over the presumptuous functionary. He relayed the details to Marriott, and spent a few moments filling his pipe. 'I think we'll go to the Ministry of Munitions and have a word with this young whippersnapper of a secretary, Marriott. In my experience, secretaries pick up all sorts of scuttlebutt. Even more than the custodians what's supposed to be guarding the front door.'

The day-duty custodian demanded to see the detectives' warrant cards before admitting them to the building. They were then required to wait until a messenger could be found to escort them to Rawlings's office.

'They seem to have tightened up on security, sir,' said Marriott.

'Fat lot of good that'll do,' growled Hardcastle. 'Talk about shutting the stable door after the horse has bolted.'

Eventually a messenger appeared. 'I understand you wish to see Mr Rawlings, sir.'

'Yes, and I haven't got all bloody day, either.'

The young man into whose office the two detectives were shown was about twenty-five years of age. He was immaculately dressed, and sported a carnation in his buttonhole.

'How may I help you, Inspector?' drawled Rawlings, once introductions had been effected.

'I'm investigating the murder of Sir Nigel Strang, Rawlings.'

'Ah, of course,' said Rawlings, somewhat taken aback at being addressed by his surname without the courtesy of a prefix. He brushed at the beginnings of a fair moustache.

'Can you suggest any reason why Sir Nigel should have been in his office between half past three and twenty to six last Tuesday morning?'

'It's a mystery,' said Rawlings.

'Yes, I'm aware of that,' snapped Hardcastle. 'Have you ever known him spend the night in his office before, or at least to arrive that early?'

'No, I can't say I have, Inspector.'

'Do you have a key to the private entrance, Mr Rawlings?' asked Marriott.

'Yes, as a matter of fact I do.'

'Where did you get that from, then?' demanded Hardcastle.

'Er, Sir Nigel lent me his, and told me to get a duplicate made.'

'Did he indeed? And why did he tell you to do that?'

'I usually went to Dulwich with his driver, to help him with his red boxes, and—'

'Red boxes? What are they?' Hardcastle knew perfectly well what they were, but disliked low-grade civil servants who spoke in their own jargon, as if trying to impress upon others how important they were.

'They're the red despatch cases, issued to Ministers and permanent secretaries, Inspector,' Rawlings said rather loftily.

'Tell me, Rawlings, what's the difference between the permanent secretary and you? You're a secretary as well, aren't you?' But Hardcastle well knew the difference, and was having a little game with Rawlings.

'To give Sir Nigel his full title,' said Rawlings airily, 'he is the permanent under-secretary of state. Mr Cresswell is the deputy under-secretary, and Mr Sinclair Cobb is the assistant under-secretary.'

'So where do you fit in?'

'I'm Sir Nigel's personal secretary. Quite a bit lower down the pecking order, so to speak.' Rawlings smiled modestly.

'So how does having a key to the back door help you to assist Sir Nigel with his despatch boxes?' asked Hardcastle, tiring of baiting the young man.

'I usually opened the door for him when we arrived, and Sir Nigel said it would be useful if he'd inadvertently left his key at home.'

'But if you went to his house to act as a porter, surely you could've reminded him to bring his key.'

Rawlings did not much care for being described as a porter. 'Yes, I suppose so, but it was Sir Nigel's idea.'

'Was the making of this extra key reported to the head of security?'

'I've no idea, Inspector. I imagine that Sir Nigel would have mentioned it to him.'

'Really.' Hardcastle frowned. 'But surely that's the sort of job he'd give to his secretary to do.'

'Perhaps, but he never asked me to do so.'

'Didn't you think it would have been a good idea to tell the security people anyway?'

'In retrospect, yes, I suppose it would've been.' Rawlings looked unhappy at the implication that he had failed in some way.

For a few moments, Hardcastle stared at the young man opposite him. Rawlings fidgeted uncomfortably.

'You see, Rawlings,' said Hardcastle eventually, 'there's a police officer on the front door twenty-four hours a day, and a custodian on duty inside.' He thought it unnecessary to mention that the policeman occasionally went round the corner for a smoke, and that the custodian had been in the habit of playing cards. 'That means that whoever murdered Sir Nigel Strang must've entered the building through the private entrance.' He paused. 'And you have one of the keys.'

'But, Inspector, surely you can't think that—'

'I don't know what to think, young man, but I shall find out who killed your boss, you can rest assured of that. And he'll be taking the eight o'clock walk.'

'Yes, I suppose so.'

'There's no suppose about it,' rejoined Hardcastle, further discomfiting Sir Nigel's private secretary.

But just when Rawlings thought the interview was over, Hardcastle started again.

'Now then, you say that you go with the driver to Dulwich to carry Sir Nigel's boxes for him.'

'That's correct.'

'So what happened when you arrived at Dulwich on the morning of Tuesday last?'

'He wasn't there.'

'I know he wasn't there, Rawlings. He was lying dead in his office,' said Hardcastle irritably. 'Did Lady Strang offer any explanation as to why he wasn't there?'

'She said she presumed that he'd stayed the night at his club.'

'When he does stay at his club, who arranges for accommodation?'

'Me usually. Sir Nigel would tell me he had a late meeting or a conference, and ask me to book a room for him.'

'At the Athenaeum?' Hardcastle was already satisfied that Sir Nigel Strang was not a member of the Athenaeum, and was interested to hear what Rawlings had to say.

'Oh no. Sir Nigel is – er, was – a member of the Royal Automobile Club. It's in Pall Mall.'

'I know where it is, Rawlings, but he made no such request last Monday, is that correct?'

'No, he didn't.'

'And he didn't mention that he wouldn't be going home?'

'No, he didn't. Otherwise I wouldn't have gone to Dulwich on Tuesday morning.'

'What time did you last see Sir Nigel on the Monday?'

'It must've been about six o'clock in the evening.'

'Did he say anything about working late?'

'Not exactly. He rang for me and said that he had one or two papers to deal with, and that I should go home. Oh, and he said what he usually says: "I'll see you in the morning".'

'So you were fully expecting him to be at Dulwich when you called there on the Tuesday morning.'

'Yes, I was.'

'How does this arrangement about going with the driver work, Mr Rawlings?' asked Marriott.

'He picks me up at about eight o'clock, and—'

'Picks you up from where?' asked Hardcastle sharply.

'I've got rooms in Old Pye Street. He calls for me there, and we drive to Dulwich.'

'Are you married?' asked Marriott.

'No.'

Hardcastle took out his pipe and began to fill it, ignoring the expression of distaste on Rawlings's face. 'As Sir Nigel's private secretary, you must be privy to all sorts of secrets, Rawlings,' he said.

'Of course, but I'm not permitted to discuss any of them,' said Rawlings triumphantly.

'Oh, I'm not talking about the work you do. We all know what you get up to here,' said Hardcastle airily, as he waved away a cloud of pipe smoke. 'But what about Sir Nigel's private life? Happily married, was he?'

Rawlings gave the appearance of being shocked by the question. 'I don't really think it's any of your business, Inspector,' he said.

'Now just you listen to me, young man. I'm investigating his murder. Someone saw fit to kill him. And whoever topped him must've had a reason. Screwing around was he?'

Rawlings blinked at the somewhat ferocious and earthy way in which Hardcastle had posed his question. 'As far as I know, he's happily married, Inspector.'

'Any children, has he?' Once again, Hardcastle was asking a question to which he already knew the answer.

'He and his wife have two sons: Guy and Hugo. They're both in the Grenadier Guards, serving at the Front, I believe.'

Hardcastle stood up suddenly. 'Thank you, Rawlings, that'll be all. I'll probably need to see you again at some time. And now, perhaps, you'd be so good as to show me to this here Mr Cobb's office.'

'Er, he may be busy, Inspector,' said Rawlings, also standing up.

'Well, if he is, he can tell me, can't he?'

Sinclair Cobb was a man in his early thirties. He had wavy hair, worn rather longer than Hardcastle thought was seemly, and was reclining in his chair with his feet propped up on the open bottom drawer of his desk.

'This is Inspector Hardcastle, sir,' said Rawlings deferentially.

'Come in, m'dear fellow, come in.' Cobb rose from his chair, skirted the desk and held out his hand. He looked at Strang's private secretary. 'Thank you, Rawlings, that'll be all,' he said curtly.

'Thank you, sir,' said Rawlings, withdrawing from the office. Hardcastle had half expected him to walk out backwards and bow, as though in the presence of royalty.

'Do sit down, Inspector, and you too, er . . .'

'This is Detective Sergeant Marriott,' said Hardcastle, as they sat down.

'Shocking business, this murder of Sir Nigel, ain't it? I mean to say, here we are at the very heart of government, and someone comes in and murders the poor fellow. Any idea who was responsible? No, I suppose not, otherwise you wouldn't still be here.'

'It's been hinted in certain quarters that an agent of the enemy might've been responsible,' said Hardcastle.

Cobb scoffed. 'I doubt that somehow. Are you seriously suggesting that some damned spy could've gained access to this building and murdered Sir Nigel? You've got one of your policeman outside, and there's a custodian always on duty at the main door, night and day.'

'When he's not playing cards,' observed Hardcastle.

'Playing cards?' Cobb sounded shocked at this revelation.

'I questioned the man Bowles at some length, Mr Cobb, and he admitted a weakness for playing brag during the night hours.'

'Did he, by Jove?' Cobb scribbled a brief note on his blotter. 'I'll speak to the head of security about that. It strikes me that some people here seem unaware that there's a war on.'

'Well, if it wasn't an enemy agent, we're looking at a domestic murder,' commented Hardcastle.

'Mmm! I suppose so,' said Cobb, 'but who on earth would've wanted to do for poor old Strang?'

'What d'you know of his private life, Mr Cobb?' asked Marriott, looking up from the notes he had been making.

An impish smile crossed Cobb's face. 'I do know that Sir Nigel had a weakness for the ladies, Inspector. So it might be a case of *cherchez la femme.*'

'Oh, you think so, do you?' Hardcastle was unfamiliar with the phrase, but knew that he could rely on Marriott to translate it for him later. 'D'you happen to know of any liaisons Sir Nigel might've had?'

Cobb laughed. 'We might not be too good at keeping military secrets, Inspector, but you can rest assured that information of that sort rarely becomes public knowledge. In short, no, I can't help you there.'

'I shall need to have a word with the Minister, Mr Cobb,' said Hardcastle. 'Could you arrange that?'

'Yes, indeed, but I'll have to let you know. Dr Addison is a very busy man, and he seems to spend as much time at Downing Street as he does here.' Cobb made another note on his blotter. 'I'll let you know as soon as it's been arranged.'

FIVE

Much to Hardcastle's surprise, he received a telephone
call from Sinclair Cobb the very next morning.

'Dr Addison is able to see you at half past two
this afternoon, Inspector. I trust that is convenient for you.'

'Indeed it is, Mr Cobb. I'm much obliged.'

Once again, Hardcastle and Marriott went through the rigma-
role of having their warrant cards examined by the same
custodian who had examined them only yesterday.

After some minutes had elapsed, during which time
Hardcastle's blood pressure continued to rise, an effete young
man appeared in the entrance hall.

'Inspector Hardcastle?'

'Yes,' growled Hardcastle.

'I'm Edward Lines, the Minister's private secretary.
Perhaps you'd be so good as to come with me, please, and
I'll show you to his office.'

Hardcastle and Marriott followed the secretary – he could
have been a carbon copy of Sidney Rawlings – up the stairs
and along the same corridor where Sir Nigel Strang's office
was situated.

Christopher Addison, a doctor of medicine, was an amiable
man, some forty-eight years of age, and had been Minister
of Munitions for only five months. Two months later, he
was to be replaced in that post by Winston Churchill, a
rising politician, who was destined to remain there for the
duration of the war.

'My dear Inspector, what a grave tragedy.' Addison stood
up and walked round his desk to shake hands with the two
detectives. 'A great loss to the ministry. Great loss. Do take
a seat, both of you.' He glanced at his secretary. 'Be so good
as to arrange for some coffee, Lines.'

'Of course, Minister.'

'Well now, how am I able to assist you, Inspector?'

'I'm not sure that you can, sir,' said Hardcastle. 'My seeing you is more in the nature of a courtesy.' He paused. 'I don't suppose you can shed any light on Sir Nigel's private life.'

'Why d'you ask that question, Inspector? D'you have some theory about Sir Nigel's murder?'

'I never have theories when it comes to a murder, sir. It gets in the way of the evidence.'

'I suppose so, Mr Hardcastle. In which case, I should perhaps ask what evidence you have?'

'At the moment very little, sir. But I'm worried about the matter of the keys.'

'The keys?' Dr Addison raised his eyebrows. 'What keys are these?'

'The keys to the private back entrance. There were originally ten, but I now learn that Rawlings, Sir Nigel's secretary, had a duplicate made on Sir Nigel's instructions. Unfortunately the head of security has no record of it. And that leads me to wonder whether anyone else has had a copy made. You see, sir, given that there's a constable outside, and a custodian inside, it looks very much as though whoever murdered Sir Nigel gained entrance by the private door.' Hardcastle felt no need to mention the shortcomings of those two individuals because he was certain in his own mind that entry had been effected through the private door.

'Great Scott!' exclaimed Addison. 'Are you suggesting that the murderer might've been someone on the staff here?'

'I'm not suggesting anything, sir,' said Hardcastle mildly. 'I'm merely drawing your attention to one of the facts I've discovered.'

'Good grief! I shall certainly ensure that James Cresswell looks into the matter. He's acting permanent secretary until a replacement for Sir Nigel can be found.'

Hardcastle thought that it was time to steer the Minister back to the original question. 'I wondered what you knew, if anything, of Sir Nigel's private life, sir.'

'To the best of my knowledge, Inspector, Sir Nigel enjoyed a very happy home life. He was, naturally enough, constantly worried about his two sons, both of whom are serving with the Grenadier Guards at the Front. You see we are doing exceptionally important work here, ensuring that the troops have sufficient munitions with which to prosecute the war. Someone who has an unhappy home life would tend to be distracted by it, and wouldn't be of great assistance to us.'

And with that, Hardcastle had to be satisfied. But he was sure that even if Sir Nigel's private life was not all that it seemed, the officials at the Ministry of Munitions would close ranks to protect his reputation. And that was not very helpful when it came to discovering who had killed him.

'Thank you, sir,' said Hardcastle, as he and Marriott stood up.

'You'll not wait for coffee?' queried Addison.

'No thank you, sir. I have a murder to solve.'

'Perhaps you would keep me informed of your progress, Inspector.'

'Of course, sir.' But Hardcastle was determined that he would not inform the Minister of any progress until he had Sir Nigel Strang's murderer in custody.

On Saturday morning, Hardcastle arrived at his office at half past eight. It was more out of habit than necessity; there was little he could do actively about the murder of Sir Nigel Strang until Monday. But he decided to review what little was known so far. And for that he needed Marriott as a sounding board.

'I've been thinking, sir,' Marriott began.

'You want to be careful, Marriott. Carry on like that and they'll make you an inspector,' said Hardcastle, as he filled his pipe. 'Anyway, what've you been thinking about?'

'James Cresswell, sir, the deputy secretary at the ministry. Well, acting permanent secretary now.'

'What about him?'

'If he gets the job permanently, he'll get the knighthood that goes with it.'

Hardcastle stared at his sergeant in disbelief. 'Are you really putting that forward as a motive, Marriott? I've come across all sorts of reasons for murder, but not that one.'

'He does have a key to the rear entrance, sir.'

'Yes, and so does everyone else, it seems. But d'you really think that a man like Cresswell can be so desperate to be called "Sir James" that he'd commit murder for it?'

'It might be more of a case that his wife is desperate to be called *Lady* Cresswell, sir.'

Hardcastle smiled. 'That might be so, Marriott. Come to think of it, I've known some sergeants' wives who were very keen for their husbands to become inspectors. They like to know that their husbands are called "sir".'

Marriott laughed. 'Well, my wife's not one of them, sir. In fact, she'd rather I wasn't a policeman at all.'

Abandoning Marriott's baseless theory, Hardcastle sat back in his chair contentedly smoking. 'The trouble, Marriott,' he said, leaning forward again, 'is that this is no ordinary murder.'

'No, sir.' After all the years he had worked with Hardcastle, Marriott was accustomed to his DDI stating the obvious.

'I'm interested in those fingerprints that Mr Collins found.'

'The ones on the doorplate, sir?'

'Yes. I think I'll have another word with that young lass who does the cleaning.'

'Why, sir?'

'I want to know if she always cleans that brass fingerplate when she does Sir Nigel's office, because if she did it on Monday morning, but not Tuesday morning, on account of her being shocked, it might be that those dabs belong to the murderer.'

'Mightn't they be Bowles's prints, sir, or even Mrs Johnson's herself.'

'No. Mr Collins has eliminated them.' Hardcastle took out his chromium hunter, stared at it, wound it, and dropped it back into his waistcoat pocket. 'No time like the present, Marriott. We'll take a turn up to Wild Street, and have a word with her.' But he stopped in the doorway. 'On second thoughts, there's no point in having a dog and barking yourself.' He opened the door to the detectives' office. 'Come here, Catto.'

Detective Constable Henry Catto sprang to his feet, and put on his jacket, wondering what he had done wrong this time.

'You know where Bow Street police court is, don't you, Catto?'

'Yes, sir, of course.'

'I should hope you do. Round the back of it is Wild Street where you'll find Peabody Buildings. Sergeant Marriott will give you the number. There's a Mrs Johnson living there, along with her harridan of a mother, name of Mrs Harding. Have a word with this Daisy Johnson and ask her if she always cleans the fingerplate on the inside of the door to Sir Nigel Strang's office. And then ask her if she cleaned it on Tuesday morning before she found Sir Nigel's body. She's a pretty lass, so don't try it on with her. Her husband's a lance-sergeant in the Grenadiers, and he'd probably have you for breakfast. Got that, Catto?'

'Yes, sir. What shall I do if she says she doesn't clean it?'

'You come back here and tell me. It's a simple enough job, Catto, so don't stand there looking blank, and don't waste all day getting there. Report back to me when you've done, and if I'm not here I'll be in the downstairs bar of the Red Lion.'

'Yes, sir,' said Catto, and still failing to see the point of the DDI's instruction, he fled.

'By the way, Marriott, where's that bold detective Drew? Do they have Saturdays off, these Special Branch chaps?'

'No, sir, he was in earlier, but he said he had to report to Superintendent Quinn at nine o'clock.'

Catto eventually returned at gone midday, by which time Hardcastle and Marriott were ensconced in the Red Lion.

'I've been to see Mrs Johnson, sir,' said Catto, pushing his way through the Red Lion's clientele, most of whom were detectives from Scotland Yard.

'I should hope you have, lad. Well?'

'Mrs Johnson said that she always cleans the fingerplate, sir, but she didn't do so on Tuesday morning, on account of having been overcome at finding Sir Nigel lying there dead, sir.'

Hardcastle took a deep draught of his ale, and surveyed the young detective. 'That all?'

'Only one thing, sir.'

'Well, spit it out, or do I have to guess?'

'Er, no, sir. She said as how she always cleans the finger-plates on both sides of the door last of all. It's because she said that she goes out of the room by Sir Nigel's main door, and cleans them on the way out.'

'Good,' said Hardcastle. 'Well, don't stand there, lad. You must have work to do. And if you think I'm going to buy you a pint, you're sadly mistaken. It ain't Christmas.'

'Does that help, sir?' asked Marriott, once Catto had departed.

'It might do,' said Hardcastle. 'It might mean that the fingerprints are those of our man, but I'm not one to count my chickens before they're hatched.'

'No, sir,' said Marriott, well knowing this to be true.

'Right,' said Hardcastle, finishing his beer, 'I think we'll have the rest of the weekend off. I'll see you on Monday. My regards to Mrs Marriott.'

'Thank you, sir, and mine to Mrs H.'

Hardcastle caught a tram from Bridge Street, and arrived at his home in Kennington Road at just after two o'clock. But a quiet afternoon was not to be.

He let himself in with his latchkey, hung his bowler and umbrella on the hatstand in the small hall, and glanced in the mirror to smooth his hair.

'You're home early, Ernie,' said his wife Alice, as he entered the sitting room.

'Yes, well I—' Hardcastle stopped in mid-sentence, and stared at the woman seated in his armchair. She was at least seventy, and was attired in a black bombazine dress and a black straw hat. Her feet were shod in what were plainly army boots.

'This is Madame Tondeleir, Ernie.'

'Oh, how d'you do,' said Hardcastle, wondering what the hell this woman was doing in his house, and more particularly in his chair.

'How do you do, *m'sieur*?' said Madame Tondeleir haltingly, and gravely nodded her head.

'Madame is Belgian, father,' said Hardcastle's daughter Kitty. She was still wearing her uniform, having taken a job as a conductress with the London General Omnibus Company, much against her father's wishes. 'She speaks Flemish, but manages quite a bit of English. She is also able to understand some of my schoolgirl French.'

'What schoolgirl French?' demanded Hardcastle. 'What are you talking about?'

'I learned French when I was at school, father,' said Kitty.

'Did you? I didn't know that.'

'You're never here to find out, are you, Ernest?' said Alice, the use of his full name implying a mild reproof. 'Madame Tondeleir lived in Ypres originally, but she was forced to move when the shelling started.'

Madame Tondeleir nodded. 'I carry my possessions on old pram and go to Vlamertinge,' she said in heavily accented broken English. 'But the Boche starting reaching there with their guns. You understand?'

'Yes, I do,' said Hardcastle, who had closely followed the progress of the war on a map that had been provided by the *Daily Mail*.

'So then I move again to Poperinge. You know this place?'

'I know *of* it, Madame,' said Hardcastle, but the difference between knowing a place and knowing of it eluded the Belgian woman. 'It's where the Reverend Clayton has his Toc H.' An Australian clergyman, Captain the Reverend Philip Clayton – better known as 'Tubby' – had set up an interdenominational meeting place in Poperinge called Talbot House. But it soon became known universally as Toc H, from the signallers' phonetic alphabet for TH, and is there to this day.

'Yes, yes, the Toc H,' said Madame Tondeleir nodding, and smiling for the first time. 'But I think the war gets closer, so I manage to get to England as refugee.'

'Well done,' said Hardcastle, for want of a better thing to say.

'There are quite a few Belgians here now, Ernie, in a hostel near Lambeth town hall,' said Alice. 'The vicar of St Mark, down the road, asked us to entertain some of them for a meal whenever we could. Madame Tondeleir, Kitty and I have just had lunch. Have you eaten, dear?'

'Had a pie and a pint at the Red Lion,' said Hardcastle tersely.

'That's all right, then.'

The conversation, difficult though it was, carried on for an hour or so, with Alice telling Madame Tondeleir about London.

'Is your husband with you, Madame?' asked Hardcastle.

Madame Tondeleir looked immeasurably sad, and shook her head. 'He died before the war,' she said. 'I have a son, but I do not know where he is. He is a lawyer in Ypres, but the law courts have been smashed down. I have not seen him since.' But there was no other sign of grief, and the old lady sat staring at the empty fireplace.

'Madame's daughter is here though, Ernie,' said Alice. 'She's working with the Belgian Surgical Depot at Mulberry Walk in Chelsea.' She glanced at her own daughter. 'Perhaps you'd make us a cup of tea, Kitty.'

'I'll go out and get a paper,' said Hardcastle. 'I'll be back for tea.'

Ten minutes later, Kitty came into the room bearing a large tray on which there were tea things and a large fruitcake.

'We were lucky to get the makings for that,' said Alice, but immediately regretted it. Such shortages were nothing compared with the privations that Madame Tondeleir and her family had suffered.

The awkward silence was broken by the return of Hardcastle.

'Anything fresh in the paper, Ernie?' asked Alice.

'They're proposing to give the Irish home rule,' said Hardcastle, 'and set up a government in Dublin. It'll be for the whole of Ireland except the six counties of Ulster, and it's only going to last until the end of the war.' Holding the newspaper in one hand, he gestured at the article with the other. 'After that, they'll make permanent arrangements.' He scoffed and tossed the newspaper on to a table. 'If that's not storing up trouble, I don't know what is,' he said scathingly. 'Oh, and the Americans have arrived. At least, their flotilla has been sighted offshore, on their way to France.'

'Americans?' Madame Tondeleir took a sudden interest.

'Yes, Madame,' said Hardcastle, 'they're joining in the war, thank God. With them on our side, it won't be too long before we beat old Fritz. They've got a good army.' He rubbed his hands together, and glanced at the tea tray. 'Ah, I see you've managed to get some ginger snaps, Alice.'

'So,' cried Kitty. 'The Yanks are coming.'

'Where on earth did you get an awful expression like that, Kitty?' Hardcastle frowned at his eldest daughter.

Kitty laughed gaily. 'Oh, father, don't you know? It's from a new song that's come out, called *Over There*. I've got the sheet music upstairs.' She gestured towards the piano. 'I'll play it for you if you like.'

'I don't think that'll be necessary,' said Hardcastle, trying to be the stern father, but his attempt at paternal severity was ruined somewhat by Alice's laughter.

SIX

Hardcastle and Marriott arrived at West Norwood at two o'clock on the Monday afternoon, thirty minutes ahead of the time scheduled for Sir Nigel Strang's burial. The DDI always liked to watch what he described as the 'comings-and-goings' at funerals.

At exactly half past two, a glass-sided hearse, drawn by four horses, entered the cemetery. The hearse was followed by four broughams, each with a pair of horses. It was obvious that no expense had been spared.

The mourners – a substantial number of the great and the good – filed along the broad path into one of the two chapels that were set among trees at the top of sloping lawns. It was a beautiful sunny day, with sufficient breeze to keep everyone cool without ruffling the hats of the ladies.

Bringing up the rear of the main party, Hardcastle and Marriott were given an order of service by Hobson, the butler, who was acting as one of the ushers.

'This here planting must've cost a pretty penny, Hobson,' said Hardcastle irreverently.

'Nigh on sixty pounds, sir,' whispered Hobson in reply. 'The very best that Harrods could provide.'

The two detectives found seats in the back row of pews, and carefully surveyed those who had come to pay their last respects.

'Don't see anyone who looks out of place, sir,' said Marriott.

'Nor me,' said Hardcastle. 'Just a group of friends, relatives and civil servants, I suppose.'

'That's interesting though, sir,' said Marriott, glancing sideways. 'Unless I'm much mistaken that's Daisy Johnson.'

The woman, suitably dressed entirely in black, but nonetheless attractive for all that, was tiptoeing past the end of the pew occupied by the two police officers. After some hesitation, she seated herself a row or two behind the main body of mourners.

'Well, well,' said Hardcastle, 'for a woman who's probably never set eyes on Sir Nigel – apart from when he was dead – it strikes me as great devotion to have travelled all the way here from Wild Street by tram.'

'If she came by tram, sir,' said Marriott.

'Well, I don't see the high and mighty Lady Strang offering her a lift in one of them fancy carriages, do you, Marriott?'

Marriott smiled at Hardcastle's customary perversity, but remained silent. What the DDI had said, however, was true; there was no way a carriage would have gone from Dulwich Village to West Norwood via Wild Street.

The service seemed interminable, and Dr Addison's eulogy went on for some time. But at last the pallbearers were able to carry the coffin out to the cemetery, and to the place where Sir Nigel was, at last, to be laid to rest.

The clergyman intoned the usual words as the coffin was lowered, and the obligatory handful of earth was thrown on to it, and at last the congregation began to disperse. During the final part of the ritual, Hardcastle spotted Daisy Johnson standing alone at some distance from the official party, a handkerchief to her face.

'She seems a bit upset about this business, sir,' said Marriott.

'Perhaps he was in the habit of giving her a good Christmas box,' said Hardcastle cynically.

The two detectives walked to the cemetery gates, and stood to one side, waiting until the mourners drove past in their carriages. With a disdainful lift of her chin, the heavily veiled Lady Strang glanced out of the window, and stared at Hardcastle.

The last to leave was Daisy Johnson.

'Hello, Mrs Johnson,' said Hardcastle, as the ministry cleaner walked past him.

'Oh!' Daisy seemed surprised to see the two police officers.

'I didn't think I'd see you here.'

'It's only right and proper that I should pay my last respects, Inspector.' Daisy paused only briefly, making it obvious that she had no desire to engage in a lengthy conversation.

'Yes, I suppose so,' muttered Hardcastle, half to himself,

as he watched the trim figure walk out of the gates. But
turning to Marriott, he added, 'There's more to her than
meets the eye. She's a voluptuous little hussy.' And with that
enigmatic statement, he strode out to Norwood High Street,
and hailed a cab.

'What d'you reckon was the reason for her coming here,
sir?' asked Marriott, somewhat confused by what the DDI
had said.

'Time will tell, time will tell,' said Hardcastle, further
confusing Marriott, as they clambered into the taxi. 'Scotland
Yard, cabbie,' he said, and turning to Marriott, added, 'Tell
'em Cannon Row and half the time you'll finish up at Cannon
Street in the City.'

'Yes, sir,' said Marriott wearily.

'I'm wondering what she was doing there, Marriott,' mused
Hardcastle when he and Marriott arrived back at Cannon
Row police station. It was obvious that Daisy Johnson's atten-
dance at Sir Nigel's funeral was still vexing him.

But Marriott had known his DDI to go off at an irrelevant
tangent many times in the past. And only rarely had he been
able to draw him back to the main line of enquiry.

'Perhaps what she said was the truth, sir,' suggested
Marriott. 'She might be deeply religious for all we know,
and thought it was the right and proper thing to do.'

'Maybe she's one of those people who make a habit of
going to funerals,' growled Hardcastle, 'but I think we'll have
another chat with her tomorrow morning.'

However, by next morning, Hardcastle had changed his mind
about interviewing Daisy Johnson again.

'I've come to the conclusion that we're not going to get
much out of the civil servants in Strang's department,
Marriott,' said Hardcastle thoughtfully, as he filled his pipe.
'Leastways, to find out what sort of man he was.'

'I don't see who else we can ask, sir.'

'If it's anything like the Metropolitan Police,' began
Hardcastle, having got his pipe well alight, 'they'll get a
transfer every time they get made up. When you got made
first-class sergeant, you were transferred here from Bow

Street on E Division. And that,' he added jocularly, 'gave you the opportunity of working with me and learning how to solve murders.'

'Yes, sir.' Marriott was unsure whether that had been to his advantage.

'Now then, if we can find out where Sir Nigel was stationed, so to speak, before he turned up at the Ministry of Munitions, we might just find out a bit more about him.'

'But how do we go about that, sir?'

'I reckon a word with that Sinclair Cobb fellow. He seemed more human than the rest of 'em.'

The affable Sinclair Cobb stood up as the detectives were shown into his office. 'I suppose we'll have to get used to you chaps showing up here, Inspector.'

'You will, Mr Cobb, at least until I see the murderer dangling at the end of a rope,' said Hardcastle bluntly, 'but I shan't take up too much of your time this morning. In fact I have just one question.'

'Fire away,' said Cobb.

'Which department was Sir Nigel in before he came here?'

'Oh, that's easy. He was deputy secretary at the Home Office and came here on promotion when this ministry was formed.' Cobb hesitated briefly. 'That would've been in May 1915. Got his K a year later.'

'K is short for knighthood, Marriott.' Hardcastle had noticed the perplexed look on his sergeant's face. Turning back to the assistant secretary, he said, 'Thank you, Mr Cobb, we'll take up no more of your time.' But he stopped at the door of Cobb's office. 'Can you suggest someone I could speak to at the Home Office? Someone who might've known Sir Nigel well, and I don't mean just how good he was as a civil servant.'

'Yes, as a matter of fact, I can. There's a fellow over there by the name of Endicott, Adrian Endicott. He's an assistant secretary, and he and I were at Oxford together. Tell him I sent you, and he'll give you any help he can.'

'I'm much obliged, Mr Cobb.'

*   *   *

It was only a short walk from the Ministry of Munitions to the Home Office in Whitehall. It was an imposing building that had, at the pinnacle of its facade, a statue of Queen Victoria, a smaller version of the one in Queens Gardens opposite Buckingham Palace.

After the usual delay that they always seemed to experience in trying to enter a government building, Hardcastle and Marriott were eventually shown into Adrian Endicott's office.

'Mr Cobb at the Ministry of Munitions suggested you might be able to assist,' said Hardcastle, once he had explained to Endicott the reason for his interest.

'But what can I possibly tell you that Sinclair wasn't able to?' Endicott was about the same age as Cobb, which was not surprising seeing that they had been up at Oxford together. And like Cobb, wore similar clothing: black jacket and striped trousers being the prescribed form of dress.

'I'm interested in what sort of man he was, Mr Endicott. For instance, I'm puzzled as to why Sir Nigel was in his office at twenty to six on Tuesday morning.'

'I don't really see how I can help you over that, Inspector.' Endicott's face assumed a puzzled expression.

Hardcastle related what little he knew of the sequence of events that had resulted in the finding of Sir Nigel's dead body in his office. 'To the best of my knowledge, Mr Endicott, he'd never before worked all night in his office, and, apart from anything else, no one at the ministry knew he was there. Until a cleaner found his dead body, that is.'

'A bit of a rum do, Inspector.'

'Indeed, sir, but I'm trying to find out something about his private life. All I've heard so far is that Sir Nigel was happily married, lived in Dulwich Village, and had two sons in the Grenadier Guards who are at the Front.'

Adrian Endicott looked down, and spent some seconds straightening his blotter so that it aligned with the edge of the desk. 'I think that Nigel was a bit of a ladies' man, Inspector,' he said hesitantly, at last looking up. Although the door to his office was firmly closed, he spoke in hushed tones as though fearful of being overheard.

'What led you to believe that, Mr Endicott?'

'I happened to see him one day walking in St James's Park. It was lunchtime, and he had this charming looking girl with him. They seemed to be enjoying an animated conversation, but I can tell you that the girl was definitely not Rosalind Strang. I've met her two or three times, you see.'

'Have you any idea who this woman was?' asked Hardcastle.

'No, I'm afraid not, other than to say that she appeared some years younger than Nigel.'

'And is that the only occasion you saw Sir Nigel out with a woman who was not his wife, Mr Endicott?'

'Yes.'

'Are you basing your opinion of Sir Nigel being a womaniser on that one sighting of him with another woman?' asked Marriott.

'Not entirely, no.'

Inwardly, Hardcastle was exasperated at Endicott's reluctance to embellish his original allegation, but realised that if he displayed too much impatience, the assistant secretary might clam up altogether.

'So, there's been something else, has there?' asked Hardcastle.

'Nothing that I can put my finger on, Inspector, but generally speaking it was fairly common knowledge around the office. There was another chap here who told me he saw Nigel out with a girl, but from the description it sounded like a different girl.'

'Who was this man?' asked Hardcastle. 'I'd like to have a word with him.'

'I'm afraid that won't be possible, Inspector.'

Hardcastle was about to lose his temper with what he saw as civil service intransigence. 'I should perhaps explain, Mr Endicott—'

'I'm afraid he's dead,' said Endicott. 'He joined the Colours in late nineteen-fifteen and was killed at the Battle of the Somme.'

'I see.' Hardcastle stood up. He had added a little more to his knowledge of Sir Nigel Strang, but nowhere near enough. Furthermore, there could be an innocent explanation for Sir

Nigel having been accompanied by a young woman. She could have been a niece or even a goddaughter. 'Thank you, Mr Endicott. I'll not detain you any longer. If you should remember anything else that might assist me, perhaps you'd let me know at Cannon Row police station. Turn right out of the Home Office and take the first left into Derby Gate. It's opposite New Scotland Yard.'

'Yes, Inspector, we at the Home Office do know where New Scotland Yard is.' Endicott stood up and shook hands.

'We're not getting anywhere with this damned murder, Marriott,' said Hardcastle, once again stating the obvious.

'D'you think there's anything in this suggestion that Strang had an eye for the ladies, sir?'

'Anybody's guess, Marriott. Maybe he had, and that Lady Strang knew about it. She certainly didn't show much sign of grief, either when we told her he'd been topped, or at the funeral. On the other hand she might've enjoyed a bit of nookie herself, not that I can imagine anyone taking a fancy to her. Funny people, the upper classes. I wonder if Hobson kept a list of the people who attended the funeral.'

'What d'you think that might tell us, sir? If he did have a list, that is.'

'We might learn a bit more about Sir Nigel if we talked to some people who were social acquaintances rather than work colleagues.'

Rather than trust what he saw as a delicate enquiry to the telephone, Hardcastle decided to journey once more to Dulwich Village.

'Good afternoon, sir.' Hobson was his usual deferential self. 'Did you wish to see her ladyship?'

'No, it's you I want a word with, Hobson.'

'Very good, sir. Perhaps you'd care to follow me.' Hobson led the two detectives through a door in the corner of the hall, and down a flight of stairs to the kitchen. Opening another door, he showed them into his pantry. 'I hope you don't mind coming in here, sir, but it's out of the way.' It seemed that he had already worked out that Hardcastle wanted to discuss something of a confidential nature.

'Perfectly all right, Hobson,' said Hardcastle, as he and Marriott settled themselves in the armchairs with which Hobson's small office was furnished.

'Perhaps I could interest you in a small libation, gents,' offered Hobson. 'I have a rather fine malt here.'

'That's very generous of you, Hobson,' said Hardcastle, under no illusion but that the whisky came from the stock paid for by Sir Nigel.

The butler busied himself pouring three large measures of Glenlivet, and took a seat behind his desk. 'Now, gentlemen, how may I help you?'

Hardcastle took a sip of his whisky, enjoying it all the more in the knowledge that it would have cost at least five shillings a bottle. 'Did you by any chance make a list of the people attending Sir Nigel's funeral, Hobson?'

'I did indeed, sir. Her ladyship wants to write to each of the mourners expressing her gratitude for their attendance and condolences, and, of course, for the floral tributes.' Hobson opened a drawer of his desk and took out a sheaf of paper. 'Would you care for a copy, sir?'

'Thank you, Hobson, most helpful.' Hardcastle handed the list to Marriott. 'There is one other thing you might be able to help me with,' he said.

'What's that, sir?'

'It's a rather delicate matter, but I've heard that Sir Nigel was seen on occasions in St James's Park with a young lady. I was wondering . . .'

Hobson laughed. 'It was well known that Sir Nigel had an eye for a pretty girl, sir.'

'And did Lady Strang know about it?'

'I daresay she did, sir, but that's the sort of thing that goes on. Even with the royal family, I'm told. But so long as it's kept under wraps, so to speak, there's no harm done, I suppose.'

Hardcastle was surprised that Hobson was so open, but then he wondered if the butler was under notice, given that there would be a radical change in the structure of the household now that Sir Nigel was dead. And that prompted his next question.

'Will you be staying on here, Hobson?'

'I somehow doubt it, sir. As a matter of fact I've allowed my name to be circulated among fellow butlers. It's a sort of freemasonry, you see. Someone somewhere will be wanting a butler, and word of mouth, and the implicit reference that goes with it, is a much better way of securing a position.'

'Is there no danger of you being called up under Lord Derby's conscription scheme?'

'Ah, Lord Derby . . .' Hobson paused to take a sip of his whisky. 'I think it was Field Marshal Haig who likened him to a feather pillow: always bore the mark of the last person who sat on him. But to answer your question, sir, I very much doubt it. I'm getting on for fifty years of age, and I'm married to the cook here, so I'm exempt on two counts.'

'D'you happen to know the names of any of the women with whom Sir Nigel was acquainted, Hobson?'

'If you mean someone he was having an affair with, I could possibly . . .' Hobson paused again. 'If you care to give me that list back, Mr Marriott . . .'

Marriott handed over the list of those who had attended Sir Nigel Strang's funeral.

For a few moments, Hobson studied the list before taking a pencil in a silver case from the pocket of his waistcoat, and putting crosses by two of the names. He handed the list back to Marriott. 'Both married ladies, sir,' he said to Hardcastle, 'but if anyone asks me, I haven't the faintest idea how those crosses got on the list.'

Hardcastle and Marriott finished their whisky, and stood up.

'I'm much obliged to you, Hobson,' said Hardcastle, 'and I hope you find a suitable position.'

'Should you hear of anything, sir, perhaps you'd put in a word. And if it so happens that a butler *and* a cook are required, so much the better.'

'I'll bear it in mind, Hobson, and thank you for the whisky.'

'My pleasure, sir,' said Hobson, and conducted the two detectives back upstairs to the front door.

SEVEN

It was unfortunate that Hardcastle had decided not to interview Daisy Johnson yesterday, but had instead been to see Adrian Endicott at the Home Office.

On Wednesday morning, at about ten thirty, Hardcastle and Marriott were at Bow Street police court in connection with a matter quite unrelated to the murder of Sir Nigel Strang.

It did not take long for their prisoner, a burglar with a lengthy record of previous convictions, to be remanded in custody for a further eight days.

'Now seems to be an opportune moment to call on Mrs Johnson,' said Hardcastle. 'It's only round the corner, and I daresay she's done with cleaning and polishing at the ministry.'

The two detectives walked round to Wild Street, and were confronted by a constable standing at the foot of the staircase that led to the flat in Peabody Buildings shared by Daisy Johnson and her mother, Mrs Harding.

The policeman stepped into Hardcastle's path. 'Can I help you, sir?' he asked.

'I'm DDI Hardcastle of A Division. What are you doing here?'

'May I see your warrant card, sir?'

Hardcastle produced the document, and the policeman saluted. 'All correct, sir.'

'Well, if it's all correct what the blue blazes are you doing here, lad?' Hardcastle asked again, as ever irritated by the obligatory but meaningless form of reporting.

'There's been a murder, sir.'

Hardcastle frowned. 'Who's been topped?'

'A Mrs Daisy Johnson, sir. Quite messy so they tell me. The divisional surgeon and the DDI's up there now.'

Despite his bulk, Hardcastle took the stairs two at a time, pausing only to wave his warrant card at another policeman stationed outside the door of the Johnson flat.

Frederick Metcalfe, E Division's divisional detective inspector, looked up as Hardcastle and Marriott entered the room. 'Hello, Ernie. What brings you here?'

'Your murder, Fred.' Hardcastle outlined his interest in Daisy Johnson.

Metcalfe ran a hand round his chin. 'D'you reckon there's a connection, Ernie?'

'It's a damned funny coincidence if there isn't,' said Hardcastle. 'What are the circumstances?'

'The dead woman's mother went out to do a bit of shopping at just before eight this morning. When she got back she found Daisy Johnson dead on the floor of the kitchen, and Mrs Johnson's two kids yelling their heads off.'

'What happened next, sir?' asked Marriott.

'Ah, Marriott, I didn't see you there. Any time you want to come back to E Division, you'll be welcome.'

'You can't have him,' said Hardcastle bluntly. 'But you were going to tell me what happened, Fred.'

'Mrs Harding,' said Metcalfe, 'that's the girl's mother, went screaming out of the flat, shouting for a copper. The PC reports that he was called by her at ten minutes to nine.'

'Where is she now, Fred?' asked Hardcastle.

'Charing Cross Hospital,' said Metcalfe. 'No sooner had a PC come running than she collapsed with the shock. Suspected heart attack apparently. I've had the two children taken to the nick for the matron to look after.'

'Was Mrs Johnson here when Mrs Harding left the flat to go shopping?' Hardcastle asked.

'No. I gather from neighbours that she normally got in from her cleaning job at about half past eight.'

'So whoever topped her either struck lucky or knew her timetable,' commented Hardcastle.

He's stating the obvious again, thought Marriott.

'Looks like it, Ernie. He was lucky not to meet Mrs Harding on the stairs, given that it all happened within a twenty-minute bracket, so to speak.'

'Perhaps she did,' said Hardcastle drily. 'Any indication how the murderer got in?'

'There's no sign of a forced entry. Either he had a key, or Daisy let him in, whoever he was. On the other hand perhaps they're the sort of trusting people who never locked their door anyway.'

'I suppose you've not been able to question Mrs Harding, Fred.'

'No, and it doesn't look as though we'll be able to. They reckon she's unlikely to survive.'

'Has she got a husband?'

'There's no sign of one, but I've got a couple of DCs knocking on doors, to see what they can find out.'

Hardcastle glanced into the kitchen. It was obvious that whoever had murdered Daisy Johnson had launched a savage attack. There was a considerable amount of blood on the floor, and the dead woman's white blouse was almost completely crimson.

'Any weapon, Fred?'

'Haven't found one yet. It looks like whoever done for her took it with him. And I doubt we'll have any useable fingerprints to go on either. The bugger probably wore gloves. He must've been covered in Daisy's blood, and I've alerted E Division and surrounding stations to look out for a blood-soaked man, but I doubt they'll find him. Could be miles away by now.'

'Well, the best of luck, Fred. Keep me informed of any developments, will you?'

'Yes, and if you come across anything in your topping that might help me in mine, let me know.' Metcalfe stuck his hands in his pockets and looked round the room, a hopeless expression on his face.

By the time that Hardcastle and Marriott returned to Cannon Row police station, Detective Sergeant Drew was waiting.

'Ah, Drew, I've got another titbit for you to tell your guv'nor,' said Hardcastle, and went on to give the Special Branch officer the details of the murder of Daisy Johnson.

'D'you think there's a connection, sir?' asked Drew, posing the same question that DDI Metcalfe had asked.

'Anyone's guess,' said Hardcastle, 'but maybe Mr Quinn and you clever fellows over at the Yard can come up with something that'll help me.'

'Seems a strange business, sir,' said Marriott, once DS

Drew had departed. 'Coming so soon after Sir Nigel was killed, I mean.'

'It certainly ain't the straightforward sort of topping I'm used to, Marriott. I don't know what it is about this war, but I'll be bloody glad when it's over. Then we can get back to dealing with ordinary decent murders.' Hardcastle took off his spats and shoes, and began to massage his feet. 'This one looks as though it's shaping up like the topping of that bloody woman Rose Drummond last year. Every time Special Branch puts their oar in, it starts to get complicated.'

Marriott remained silent; he had no desire to encourage one of his chief's diatribes.

'Right, Marriott,' continued Hardcastle, 'I think it's time we had a look at those two women that our friend Hobson marked up on the list of people who were at Strang's funeral. Got it there, have you?'

'Yes, sir.' Marriott produced the list and handed to the DDI.

Hardcastle spent a few minutes poring over the names. 'Mrs Selina Tait and Mrs Catherine Chandler,' he said. 'Now I wonder why they turned up at Strang's planting on their tod, Marriott.'

'A lot of husbands are serving, sir. Perhaps they're at the Front.'

'And that would make it very easy for Sir Nigel to visit them without the husbands interfering, and without any eyebrows being raised. Particularly after dark. I think we'll have some enquiries made, Marriott. Who have we got available?'

As the first-class sergeant, Marriott oversaw the day-to-day work of the detectives, and knew the whereabouts of each officer at any given time. 'I'm afraid Catto's the only one in the office at the moment, sir.'

'Oh well, I suppose he'll have to do. Fetch him in here,' said Hardcastle, as he replaced his shoes and spats.

Moments later the nervous figure of Detective Constable Henry Catto hovered in the doorway of Hardcastle's office.

'Come in, Catto, for God's sake. I'm not going to eat you.'

'Yes, sir. Er, no, sir.'

'Now then, Sergeant Marriott will give you two names

and addresses. Find out as much as you can about them, and as soon as you can. But don't go asking their neighbours. Understood?'

'Yes, sir.'

'Well, don't stand there, boy, get on with it.'

Fifteen minutes after Catto's departure, DS Drew returned.

'Well, Drew, and what did Mr Quinn have to say about our latest topping?'

'He was very interested, sir,' said Drew guardedly, 'and he'd like to see you at your earliest convenience.'

When a superintendent demanded to see a DDI at his earliest convenience, it meant immediately. With a sigh, Hardcastle took his bowler hat from the hatstand, and picked up his umbrella.

'It's not raining, sir,' ventured Drew.

'But it might be on my way back,' snapped Hardcastle.

'A pretty kettle of fish, Mr Hardcastle,' said Quinn. 'What d'you make of it?'

'I'm sure there's a connection, sir, but at the moment I can't for the life of me see what it is.'

'Colonel Kell of MI5 is interested in the outcome, as I told you the last time you were here.' Quinn stroked his beard. 'He seems to think there is some espionage involvement in Sir Nigel's murder. What's your view?'

'It's a possibility, sir, but nothing was taken. The safe was still locked when Sir Nigel's body was found, and no documents of any description were missing from anywhere else.'

'Have you considered the possibility that your murderer was disturbed, possibly by this cleaning woman, Daisy Johnson. Fearing being identified, he might have made a point of searching her out and killing her.'

'I have to admit that the thought had crossed my mind, sir,' said Hardcastle who, until then, had not thought of it at all. 'Unfortunately we aren't able to interrogate Mrs Johnson now.'

'No, but perhaps that should have been put to her the first time she was interviewed by your Detective Sergeant Marriott.'

It was a mild form of censure that did not please Hardcastle. He was tempted to comment that it was easy to be wise with hindsight, but did not think that Superintendent Quinn would be amused by such an impertinent comment.

'Mrs Johnson was adamant that she found Sir Nigel Strang's dead body at twenty minutes to six, sir, and Dr Spilsbury assured me that Strang had probably been dead some two hours or so before the discovery of the body.'

Quinn appeared unimpressed by the pathologist's opinion, mainly because it conflicted with his own theory. 'Very well, Mr Hardcastle, but make sure that Drew is privy to anything that might be of interest to Special Branch.'

'Yes, sir.' Hardcastle left Quinn's office quietly simmering with rage at the superintendent's criticism. 'I wonder when he last investigated a murder,' he muttered, as he descended the broad steps of New Scotland Yard, and returned to his police station.

Much to Hardcastle's surprise, Catto knocked on the DDI's office door at half past eight the following morning, just as the DDI was starting a discussion with Marriott about what to do next.

'Well?' barked Hardcastle.

'I thought I'd better report what I've found out so far about the two addresses, sir,' said Catto hesitantly.

'Then report, Catto. I haven't got all day.'

'Mrs Catherine Chandler lives at seventeen Belgrave Square on Gerald Road nick's ground, and is married to Major Vernon Chandler of the Royal Garrison Artillery. Mrs Selina Tait's address is number five Heath Road, Hampstead. Her husband is Lieutenant Commander Archibald Tait of the Royal Navy.'

Hardcastle leaned back in his chair, and for a few seconds gazed at the DC. 'You're coming on quite well, Catto,' he said, and that, from Hardcastle, was praise indeed. 'Did you happen to find out whether these two women's husbands were at home, or are they off fighting the Hun?'

'I'm afraid I don't know that, sir,' said Catto, fearing that he was to be admonished for not having done his job thoroughly.

'No, I suppose not,' said Hardcastle mildly. 'All right, lad, that's all.'

'Thank you, sir,' said a relieved Catto, and fled to the comparative safety of the detectives' office.

'He found that out a bit *jildi*, Marriott,' said the DDI. 'And I'll bet he chatted to the neighbours despite me telling him not to. Fetch him back in here.'

'You wanted me, sir?' Catto reappeared, now more nervous than ever.

'How did you find that information so quickly, Catto? Did you interview the neighbours despite me telling you not to?'

'No, sir, I called at the two addresses Sergeant Marriott gave me, sir. But I didn't make enquiries as a police officer, sir. I pretended I was from the local council collecting names in case of an air raid, sir. So we'd be able to discover who was missing like. If their house got Zeppelined, sir.'

Hardcastle remained silent for some seconds, during which time Catto thought he was about to be despatched to the clothing store at Lambeth to be kitted out with uniform. 'Right, Catto, clear off,' he said eventually.

'Yes, sir.' And once again Catto removed himself from the DDI's presence as quickly as possible.

'What d'you think about that, Marriott?' asked Hardcastle.

'Well, sir, you didn't tell him not to call at the subjects' addresses, only not to call on the neighbours.'

'Yes, so I did. He's a cunning bugger is Catto, and resourceful, too. But don't tell him. It don't do to have detectives with swollen heads.' And Hardcastle roared with laughter.

Hardcastle decided to call first at the Belgrave Square address of Catherine Chandler, on the grounds that it was nearer – much nearer – than the Taits' address in Hampstead. It turned out to be a good decision.

It was half past seven when Hardcastle knocked at number seventeen.

A trim housemaid opened the door. 'Good evening, sir.' She glanced nervously at the two detectives.

'Is Mrs Chandler at home, lass?' asked Hardcastle.

'I'll enquire, sir. Who shall I say it is?'

'The police, but tell her there's no need for alarm.'

Hardcastle was aware that the unexpected arrival of police often heralded news of a death, particularly now that the war had been going on for two and a half years.

Hardcastle and Marriott were eventually shown into the sitting room.

Mrs Catherine Chandler was an attractive woman of about thirty with long Titian hair, and wore a full-length, black velvet dress unrelieved by any colours at all. Hardcastle wondered briefly if she was in mourning for her husband.

'Good evening, ma'am. I'm Divisional Detective Inspector Hardcastle of the Whitehall Division, and this here is Detective Sergeant Marriott.'

Catherine Chandler inclined her head, and raised an eyebrow. 'If it was my husband you were hoping to see, Inspector, I'm afraid he's with the army in Flanders.'

'No, ma'am, it was you I wanted to talk to.'

'Oh, how intriguing.' She laughed gaily at the thought that the police wanted to interview her, rather than her husband. 'Do sit down, both of you. May I offer you something to drink?'

'No thank you,' said Hardcastle.

'Well now, what can I do for you?'

'I'm investigating the murder of Sir Nigel Strang, ma'am.'

'Oh, of course. I was at his funeral.'

'Yes, I know.'

'And I suppose you're speaking to everyone who was there, are you?'

'That's correct, ma'am,' said Hardcastle, although he had no intention of interviewing anyone else but Selina Tait. At least, not yet. 'How well did you know Sir Nigel?' he asked, and was gratified to see that Catherine Chandler coloured slightly.

'I, er, well, that is to say my husband and I met him at a dinner party arranged by a mutual friend.' The woman flicked open a fan and waved it languidly in front of her face.

'But you said your husband was in Flanders.' It was obvious to Hardcastle that he had asked an embarrassing question. But he was a shrewd interrogator, and knew that if he waited long enough, the woman would feel impelled to say something further. Probably something that would implicate her.

'Yes, but he was home on leave at the time.' Mrs Chandler dropped the fan on to the seat beside her.

'And when was this?'

'About a year ago, I suppose. I can't really remember precisely.'

'And has your husband been home since then?'

'No, but I don't really see what this has to do with Sir Nigel's murder, Inspector.'

'I was merely wondering if he would be able to tell us anything about Sir Nigel,' said Hardcastle smoothly. 'But failing that, what do you know about him?'

'Such as?' Catherine Chandler adopted a haughty attitude.

'If I might take you into my confidence, Mrs Chandler, I've heard that Sir Nigel . . . how can I put it, now? Yes, that he enjoyed the company of ladies.' Hardcastle looked at Catherine Chandler with an unwavering gaze.

'I believe that's so.'

Again Hardcastle waited silently, his face betraying a questioning expression.

'All right, so I had an affair with him. Is that what you wanted to hear? That's what this is all about, isn't it?' Her face remained expressionless, but the tension in her clasped hands indicated hostility.

'How long did it last, Mrs Chandler?'

'About six months.'

'From when to when?'

'It finished last month.'

'Did Sir Nigel tell you how he explained his absences to his wife?' asked Hardcastle.

'He told her he was working late at the office. Apparently it happened quite often. Sometimes he was so late that he would stay at his club. At least, that's what he told Rosalind.'

'You knew his wife, did you?'

'Of course. I told you that my husband and I met the Strangs at a dinner party arranged by mutual friends.'

'Might I ask who those friends were?'

'If you must. They were Archie and Selina Tait. They live in Hampstead. Archie's in the navy.'

'And Mrs Tait was at the funeral too,' said Hardcastle.

'How did you know that?' demanded Catherine.

'I was there,' Hardcastle reminded her, but wondered whether she was being deliberately obtuse.

'Oh really?' she said offhandedly. 'I didn't see you.'

'Can you think of anyone who might've wanted to kill Sir Nigel, Mrs Chandler?' asked Hardcastle. 'Did he ever mention anyone?'

'I can't imagine that anyone would've wanted to harm him. He was a sweet man.'

Yes, thought Hardcastle, *sweet he may have been, but he was not above taking advantage of your husband's absence while he was fighting for his country.*

'One other question, Mrs Chandler,' asked Marriott. 'How often did you meet Sir Nigel?'

Catherine seemed surprised that the question had come from the sergeant, and glanced at him with a look of disdain. 'About once a week,' she said.

'And he came here, did he?'

'Yes, of course he did.' Catherine withdrew a handker-chief, dabbed lightly at her lips and faced Hardcastle again. 'Now, if that's all, Inspector, I'm expecting a visitor.'

'Yes, ma'am, that's all, thank you,' said Hardcastle, as he and Marriott stood up. 'For the present.'

Catherine leaned across to a side table, and rang a small brass bell. 'These gentlemen are leaving, Beryl,' she said brusquely, when the maid appeared.

'That's ruffled her feathers a bit,' said Hardcastle wryly, as he and Marriott walked across Belgrave Square.

'D'you reckon she'll be on the telephone to her friend Selina Tait, sir?'

'Only if she knows that Mrs Tait was having an affair with Sir Nigel as well, if she was,' said Hardcastle. 'But she's hardly likely to tell Mrs Tait what she's just told us.'

'When d'you propose seeing Mrs Tait, sir?'

'Tomorrow evening, I think. That'll give her time to cook up an interesting story, providing Mrs Chandler has been on the telephone to her by then. And somehow, I don't think she could resist a bit of gossip.'

'D'you think that Major Chandler might have topped Strang, sir?' suggested Marriott. 'I should think any soldier in Flanders who'd been cuckolded would take it pretty hard.'

Hardcastle stopped, and turned to face his sergeant. 'I was just thinking that myself, Marriott,' he said.

EIGHT

L ate on Thursday morning, Hardcastle received a surprising telephone call from Joshua Harvey, the DDI of the P or Camberwell Division.

'It's about the murder you're dealing with, Ernie. This morning a PC patrolling Dulwich Village was stopped in the street by a Lady Strang who lives nearby. The PC ascertained that it was a house called The Lodge.'

'What did she want, Josh?' asked Hardcastle.

'She said she had important information to give to police about the murder of her husband. The PC reported it at East Dulwich police station, and it eventually reached me. I went to see her and told her that the matter was being dealt with on A Division, and that she needed to go to Cannon Row to speak to you.'

'What did she say to that?'

'She said she had no intention of travelling to Westminster, and if you were interested you should call on her at Dulwich.'

'Did she indeed? In that case, I suppose I'd better go and see her ladyship.'

'Good afternoon, sir,' said Hobson, a black armband on his sleeve. 'If you'd be so good as to follow me, her ladyship is expecting you.' He opened the door of the sitting room. 'Inspector Hardcastle and Sergeant Marriott, m'lady,' he announced.

It was almost as if Lady Strang had not moved from where she had been sitting on the occasion of Hardcastle's last visit. The only variation in her apparel was that she was now dressed in unrelieved black.

'Good afternoon, gentlemen. Do take a seat.'

'I understand you have something to tell me about the murder of your late husband, Lady Strang.'

'My husband was a philanderer, Inspector.' Rosalind Strang's face betrayed no emotion at this revelation, and it was obvious that there was to be no small talk before she got to the matter in hand.

'Really, ma'am?' Hardcastle contrived an expression that implied this was news to him. But looking at Lady Strang, he was not at all surprised that her husband looked elsewhere for sexual pleasure.

'I was always aware of his affairs, even though he thought I knew nothing of them. I didn't mind as long as he was discreet about them. But a woman can always tell, you know.'

'I'm sorry to hear that, ma'am.' But Hardcastle believed her; he knew that his wife Alice would be instantly aware if he started playing fast and loose. Not that there was much chance of that.

'But when I saw Catherine Chandler and Selina Tait at the funeral, I realised that they were probably two of his fancy women.'

'How can you be so sure?' asked Hardcastle.

'But why else would they have been there, Inspector? They weren't close friends of ours. In fact, we only met the Chandlers once. As for the Taits, Mrs Tait and I met through a knitting circle that was making socks and mufflers for the troops, so you couldn't really call us friends. Nevertheless, Selina Tait invited Nigel and me to dinner one evening, and the other guests were Vernon and Catherine Chandler. It was quite a jolly little party but, later on, I noticed how much attention my husband was paying to both Mrs Chandler and Mrs Tait. He was flirting and making slightly risqué comments to them when he thought I couldn't hear.'

'When did this dinner take place, ma'am?' asked Marriott, looking up from his pocketbook.

'About a year ago, young man.' Rosalind Strang afforded Marriott but a fleeting glance. 'At the Taits' house in Hampstead.'

'But why d'you think this has anything to do with your husband's murder, Lady Strang?' asked Hardcastle, trying hard to look taken aback by what the woman was telling him.

'I should have thought that fairly obvious, Inspector. Vernon Chandler is in the army in Flanders, and Archie Tait is at sea in an ironclad. I can tell you this much: soldiers and sailors who are on active service do not look kindly upon civil servants in any event; they think they're scrimshankers, and derisively call them "frockcoats", along with politicians who they class in the same category. And if one of them discovers that his wife is having an affair with a civil servant or, for that matter, anybody who is serving his country at home, he is likely to take some extreme action.'

'Are you suggesting that—?'

'I most certainly am, Inspector. I suggest you speak to Vernon Chandler and Archie Tait, because I'm sure you'll find that one of them murdered my husband.'

'How can you be so sure that your husband was having an affair, particularly with the two women you mentioned?'

'Nigel frequently worked late, Inspector, and when he did, he stayed at his club – the Athenaeum – or so he said. But several times I telephoned him there, only to be told that he was *not* staying at the club that night. Furthermore, they said he was not a member.' Lady Strang paused to make clear her next point. 'Neither was he at the office. In fact, young Rawlings, my husband's secretary, told me on some of those occasions that my husband had actually gone home. Well, that was nonsense, of course.'

'Did you challenge your husband about it?'

'Certainly not. There was no point. Having affairs is something that men do. As I said just now, one expects discretion in these matters, and fortunately there was never any hint of scandal. Nigel knew only too well that the slightest indication of an affair with a married woman would have spelt the end of his career.' Lady Strang let out a sigh. 'It happens, Inspector,' she said. 'After all, the late king was doing it all the time. Did you know that Rules Restaurant in Maiden Lane even had a private entrance constructed so that when King Edward and his paramour of the moment were on their way up to a private room, they would not be subjected to the gaze of the restaurant's clientele?'

'No, I didn't know that, ma'am,' said Hardcastle, and did not believe it anyway. But talk of private entrances caused him to wonder whether Sir Nigel Strang had ever been foolish enough to entertain a lady in his office. 'Well, thank you for being so candid, Lady Strang, and I will certainly act on the information you have given me.'

'Hobson will see you out, Inspector.' Lady Strang swept across the room and tugged at the velvet cord that would summon the butler.

As the two detectives left Lady Strang's house, Hardcastle flagged down a cab. 'Heath Road, Hampstead, cabbie,' he said.

'D'you reckon there's anything in the widow's suggestion, sir?' asked Marriott, as he and the DDI settled themselves.

'There might be, Marriott, but there again there might not be. But there's one way of finding out. If, at the time of the murder, Major Chandler was in Flanders, and Lieutenant Commander Tait was at sea, that rules them out, don't it? But at least what Lady Strang told us makes interviewing Selina Tait that much easier.'

When her maid announced the arrival of the police, Selina Tait crossed the room with hand outstretched. In a 'princess' robe of peach silk with a daring décolletage, she looked to be in her mid-thirties. With blonde hair that was bobbed and loosely waved in a style that was becoming increasingly popular, she seemed to epitomise what some fashion magazines were calling 'the modern woman'. Hardcastle knew instinctively that his wife Alice would not have approved.

'Good afternoon, gentlemen.' Selina Tait shook hands with the two detectives.

'Good afternoon, ma'am. I'm Divisional Detective Inspector Hardcastle of the Whitehall Division, and this here is my assistant, Detective Sergeant Marriott.'

'How d'you do? Please sit down, and tell me how I can help you. Would you care for some tea? Yes, I'm sure you would.' Selina did not wait for an answer, and looked at the maid. 'Some tea, please, Kitty, and I'm sure these gentlemen would like some biscuits.'

'Very good, ma'am.' The maid bobbed and left the room.

'I suppose you've come to see me about poor Nigel Strang.'

'Yes. I understand you had an affair with him.'

In contrast to Catherine Chandler's reluctant admission of adultery, Selina Tait merely smiled. 'How did you know?' she asked.

'Lady Strang told me,' said Hardcastle.

'Did she really? The bitch. But how did she know?'

'She said that a woman always knows,' responded Hardcastle.

Selina Tait gave a gay little laugh. 'It's true that Nigel and I did have an affair.' She paused to look at Hardcastle under lowered eyelashes. 'I think you'll find that he had an affair with Catherine Chandler, too. And probably quite a few more. He was very much the Lothario, was Nigel.'

'I take it that your husband was away, Mrs Tait.'

'Of course he was. Archie's in the Royal Navy on one of those ghastly ironclads. I haven't seen him for, what, about ten months? Maybe a year. And a girl does have needs, you know.'

Kitty arrived with a tray of tea, and placed it on an occasional table that she moved closer to her mistress.

'Shall I serve it, ma'am?'

'No, Kitty, I'll take care of it, thank you.' Selina busied herself pouring the tea and handing it round. 'But I suppose that, as a policeman, you don't regard that sort of thing as acceptable behaviour.'

'It's of no concern to me, ma'am,' said Hardcastle. In fact, he had often been obliged to point out that the police were not judges of morals. 'But finding out who murdered Sir Nigel Strang is. You say that your husband has been away for ten months or so.'

'That's correct.' Selina took a sip of her tea and placed the cup and saucer on the table. 'Good heavens,' she said suddenly, 'you don't think that Archie had anything to do with it, do you?' She laughed at the idea.

'I can see that he didn't,' said Hardcastle, but he had no intention of taking Selina Tait's word for it.

'Did Sir Nigel always come here for his assignations, Mrs Tait?' asked Marriott.

'Yes.' Selina looked at Marriott with a dreamy expression on her face, but it was unclear whether she was recalling happier times, or considering the good-looking Marriott. 'I often wished we could go to a decent hotel – Brighton perhaps, or somewhere romantic like that – but Nigel said that he couldn't afford to take any time off from his job at the Ministry of Munitions. But I suppose what he really meant was that that harridan of a wife of his would smell a rat. Not that she would know much about having affairs.' Selina laughed. 'But as it was she who told you he was having an affair with me, she obviously knew.'

'And when did your affair end?' asked Hardcastle.

'When Nigel was murdered.' Selina looked sad, but Hardcastle guessed that her regret was at losing an available man, rather than that particular one.

'How did you meet Sir Nigel, Mrs Tait?' asked Hardcastle. He knew where and when they met because Lady Strang had told him. But it might shed some light on how Sir Nigel made the acquaintance of women who became his conquests.

'It was at a dinner party, actually. Rosalind and I had been involved in setting up little groups of women who were prepared to knit socks and mufflers, and that sort of thing, for the boys in the trenches. I invited Rosalind and Nigel to dinner one evening, and also invited some friends of ours, the Chandlers. Nigel made it very obvious, when his wife was being shown around the garden, that he was interested in Catherine and me, and even went so far as to ask when our husbands were returning to duty. Such a naughty man, but gallant with it.'

'And then he got in touch with you, I suppose,' said Hardcastle.

'Yes, he telephoned and asked me out for dinner, but I suggested he came here.' Selina smiled at the recollection. 'And, well, one thing led to another,' she added, her gaze dropping fetchingly.

'I see,' said Hardcastle, as he and Marriott rose. 'Thank you for the tea, Mrs Tait. I doubt that I'll need to see you again.'

'I'm always here should either of you need to, Inspector,' said Selina, casting a final glance in Marriott's direction as she spoke.

It was gone six o'clock by the time Hardcastle and Marriott arrived back at Cannon Row.

'Fetch Wood in here, Marriott.'

Seconds later Detective Sergeant Herbert Wood came into the office. 'You wanted me, sir?'

'Yes, Wood. Tomorrow morning cut along to the Admiralty and find out where Lieutenant Commander Archibald Tait is at the moment, and when he was last in this country. His wife said that he's at sea, and has been for the past ten months, but I want to make sure. When you've done that, go and see the assistant provost marshal, Lieutenant Colonel Frobisher. You'll find him tucked away in an office in Horse Guards Arch. Give him my compliments, and ask him where Major Vernon Chandler of the Royal Garrison Artillery is stationed and when he was last over here. Got that?'

'Yes, sir.' Wood finished scribbling notes in his pocket book and departed.

'D'you think there's anything in what Lady Strang alleged, sir?' asked Marriott.

'No,' said Hardcastle. 'If we'd found Strang's body in either Catherine Chandler's place, or Selina Tait's, I might've been tempted to feel their husbands' collars. But he was found in his office, and I don't think that either of those cuckolded husbands would've put themselves on offer by gaining access to the ministry to top him.'

By lunchtime on Friday, Hardcastle's dismissal of the two service officers as suspects was confirmed with the return of DS Wood.

'Lieutenant Commander Tait is in a destroyer on convoy duty in the Atlantic, sir,' said Wood. 'The Admiralty wouldn't give me the name of the ship for security reasons.'

'Thank God someone's worried about security,' commented Hardcastle. 'When was Tait last at home?'

'His last leave was nine months ago, since when he's been sailing out of Liverpool to Halifax and back.'

'You're sure it was nine months? Mrs Tait suggested ten, or even a year.'

'No, it was definitely nine months, sir. A commander at the Admiralty told me the crews have a very quick turn-around, and they can't be afforded for leave. They only started the convoy system this year, and they still haven't got enough destroyers.'

'And Chandler?'

'Major Chandler is a regular officer in the Royal Garrison

Artillery, serving with the BEF. Colonel Frobisher wouldn't tell me exactly where.'

'Probably doesn't know,' observed Hardcastle drily.

'Last leave was six months ago, sir.'

'Thank you, Wood,' said Hardcastle, and turned to Marriott. 'Well, that seems to rule them out.'

'Looks like we're back to the beginning again, sir,' said Marriott.

'Not quite,' said Hardcastle. 'Get on to the first-class sergeant at Bow Street nick, and find out what's happening about Daisy Johnson.'

Ten minutes later, Marriott reported back. 'The inquest's on Monday, sir, and Mr Metcalfe's not going to object to release of the body for burial. I've asked Bow Street to let us know when and where the funeral's to be. I thought you might want to take a look.'

'Yes, I do, Marriott.'

'I was also told that Mrs Harding is making a recovery, sir.'

'Who's Mrs Harding?' asked Hardcastle.

Marriott suspected that Hardcastle was being his usual obtuse self, and that he knew fine who she was. Nevertheless, he played along with it. 'Mrs Harding is Daisy Johnson's mother, sir.'

'Ah yes, of course.'

'Apparently the medical people at Charing Cross Hospital were surprised that she pulled round. They'd more or less given up hope.'

'I wonder what she'll be able to tell Mr Metcalfe,' mused Hardcastle.

'I doubt it'll be much, sir,' said Marriott. 'Incidentally, sir, the clerk-sergeant's waiting to see you.'

'What's he want. Going on about expenses again, is he? Tell him we're dealing with a murder, and we don't have time to worry about his bits of paper.'

'He didn't say what he wanted, sir, but shall I ask him to come in?'

'Yes, do that, Marriott.'

The clerk-sergeant, a youngish man called Weston, entered the office.

'What can I do for you, Weston?' asked Hardcastle.

'Discipline board, sir,' said Weston, flourishing a piece of paper. 'The superintendent is hearing the case of neglect of duty and absence from his post against PC 602A Lewis on Monday morning at ten thirty, and has directed your attendance.'

'D'you mean that Lewis isn't pleading guilty?'

'I've no idea, sir,'

'You must've seen the discipline papers.'

'Yes, sir, but there was no indication of a plea.'

'I suppose that means the bugger's pleading Not Guilty. Yes, all right, Weston. Mark me up warned.'

'Very good, sir,' said the clerk-sergeant, and made his way back to his office.

'Never rains but it bloody pours,' muttered Hardcastle. 'We both heard Lewis confess to being off his post. Well, if he thinks he can get away with it, he's got another think coming.'

NINE

Despite having a murder to solve, Hardcastle spent Friday afternoon doing what he usually did on a Friday afternoon: checking the expenses of all the detectives on A Division. From time to time, he made comments in red ink, such as: 'No need for a taxi on this occasion, claim disallowed.' In some cases he returned unsatisfactory claims for resubmission.

For the remainder of the day, and all of Saturday morning, he and Marriott examined what little evidence they had. Sir Nigel Strang had been a womaniser; that was evident from the testimonies of Lady Strang, and Mesdames Chandler and Tait. However, Strang had been performing a vital role as permanent secretary at the Ministry of Munitions, presumably to his master's satisfaction. That Strang's personal secretary possessed a key to the private entrance – a key the existence of which had not been reported – led Hardcastle to believe that there may be other members of staff who also possessed one. He thought about investigating that unsatisfactory state of affairs, but at once realized that if the murderer was a civil servant at the ministry, he would be unlikely to admit to the possession of such a key, and indeed would most probably have disposed of it by now.

'Oh bugger it!' exclaimed Hardcastle, throwing down his pen and picking up his pipe. He glanced at his watch. 'Quarter past one. I'll let you buy me a pint at the Red Lion, Marriott, and then we'll go home. By the way, have you been warned for Lewis's disciplinary hearing on Monday?'

'Yes, sir.'

It was just past three o'clock by the time Hardcastle arrived home in Kennington Road. As he hung up his hat and umbrella he heard strange voices coming from the parlour. 'Not more bloody refugees, I hope,' he muttered to himself. 'Is this family never going to have the house to itself?'

But when he opened the door to the parlour, he was faced not with refugees, but two soldiers in the army's convalescent uniform known as 'hospital blues'. Both appeared to be in their early twenties.

'Hello, Pa.' The Hardcastles' youngest daughter Maud, her nurse's uniform giving her the appearance of being much older than her nineteen years, was sitting next to her mother.

'Hello,' responded Hardcastle. 'What's all this, then?' It was then that he noticed that one of the men had only one arm, while the other was missing a leg.

'Meet John Gould and Joseph Lynch, Pa. They're convalescing at the home where I'm working. I've brought them back for tea, and a bit of a chat.'

For a year now, Maud Hardcastle had been working as a VAD at one of the big houses in Mayfair that its owner had given over to the care of wounded soldiers.

'Don't stand up.' Realising that it had been a stupid thing to say in the circumstances, Hardcastle hurried across the room and shook hands with John Gould. He turned to do the same with Joseph Lynch, but too late realised that it was Lynch's right arm that was missing.

'Sorry, sir,' said Lynch, with a laugh, and offered his left hand. 'I suppose I'll have to get used to that now.' He spoke with a broad Irish brogue that was almost unintelligible to Hardcastle's London ear.

Hardcastle was ill at ease to be confronted, in his own home, by the realities of total war. He had seen some of the graphic photographs in the *Daily Mail*, and he had seen casualties being unloaded at Waterloo railway station, but had never actually spoken to anyone who had been in the fighting. Uncertain what to say next, he fidgeted with his pipe for a few moments, and then filled it with tobacco.

'Do smoke if you want to, lads.'

Joseph Lynch took a pipe from his pocket. 'I wonder if you'd mind, sir,' he said. 'I haven't quite got the hang of it yet, and usually one of my mates in the home'll fill it for me.'

Glad of something to do, Hardcastle took the man's pipe and began filling it with his own tobacco.

'There's no need for that, sir,' said Lynch. 'I've got a pouch here somewhere.'

'That's all right,' said Hardcastle. 'Does St Bruno suit you?'

Lynch laughed. 'We'll smoke anything in the trenches, sir. There was one fellow who smoked nettle leaves, would you believe? I told him it would kill him. Sure enough, a sniper got him the very next day.' He laughed again, but this time it was a coarse, bitter laugh.

'You've been in the thick of it, then,' said Hardcastle.

'That we have, sir,' volunteered Lynch. 'In the Arras sector, down near Albert and Thiepval, and I can tell you it's blue bloody murder.' He glanced at Alice and Maud Hardcastle. 'Begging your pardon, ladies. Half our battalion – the Royal Irish Fusiliers – were wiped out. I suppose I'm one of the lucky ones. There'll be no more war for me.'

'Nor me,' put in Gould, laughing as he waved the empty leg of his trousers.

'Are you two friends?' asked Hardcastle.

'Only since we got our Blighty one, sir,' continued Gould. 'I was with the North Staffordshire Regiment. There's not many of us left in our battalion.' He took out a packet of Woodbines and lit one. 'Joe and me somehow found ourselves on the same hospital train, and the same hospital ship. Then, would you believe, we fetched up in the same ward at Frensham Hill Military Hospital. Finally, we were sent to this big house in Park Lane, and had your lovely daughter looking after us. Can't get much better than that, can it, sir?'

'Now, now, that's enough of that,' said Maud, blushing coyly.

'I expect you'd like something a bit stronger than tea,' suggested Hardcastle, still at a loss to find a suitable subject for conversation.

'They're not allowed alcohol while they're convalescing, Pa,' said Maud.

'Well, if they don't tell the matron, I won't,' said Hardcastle, forcing a laugh. And he went to the cabinet and took out a bottle of Scotch. 'Anyway, you can tell her that it was a policeman who gave it to you,' he added, 'so that's all right.'

'Are you a policeman, sir?' asked Gould.

'For my sins, yes.'

'I was hoping to join the Force when this lot was over,'

said Gould sadly, 'but there's not much hope of that now. I shan't be playing any more football, neither.'

'Is there any sign of it all coming to an end?' asked Hardcastle.

'When the Madonna falls, sir.'

'What?' Hardcastle looked from one soldier to the other. 'What's the Madonna got to do with it?'

'It's the basilica at Albert, sir,' said Gould. 'It's been shelled something awful, and the Madonna on top of the steeple's leaning over at right angles. They reckon that when the Madonna falls, the war'll end.'

'Oh, I see,' said Hardcastle, imagining that he was being made the butt of some macabre army joke. In fact, it was a popular myth among the troops in that theatre of war. But what they did not know – nor did most other people – was that the Royal Engineers had secured the Madonna with cables to ensure that it would not be damaged by falling to the ground. Neither could they know that once the war was over the basilica at Albert would be restored to its former splendour.

When Hardcastle reached his office on Monday morning, he was still thinking about the two young soldiers who Maud had brought home. He was amazed by their cheerfulness despite their appalling wounds, and wondered how they, and the thousands of others, would cope with life, being maimed as they were. As a result he was in no mood to afford any degree of sympathy to the idle policeman who, at the DDI's behest, was to face disciplinary proceedings later that morning for neglect of duty. Not that the outcome rested with him.

At half past ten precisely, PC Lewis was arraigned before Superintendent Arthur Hudson, who had charge of the A or Whitehall Division of the Metropolitan Police. Seated beside Hudson was his deputy, Chief Inspector Charles Curtis.

'Are you Police Constable 602A Herbert Lewis of Cannon Row police station, A Division?' The regulations obliged Hudson to pose the formal question, even though he knew well who Lewis was.

'Yes, sir.'

'You are charged in that at divers times between ten p.m. on Monday the fourteenth and six a.m. on Tuesday the fifteenth of May nineteen-seventeen, you did absent yourself from your fixed post at the main door of the Ministry of Munitions. How do you plead?'

'I wasn't absent, sir. I was round the corner, but I could still see the door.'

Hudson turned to the chief inspector. 'What are the directions for that post, Mr Curtis?'

Curtis coughed affectedly and read from a sheet of paper. 'The post at the door of the Ministry of Munitions shall be covered at all times by an armed constable, sir. He may patrol to a maximum distance of five yards in either direction from the door, but will not leave his post until properly relieved.'

'Well, Lewis,' said Hudson, 'being round the corner is not patrolling five yards on either side of the door, is it?'

'No, sir,' admitted Lewis.

'You were therefore absent from your post, weren't you?'

'Yes, sir.'

'Very well,' said Hudson, and turned to Lewis's sub-divisional inspector. 'Any previous misconduct matters regarding this officer, Inspector?'

'No, sir. Lewis is a man of previous good character.'

'PC Lewis, it was nothing short of wilful and gross neglect of duty to leave your post at an important government office, especially in time of war. You will be fined three days' pay, and transferred to the Dockyard Division at Chatham with effect from next Monday. Understood?'

'Yes, sir,' replied the miserable Lewis. It was not so much the fine that disturbed him, but the transfer to Chatham, miles from the section house where he lived. And that would entail finding digs locally. But that was not all. He knew that the Dockyard Divisions had a fair complement of defaulters, among them some inspectors and some sergeants. The prospect of patrolling the remote areas of a dockyard in wet and windy conditions without any hope of slacking did not appeal to him.

'Very well,' said Hudson, 'dismiss.'

*　　*　　*

'Well that was a waste of time,' muttered Hardcastle, once
he was back in his office. 'Didn't bloody well need me there
at all, nor you, Marriott.'

'No, sir.' Marriott declined to point out that had Lewis
continued to deny the allegation, his case would have had to
be adjourned if the principal witnesses to Lewis's original
confession had not been there. In the event the proceedings
had taken little more than ten minutes to resolve.

'Anything from Bow Street about Daisy Johnson's topping,
Marriott?'

'Yes, sir. The inquest was convened and adjourned *sine
die*. Mr Metcalfe raised no objections to the release of the
deceased's body. Incidentally, sir, the post mortem revealed
that Daisy Johnson was pregnant.'

'Oh? How long?'

'The pathologist put it at three months, sir.'

'I wonder whose nipper it was,' mused Hardcastle. 'Has
Mr Metcalfe been able to interview Mrs Harding, Daisy's
mother yet?'

'Yes, sir. She's making a good recovery, but was unable
to tell police anything they didn't know already.'

'Story of my life,' muttered Hardcastle. 'Keep in touch
with Bow Street and find out where and when the funeral is
to be.'

'Already been arranged, sir. It's tomorrow at St Bride in
Fleet Street. Half past ten.'

'Interesting,' mused Hardcastle. 'That's reckoned to be the
journalists' church.'

Divisional Detective Inspector Frederick Metcalfe of E
Division was already in the churchyard of St Bride when
Hardcastle and Marriott arrived.

'Are you going in, Ernie?' asked Metcalfe.

'No, Fred. I can't be doing with another funeral service
in eight days. I'll wait out here.'

'Me too,' agreed Metcalfe, filling his pipe and offering his
pouch to Hardcastle.

'I'll smoke my own, if it's all the same to you, Fred,' said
Hardcastle. 'How come Daisy Johnson gets herself buried
here in St Bride?'

'Apparently her father, now deceased, was a compositor on the *Daily Chronicle* for years. When the bosses there heard about Daisy's murder – well, they would've done, wouldn't they, being the press? – they agreed to pay for the funeral.'

While the burial service was taking place, the two DDIs stood in the churchyard, smoking. For a while they discussed their respective investigations, but it was evident that neither of them had made much progress. That subject exhausted, they moved on to the next most popular topic in the Metropolitan Police: a discussion about senior officers, usually to the latter's detriment.

At last the doors of the church opened, and the pallbearers emerged carrying the coffin, to be followed by the handful of mourners. Dressed in black, most were presumed to be friends and family, although there was no sign of Mrs Harding.

'Daisy's mother's not here, then,' observed Hardcastle.

'No,' said Metcalfe, 'she's still in hospital.'

'And that, I presume,' said Hardcastle, nodding towards a soldier, 'is Daisy's husband. Must have got leave from Ypres. At least, that's where Daisy said he was stationed.'

'I reckon so,' said Metcalfe, 'but I've not had a chance to talk to him yet.'

'I thought Daisy said he was a lance-sergeant, sir,' said Marriott.

'Well, he's got three stripes on his arm,' said Hardcastle, 'and the last time I looked that meant a sergeant.'

'But he's wearing a red sash, sir, and only full sergeants wear a sash, not lance-sergeants.'

'You're full of useless information, Marriott,' commented Hardcastle. 'But with the number of casualties in this bloody war, it's quite possible he's been promoted. Anyway, how d'you know all that?'

'My brother's a sergeant-major in the Middlesex Regiment in Flanders, sir.'

'Ah, so he is. There's no need to keep telling me, Marriott.'

'No, sir.' Marriott sighed inwardly; his chief never failed to tell him why he always told cab drivers to go to Scotland Yard every time they were returning to Cannon Row.

The three detectives waited at a distance until the coffin had been lowered into its grave.

'There doesn't seem to be anyone here who looks out of place, Marriott,' said Hardcastle, 'but grab hold of that Sergeant Johnson, and tell him I'd like a few words with him at his convenience. Tell him to call at Cannon Row.'

It was at half past two that same afternoon that Sergeant Gerald Johnson presented himself at Cannon Row police station and asked for Hardcastle. Minutes later, he was escorted to the DDI's office by the station duty constable. Marriott followed him in.

'Sarn't Johnson, Grenadier Guards, sir. I'm told you wanted to see me.' The young soldier – probably not yet thirty – stood ramrod straight, the afternoon sun glinting on his highly polished grenade cap badge, and the brass letters 'GG' on each of his shoulder straps.

'Sit down, Sergeant Johnson,' said Hardcastle. 'Smoke if you wish.' He noticed that Johnson was no longer wearing his red sash; presumably it was a ceremonial adornment only worn on special occasions, like funerals. But Hardcastle would be the first to admit that he knew very little of the army and its customs.

'Thank you, sir.' Johnson removed his cap, and sat down on the hard chair opposite Hardcastle's desk. After a moment or two, he took out a packet of Churchman's Tenner cigarettes, and lit one.

'I'm sorry about your wife, Sergeant Johnson,' said Hardcastle diffidently; he was not good at expressing sentiments of condolence.

'Thank you, sir.'

'I'm surprised you're not at the wake,' said Marriott.

'Not my scene, sir.' Johnson turned his head slightly to address Marriott. 'Family all chattering away, like nothing's happened, and drinking brown ale till it comes out of their ears. To tell the truth, I was glad to get away.'

'When did you arrive back here?' asked Hardcastle. 'From Ypres, wasn't it?'

'Yesterday morning, sir. They give me compassionate leave, special like, to bury the missus. I'm away again tomorrow morning. Still, it'll give me a chance to have a few wets down the local pub.'

'Why I've asked you to see me, Sergeant Johnson, is to ask you if you know of any reason why your wife should've been murdered.'

'No idea, sir, and that's the God's honest truth. It's a mystery to me. She was a sweet girl was Daisy. Wouldn't never harm a hair of anyone's head, she wouldn't. D'you reckon you'll find who done it, sir?'

'It's not my case,' said Hardcastle. 'It's being dealt with by Divisional Detective Inspector Metcalfe of the Holborn Division.'

'Then why—?'

'But I'm dealing with the murder of Sir Nigel Strang who your wife found dead in his office, a fortnight ago.'

'But what was my Daisy doing in this toff's office?'

'Ah!' Hardcastle took his pipe from the ashtray and lit it. 'Your wife was employed as a cleaner at the Ministry of Munitions, Sergeant Johnson,' he said, puffing clouds of smoke towards the ceiling.

'Well, bugger me, I never knew that. I wonder why she never told me.'

'Probably thought that to mention the Ministry of Munitions in a letter might be a breach of security.'

'Yes, I s'pose so,' said Johnson thoughtfully.

'Anyway, she went into Sir Nigel's office at about twenty minutes to six in the morning, and found him dead on the floor.'

'Seems a funny time for a toff like him to be in his office,' said Johnson, nipping out the tip of his half-smoked cigarette in Hardcastle's ashtray before putting the butt end in his tunic pocket, 'but I s'pose with the war and everything, people are doing all sorts of weird things these days.'

Hardcastle changed the subject. 'I suppose you know your mother-in-law's in hospital.'

'Best place for that old witch,' said Johnson forcefully. 'Always trying to set Daisy against me, was Fanny Harding. Was against our getting wed right from the start, the old bitch. What's the matter with her anyway, sir?'

'She found your wife dead on the kitchen floor at your flat in Wild Street. She apparently had a heart attack, and was taken to Charing Cross Hospital.'

'Yes, well, I shan't be wasting valuable drinking time going to hold her hand, and that's a fact.'

'Thank you for coming to see me, Sergeant Johnson. It may be that Mr Metcalfe will want to see you. He's at Holborn police station.'

'I've already had a message to that effect, sir.' Johnson stood up, and donned his cap. He paused in the doorway. 'I've sort of got used to this sort of thing across the water, but you don't expect it in spitting distance of Bow Street police court, do you, sir?' And with that philosophical comment, he left the office.

'Not much of a homecoming for that poor devil, was it, Marriott,' said Hardcastle. 'Bloody war.'

Hardcastle had further occasion to curse 'the bloody war' when he arrived home at Kennington Road that evening.

'What, no visitors, Alice?' said Hardcastle jocularly as he entered the parlour.

'Go on, Ernie, you know you don't mind.'

'What's for supper, love?'

'Good heavens, you're no sooner through the door than you want to know what's going to be on the table.' But Alice Hardcastle's gentle ragging was made in jest. 'There's a letter for you on the mantelpiece, Ernie. Looks important. Says it's "On His Majesty's Service".'

Hardcastle took the envelope. 'If Derby thinks he's going to call me up for his conscription scheme, he's got another think coming,' he said, as he tore open the envelope. He scanned it and laughed. 'It's from Lord Devonport, calling himself the Food Controller, whatever that is when it's at home.'

'What's it about?' asked Alice, wiping her hands on her apron.

'It's addressed to "the householder", and it says we're not to waste bread, Alice, and we're to wear a purple ribbon to show we're being frugal.' Hardcastle screwed up the letter and tossed it into the empty fireplace.

'Be a bit difficult to be anything but frugal these days,' said Alice, 'what with the price of bread and flour these days. And it looks like more and more things are going on the ration.'

'Bloody war!' commented Hardcastle.

'And we can do without that police station language, Ernest, thank you very much,' said Alice.

'Sorry, dear.' Hardcastle knew that the use of his full name was, of itself, a rebuke for his language.

'Anyway, I've got a nice bit of ham for your supper, Ernie, so make the most of it. Mr Squires the grocer let me have it, but he said it's getting short.'

'He only let you have it because I'm a copper,' growled Hardcastle. Settling into his armchair, he picked up the *Daily Mail*. 'See they had a Zeppelin raid down at Woolwich Arsenal again last night, Alice.'

TEN

On Wednesday morning, Hardcastle received a telephone call from William Sullivan, the DDI of C Division, who was stationed at Vine Street police station. Sullivan, a man of whom Hardcastle did not greatly approve, was renowned for his flamboyant mode of dress. Expensively suited, he was never seen without a bowler hat with a curled brim, and a Malacca cane. He also sported a monocle, an affectation that caused the local villains to dub him 'Posh Bill with the Piccadilly window'. It was rumoured that he had a small mirror affixed to the inside of his bowler so that he could ensure that his hair was immaculate whenever he took off his hat. But Hardcastle had no evidence of it.

'Ernie, old boy, it's Bill Sullivan of C Division.'

'What can I do for you, Bill?' asked Hardcastle flatly.

'It's more a case of what I can do for you, Ernie. A PC came to see me this morning. Apparently he'd seen a photograph of Sir Nigel Strang in *The Times*.'

'Really? Do all your officers read *The Times*?' enquired Hardcastle acidly.

'We have a very superior sort of constable in the St James's Division, Ernie. You should know that, having served here in the dim and distant past. However, this PC told me that he'd once stopped Sir Nigel Strang in the company of a prostitute. I don't know whether that's of any interest to you, but d'you want me to send him over?'

'Yes, please, Bill, and as soon as possible.'

The PC who entered Hardcastle's office some forty minutes later, was a man of about thirty-five.

'PC 303C Duncan Frazer of Vine Street, sir. Mr Sullivan said I was to see you.'

'Quite right,' said Hardcastle, lighting his pipe. 'Go across to the detectives' office and ask DS Marriott to come in.'

'Yes, sir.'

'This is PC Frazer of Vine Street, Marriott,' said Hardcastle, once his detective sergeant had joined him. 'He has a startling piece of information that'll help us solve this murder. Let's hear it, Frazer?' He sat back, and blew a plume of smoke towards the ceiling.

'I happened to see a photograph of Sir Nigel Strang in *The Times*, sir, and realised it was a man who I'd stopped having a bit of a barney with a tom.'

'When was this?'

Frazer considered the question thoughtfully. 'Approximately the beginning of the month, sir.'

'"Approximately" is no good to me, Frazer. When exactly?'

The PC pulled out his pocket book. 'Wednesday the second of May, sir, at twelve thirty a.m.'

'Where?'

'Shepherd Market, sir.'

Hardcastle nodded. He knew, as did any officer who had served on C Division – and even beyond – that for years Shepherd Market had been a haunt of prostitutes and those seeking their services.

'Well, don't keep me in suspense, Frazer.'

'There was a bit of a shouting match going on, sir, so I went up to the couple. The tom said that she and the man had been arguing over the price. She wanted five quid, and the man said he wasn't going to pay more than two.'

'Who was this prostitute, Frazer?' asked Marriott.

'A woman by the name of Mary Duggan, Sergeant. She's well known at the nick, and she's been arrested several times for soliciting prostitution.'

'Did you obtain the man's name?'

'For what it's worth, Sergeant, he said he was called Jack Brown, and gave his occupation as a clerk, and an address in Strutton Ground.'

'Well, that's original,' scoffed Hardcastle sarcastically. 'They usually claim to be John Smith. I don't suppose you checked that address, did you?'

'No, sir, there was no cause to. I referred them to their civil remedy, and the man departed. No breach of the peace.'

Hardcastle smiled. The phrase 'I referred them to their

civil remedy' was the entry policemen always made in their reports if there were no grounds for arrest or summons. But he knew from experience that disputants rarely sought the expensive services of a lawyer, or were prepared to endure the wearisome procedures of the civil courts.

'If it was Sir Nigel Strang, I can tell you he definitely doesn't live in Strutton Ground. And you're sure it was him?'

'Yes, sir.'

'Why did it take you so long to report this to Mr Sullivan, Frazer?'

'I bought myself some fish and chips last night, sir, and it was wrapped in this old copy of *The Times*. As soon as I saw the photograph, and details of Strang's murder, I realised he was the man I'd stopped.'

'What beat were you on when this incident occurred, Frazer?'

'Seven beat, sir. Area bounded by Piccadilly, Old Park Lane, Pitt's Head Mews, Derby Street, Curzon Street, Half Moon Street, and back to Piccadilly.'

'And Shepherd Market's right in the middle,' mused Hardcastle.

'Yes, sir.'

'Right, Frazer, sooner rather than later, get hold of this Mary Duggan and tell her I want to see her. And if she don't come, tell her I'll come looking for her, and it won't just be a half-crown fine up Marlborough Street police court, neither.'

'Yes, sir,' said Frazer with a brief grin. 'It'll likely be later this afternoon, sir. The girls don't generally show up till about four at the earliest.'

'I know that, Frazer. I used to be a detective sergeant at Vine Street nick.'

The first intimation of the arrival of Mary Duggan was raised voices that Hardcastle could hear even with his door closed.

A minute or two later, a somewhat harassed sergeant appeared on the threshold of Hardcastle's office.

'There's a street woman downstairs, sir, claiming that she was told to come here to see you.'

'Who is she?' asked Hardcastle, although he had half guessed.

'Name of Mary Duggan, sir.'

'What was all the shouting about?'

'Leaving out the swear words, sir, she said as how she was losing money, and that I'd better not waste her valuable time, but to show her to your office. Well, I said that I'd have to enquire, sir, on account of you not generally interviewing people like her.'

'You'd be surprised who you have to speak to when you're a CID officer, Skipper. Send her up, and on your way ask Sergeant Marriott to step into my office.'

The blowzy woman who appeared before Hardcastle was about twenty-three, and had the coarse allure of her profession. She wore a low-cut white sateen blouse, and a grey cloth skirt that came well above the ankles. She placed her feet well apart, and put her hands on her hips.

'Sit down, Miss Duggan.'

'I ain't got no time to waste, you know.' The woman remained standing.

'Sit down when the inspector tells you,' barked Marriott.

She mouthed an obscenity at Marriott, but nevertheless perched herself on a chair. 'What d'you want of me anyhow? I ain't done nothing wrong.'

'You're a prostitute,' said Hardcastle.

'T'ain't against the law.'

'I know far more about the law than you do, young woman,' said Hardcastle mildly. 'And I do know that being a prostitute is not against the law. But soliciting prostitution is, and that's what a constable saw you doing just after midnight on Wednesday the second of May in Shepherd Market.'

'Oh yeah? Why didn't he knock me off, then?'

'Probably because it wasn't your turn.' Hardcastle was familiar with the system operated by the police at Vine Street. They had long recognised that there was no way the oldest profession's activities would ever be curbed – it would be impossible to arrest all of them every night – and prostitutes were arrested on a rota basis, appearing before the Marlborough Street magistrate about once a fortnight. As for the prostitutes, they regarded the fine as a form of licence fee.

'I'm not the only one, you know. Why pick on me?'

'Because, Mary, you happen to have got into an argument with a man who has since been murdered.'

'Gawd Almighty, guv'nor, I never killed no one.' Mary Duggan's face paled significantly beneath her rouged face and lips, and the kohl she had used in an attempt to make her eyes more appealing.

'I didn't suggest that you did. Now then, how well did you know the man you were arguing with? It was the night that a constable spoke to you and a man who gave the name of Jack Brown.'

'Bleedin' skinflint,' said Mary. 'Wanted to have a tumble for two quid.'

'Even that's above your usual price, isn't it?' asked Marriott.

'Yeah, but he was a toff, and I didn't see why he shouldn't stump up a bit more. He could afford it, the mean bastard. You could tell by the clobber he was sporting.'

'Had you seen him before, Mary?' asked Hardcastle.

'Yeah, but he usually went with Liz, 'cept she weren't there on account of how she was turning a trick for another geezer.'

'Liz who?'

'Dunno her other name.'

'Tell her I want to see her, and tell her to make it today.'

'I dunno if she'll be there today.'

'I'm sure she will, Mary. Make certain she gets the message because I don't want to have to come up to Shepherd Market and do a bit of sorting out. Right, you can go.'

'Bleedin' hell, is that it, then?'

'For the time being.' Hardcastle deliberately left the threat hanging in the air, although he could think of no reason for needing to see the girl again.

'Bloody coppers,' complained Mary, as she flounced out of the office, slamming the door behind her.

Hardcastle sat back and hooted with laughter. 'Nothing like a good honest tart to brighten up the day, Marriott. Now all we've got to do is see what this Liz has to say for herself.'

But he did not have to wait long.

It was half past six when the station officer appeared once again in Hardcastle's office.

'There's an Elizabeth Parsons outside, sir. She says you sent for her.'

'I did, Skipper. Send her in.'

Although similar in dress and appearance to Mary Duggan, Elizabeth Parsons gave the impression of being more refined.

'Do you know a man called Sir Nigel Strang, Liz?' asked Hardcastle.

'Blimey, I don't think I know any "sirs",' said Liz, flopping uninvited into a chair. 'Why, what's he done?'

'He got himself murdered, Liz, that's what he did, and I'm told that he was one of your regular clients.' Hardcastle turned to Marriott. 'Show Miss Parsons the photograph.'

Marriott crossed to the detectives' office and returned moments later with the photograph of Sir Nigel Strang that had been obtained from Hobson the butler.

'That's the man, Liz,' Marriott said.

'Oh, him. Yeah, I knows him all right. A real gent, that one.'

'How often did you meet him?' queried Hardcastle.

'About once a week, I s'pose.'

'And where did you take him?'

Liz emitted a coarse laugh. 'It was him what took me, more like,' she said. 'Always the same place, a little hotel round the back of Westminster.'

'What was the name of this hotel?'

Liz thought about that for a second or two. 'The Britannia. It's just off Palace Street.'

'Yes, I know it. Did he tell you his name?'

'He told me to call him Jack. Jack Brown. But I don't s'pose it was his real name. Most tricks don't like telling you their proper names.'

'Presumably you went to this hotel in a taxi.'

'Course we did. Too far to walk from Shepherd Market to Westminster, mister. You ought to try it.'

'I have done, many times,' observed Hardcastle.

'Did this Jack Brown tell you what he did for a living, Liz?' asked Marriott.

'Nah, he never said. But it must've been something that paid a bit handsome, 'cos he never seemed to be short of a quid or two.'

'How long did this arrangement go on?' asked Hardcastle.

'Must've been about a year, I s'pose. He was ever so nice. Not like the usual tricks. Sometimes he give me a bottle of scent or a box of them Harrods' chocolates, and they cost five and sixpence. I had a pal what worked there, and she told me they was five-and-six. I'm sorry to hear he's snuffed it.'

'Did you spend the whole night with him on those occasions, Liz?'

'Sure I did.'

'That must've cost him.'

Liz gave Hardcastle a sly grin. 'It did. Five quid, but he never quibbled.'

'Have you got a pimp, Liz?'

'A pimp?' The question had clearly disturbed the girl.

'Let's not mess about, Liz. I've been a copper long enough to know that all you girls have got minders.' Hardcastle gazed at the woman. 'You needn't worry, I'm not going to tell him that you told me.'

'Jed Thorn's the man who looks out for me, and a few of the other girls.'

'Did he know anything about this Jack Brown?'

'Nah, I never tells him who my tricks are.'

'Did Thorn ever see you with Jack Brown?'

'Nah, he never.'

'Then there's no need to tell Thorn about our little chat, is there?'

'Don't you worry about that, Mr Hardcastle. Mum's the word.'

'What d'you make of it, sir?' asked Marriott, when Liz Parsons had left to return to Shepherd Market.

'It seems that Sir Nigel Strang was a bit reckless, Marriott. It don't chime with what Lady Strang said about him being discreet. It's one thing to have a tumble with the likes of Catherine Chandler and Selina Tait in the privacy of their own homes, but picking up toms in Shepherd Market is throwing caution to the winds.'

'I wonder if this Jed Thorn did know him, sir. Perhaps it was him who topped Sir Nigel.'

'I can't think why, Marriott. According to Liz Parsons,

Strang was a generous man. Why should Thorn kill the goose that laid the golden egg, so to speak? Anyway, I think that now might be a good time to have a stroll round to this here Britannia Hotel. See if we can pick up something useful.'

'Yes, sir.' Marriott had hoped for an early night, and could not disguise his disappointment.

Occasionally – but only very occasionally – Hardcastle recognised that his detective sergeant, a man with a young family, would like some time to spend with them. 'Where's Drew?'

'He's in the office, sir.'

'Don't seem to be doing much for his money, does he? Send him across, and I'll take him with me. Do him good to learn how real police work's done. You go home to your missus, and I'll see you in the morning.'

'Thank you very much, sir,' said Marriott.

'And my regards to Mrs Marriott.'

'Thank you, sir, and mine to Mrs H.'

'Well now, Drew,' said Hardcastle, when the Special Branch officer appeared. 'Are you keeping up with what's been going on?'

'Yes, sir. Charlie Marriott's been keeping me informed of your progress.'

'And I suppose you've been keeping Mr Quinn informed.'

'Yes, sir, although I've not had much to tell him.'

'No, well, that's the way it works out in the divisional CID, Drew. Sometimes you have a stroke of luck, and sometimes you don't. But stick with me and you'll find out how the job's done.'

'Very good, sir.' Drew turned to leave the office.

'Now don't go running off, Drew. Mr Quinn's kindly lent you to me to help out, see. And while Marriott's away on another enquiry, you can come with me.' Hardcastle saw no reason to tell Drew that he had given Marriott the evening off.

'Where are we going, sir?'

'The Britannia Hotel, just off Palace Street. And we'll walk on account of it being a pleasant evening. Oh, and pick up that photograph of Sir Nigel Strang before we leave.'

*　　*　　*

The manager of the Britannia Hotel bustled forward as the two police officers entered the foyer. Hardcastle was wearing his usual bowler hat, and Drew had on a straw boater.

'Good evening, gentlemen. A table for two for dinner, is it?'

'No,' said Hardcastle, 'not unless you're giving it away.'

The manager blinked. 'I'm not sure I understand, sir.'

'I'm Divisional Detective Inspector Hardcastle of the Whitehall Division, and this here's Detective Sergeant Drew.'

'Ah!' The manager coughed affectedly. 'How can I be of assistance, Inspector?'

'You're the manager, I take it.'

'Indeed I am.'

'And your name?'

'Goodwin. John Goodwin.'

'I want you to take a look at this photograph, Mr Goodwin.' Hardcastle held out his hand impatiently.

Drew handed him the photograph, which Hardcastle, in turn, passed to the manager.

'Is this someone I should know, Inspector?' asked Goodwin.

'He was a guest in your hotel at least once a week,' said Hardcastle.

'I really don't think that I—'

'And he usually brought a young woman with him.'

'I can't say that I recall—'

Hardcastle emitted an exasperated sigh. 'I'm not about to run you in for keeping a brothel, Mr Goodwin, although I suspect that I have the evidence. I know what this man came here for when he was accompanied by a woman young enough to be his daughter. And you know it, an' all.'

'Yes, well, I didn't imagine . . .'

Hardcastle sensed that Goodwin was about to prevaricate. 'The man was Sir Nigel Strang, and he came here at least once a week with a prostitute. And I'm sure that he greased your palm to keep your trap shut. So, shall we stop beating about the bush and get down to brass tacks.'

Drew, accustomed to the more subtle approaches of Special Branch enquiries, was aghast at Hardcastle's bluntness.

'I think you'd better come into my office, Inspector,' said Goodwin hurriedly.

'Yes, I think perhaps we should,' said Hardcastle.

Once the door to the manager's office was closed, Goodwin invited the two detectives to take a seat. 'May I offer you a drink, Inspector?' he asked smoothly. 'A whisky, perhaps?'

'No, thank you. But you can tell me how often Sir Nigel Strang made use of your hotel for what the Scots delightfully describe as lewd and libidinous practices.'

'He was very discreet, Inspector, and I did explain to him that we had a reputation to maintain.'

Hardcastle scoffed. 'Well, you haven't done too well at doing it. Half the whores in the West End of London know this is a good place to bring their wealthy clients. It's practically a knocking shop. So, how many times?'

'About twice a week.' Goodwin spoke in resigned tones, convinced he was about to be arrested or, at best, prosecuted for keeping what the law termed a bawdy house.

'With the same woman?'

'There was one woman who always came with him, usually on a Thursday. But on the other occasions it was always with a different girl.'

'What name did he use?'

'Jack Brown,' said Goodwin without hesitating.

Hardcastle laughed. 'And you believed him?'

'No, but as I said, he was very discreet. He would always take the young lady straight up to his room, and leave the next morning at about nine o'clock. He never embarrassed the hotel by making use of the dining room, either for dinner or breakfast. And he always gave the chambermaid a generous tip.'

'Did you in fact know that he was Sir Nigel Strang?'

'No, but I guessed he was someone quite important.'

'Well, that quite important man got himself murdered.'

'Good God!' The manager's jaw dropped. 'Of course. I should have made the connection. It was in all the papers. I wondered why I hadn't seen him for the last two weeks.'

'Did anyone ever come here asking for him, or otherwise making enquiries, Mr Goodwin?'

'No, Inspector, not that I'm aware of. I could ask the hall porter.'

'No, I'll do that. And before I go, I should remind you

that I'm the senior CID officer for this division, and I'll have my men keeping a sharp eye on your establishment.' Hardcastle guessed that people like Strang would be charged more for the hotel's discretion, and added, 'So you can tear up your other tariff. Come, Drew.'

On their way out, Hardcastle showed the photograph to the hall porter. 'Ever see this man before?'

'No, sir.'

'Really? I thought hall porters knew everything that went on in their hotels. How much did he give you to keep your mouth shut?'

The hall porter looked around, a hunted expression on his face. 'Five bob, guv'nor.'

'And did anyone ever come asking for him?'

'Not to my knowledge, sir, no.'

'Right. I'll tell you what I just told your guv'nor. I'm the head of the CID for this division, and I'll be keeping my minces on you from now on.'

'You can rely on me, sir,' said the hall porter.

'That'll be the day,' muttered Hardcastle, and turning to Drew added, 'Bloody waste of time.'

'Yes, sir,' said Drew. He had been advised by Marriott always to agree with the DDI's occasional outbursts.

Once in the street, Hardcastle hailed a taxi. 'Scotland Yard, cabbie,' he said, and turned to Drew. 'Tell 'em Cannon Row, Drew, and half the time you'll finish up at Cannon Street in the City.'

'Really, sir?' said Drew.

ELEVEN

In order to demonstrate his appreciation for Hardcastle's gesture in giving him the previous evening off, Marriott arrived at the police station well before the DDI's own arrival at half past eight on Thursday morning. And he had not wasted his time.

'I got Catto to go over to records section, sir, and see what he could find on Jed Thorn, Liz Parsons's pimp.'

'And what did he find, Marriott?' Hardcastle displayed no surprise at Marriott's initiative, and if asked, would have said that he expected it of a detective sergeant first-class.

'He's got quite a lot of form, sir. He's been done twice for malicious wounding. In one case he striped a tom. Went down for six months.'

Hardcastle looked up in surprise. 'Did she give evidence against him?'

Marriott referred quickly to the file he was holding. 'According to this, sir, yes, she did. He also has convictions for burglary and robbery.'

'He sounds a likely candidate for a topping, then. Of course, the question is how did he get into Strang's office. I can't see a villain like him taking a chance on getting caught in a government building.'

'His antecedent history describes him as cocky, sir, with a contempt for the law.'

'Does it now? In that case, I think we'll have a word with Master Thorn. Is there an address on there for him, Marriott?'

'Yes, sir. Farley Road, Lewisham.' Marriott was disturbed, not for the first time, that the DDI seemed to be going off at a tangent. But in the past, such deviations had often paid off.

'Good. Who have we got available?'

'Wilmot and Catto are in the office at the moment, sir.'

'Good, fetch Wilmot in.'

'You wanted me, sir?' asked Detective Constable Fred Wilmot, pausing on the threshold of Hardcastle's office.

'Yes, Wilmot. I'm interested in a nasty bastard called Jed Thorn whose record says he lives in Farley Road, Lewisham.'

'What's he do for a living, sir?' asked Wilmot.

'Nothing much.' Hardcastle smiled. 'He's working as a pimp for at least one of the Shepherd Market girls, probably more. Sergeant Marriott's got his file; have a look at it. Then, get down to Lewisham and make a few enquiries. I want to know if he's still living there. And there's no need to be too discreet about it, neither, but best not call at his drum. Just sound out the local nick and the neighbours. They'll soon let him know that the law's taking an interest in his activities. I want him to feel threatened.'

'Very good, sir.' It was the sort of job that Wilmot enjoyed.

'And now, Marriott,' said Hardcastle, once Wilmot had left to do the DDI's bidding, 'we'd better get across to the coroner's court. Not that we've anything to tell him.'

'Well, Mr Hardcastle, are we in a position to empanel a jury?' The coroner looked up enquiringly.

'Unfortunately no, sir,' said Hardcastle. 'I regret to say that I'm no nearer discovering who murdered Sir Nigel Strang, and other complications have arisen.'

'Oh? Are they matters that should concern this court?'

'I daresay the matter will be brought to your notice in due course, sir, if it has not been already.' Hardcastle explained briefly about the murder of Daisy Johnson, and his concern that the two killings might be connected.

'If that is the case, there might be some justification in holding both hearings at the same time,' mused the coroner. 'However, I shall adjourn this hearing until such time as you inform me we may proceed.'

'I'm obliged, sir,' said Hardcastle.

Shortly after Hardcastle's arrival back at Cannon Row, Wilmot returned. 'Jed Thorn's still there, sir. And he's well known to the local nick as a petty villain.'

'I thought he might be,' commented Hardcastle. 'Is Catto still in the office?'

'Yes, sir.'

'Good. I want the pair of you to go down there and feel his collar. I'd nick him myself, but I would hate for him to feel that important.'

'What shall we nick him for, sir?'

'Offences under the Breathing Act, Wilmot. God Almighty, you've both been CID officers for long enough to come up with something. On the other hand, you could just nick him and let him sweat.'

Wilmot grinned. 'Yes, sir. D'you want him brought here to Cannon Row?'

'Of course I do. I'm not traipsing all the way down to Lewisham nick to give a tuppenny-ha'penny villain a serious talking-to.'

It had turned four o'clock that afternoon before Wilmot reported that Jed Thorn was in the interview room.

'Who's with him, Wilmot?' asked Hardcastle.

'Henry Catto, sir.'

'That should frighten him,' said Hardcastle drily. He put his pipe in the ashtray, and crossed the corridor to the detectives' office. 'Come, Marriott,' he said. 'We've got Thorn downstairs. We'll give him a bit of a talking-to.'

The two detectives descended the stairs to the interview room, situated near the front of the police station. With a flick of his hand, Hardcastle dismissed Catto.

The surly figure of Jed Thorn lounged on a chair in the interview room. Despite being a prostitute's pimp – a calling that usually attracted a substantial amount of money – he was dressed in a threadbare suit, a shirt with no collar, and a red kerchief around his neck. On his head was a rather worn cloth cap.

'Take your bloody hat off in my nick, Thorn,' bellowed Hardcastle as he entered the room.

Thorn did as he was told; although he had come into contact with the police fairly regularly, he did not much care for this aggressive detective.

'I'm Divisional Detective Inspector Hardcastle of the Whitehall Division, Thorn.'

'Whatever it is, I ain't done it,' said Thorn. 'And I want

to know why I've been dragged all the way up here from Lewisham.'

Hardcastle and Marriott sat down opposite Thorn, and for a few moments the DDI gazed at him in silence. Thorn shifted about on his chair uneasily. Although he had not come across Hardcastle before, he sensed that this particular policeman was not a man to be trifled with. He also sensed that even if he had not committed a crime, Hardcastle was quite capable of stitching him up with one. And that made him nervous.

Hardcastle took the file from Marriott and opened it. He made a pretence of studying it, even though he was thoroughly conversant with its contents. Eventually, he looked up and stared at Thorn once more.

'Two malicious woundings, and a string of burglaries and robberies. Quite the villain, aren't you?'

'Them woundings wasn't down to me,' protested Thorn.

Hardcastle turned to Marriott. 'Isn't it amazing, Marriott? Every criminal who comes our way has been a victim of a miscarriage of justice.'

'Well, it was,' said Thorn, but he had the nasty suspicion that he was making no headway with this abrasive detective.

'How many prostitutes d'you pimp for, Thorn?' asked Hardcastle mildly.

'I don't know what you're talking about. Me a pimp? Someone's been telling lies about me.'

'I'm investigating a murder, Thorn.'

Jed Thorn sat bolt upright in his chair, an expression of fear crossing his face. 'Now hold on, I never done no topping.' This was getting serious. He fully expected to be 'given' a crime he had not committed, but not a murder. He began to sweat.

'Really?' Hardcastle took out his other pipe and filled it, slowly. All the time, he kept his eyes on Thorn.

'I dunno what you're on about,' protested Thorn, but from his demeanour, and the expression on his face, Hardcastle's comment had clearly unsettled him.

'You don't?' Hardcastle contrived surprise. 'Well, let me explain. A fortnight ago last Tuesday, a very important civil servant – Sir Nigel Strang by name – was murdered at the Ministry of Munitions. Now, the Prime Minister, Mr Lloyd George, is taking a great interest in this case.' He paused to light his pipe. 'And I've got to find someone who'll take the eight o'clock walk for that topping.' The DDI made it sound as though anyone would do. 'Whoever I put up for it'll appear before the Lord Chief Justice, and I've no doubt that he won't hesitate to put on the black cap. You see my problem, Thorn?'

'I've never heard of this geezer, guv'nor, and that's the God's honest truth.'

'Oh, but you have, Thorn. I happen to know that one of your girls was getting herself bedded by him at least once a week. And you were taking a handsome rake-off from the arrangement.'

'I don't know who's been telling you these wicked lies, guv'nor,' said Thorn, a nervous tic starting in his left eye, 'but it ain't true. I mean to say, if – and I'm not saying I did – but if I was getting a commission, I'd be daft to kill the goose what laid the golden egg, wouldn't I?'

'That's true,' said Hardcastle thoughtfully. It was the same point that Marriott had made. 'But it *would* make sense if you were getting an even bigger commission for topping Sir Nigel.'

Even though Sir Nigel Strang was known to be a woman-iser who consorted with prostitutes, Hardcastle had not lost sight of the fact that he had been an important civil servant in a sensitive ministry. Consequently, it did not necessarily follow that his death had been connected with his numerous extra-marital affairs. There was still the possibility that the German Intelligence Service had had a hand in the murder.

Hardcastle's observation caused Marriott to have the same thought, and he suddenly realised what Hardcastle was driving at, and why he had had Thorn arrested.

'Who's been telling you all this?' Thorn's anguished hands were twisting his cap back and forth. 'Who was it?' He remained silent for a moment. 'I'll bet it was that cow Liz Parsons.'

'Why d'you think that, Thorn?' asked Hardcastle.

'Well, it was her that was having a tumble with this here—' Thorn stopped speaking suddenly, realising that he had just displayed a guilty knowledge of Sir Nigel Strang.

'Let's start again,' said Hardcastle. 'You obviously know

about Liz Parsons and her wealthy client. So what d'you know about his murder?'

'I don't know nothing, guv'nor, so help me.'

Bearing in mind where Sir Nigel Strang's murder had taken place, Hardcastle was not altogether sure that the pathetic pimp seated opposite him would have had the wit, or the courage, to kill Strang in, of all places, his own office. But if the Germans were behind it, they might somehow have obtained a duplicate key to the back entrance. Provided they had paid enough, Thorn would undoubtedly have been prepared to take on the task. And the risk.

'Get Wilmot and Catto to take Thorn back to his drum in Lewisham, Marriott, and search it from top to bottom.'

'Have you got a warrant?' demanded Thorn.

Hardcastle laughed. 'Why do I want a warrant?' he asked. 'You've just given me permission to search your premises.' He turned to Marriott. 'You heard him give me permission, didn't you, Marriott?'

'Yes, sir, quite definitely,' said Marriott. He knew that the Bow Street magistrate would, without question, grant a warrant, but he also knew that Hardcastle did not want to waste the time of his officers by their having to go to Bow Street to swear an information.

'There's one other thing, Thorn,' said Hardcastle, as he stood up. 'You're Liz Parson's "minder", and—'

'No, I ain't,' said Thorn, in a pathetic attempt at denial.

'Don't bloody well interrupt me, Thorn,' thundered Hardcastle, leaning forward to smack the table with the flat of his hand. 'I want you to make sure that nothing happens to her. If a single hair of her head gets harmed, I shall come for you, and you'll go down for at least five years. And my friend at the Home Office will make sure you serve it on Dartmoor. So it'll be in your interests to make sure that she's safe. At all times. Got that, have you?'

'I don't see as how you can make me responsible for her safety,' complained Thorn.

'That's your problem, Thorn,' said Hardcastle dismissively. 'Lock him up, Marriott, until Wilmot and Catto are ready to take him home. Tell 'em there's no hurry, and I'll let 'em know when to go.'

Hardcastle crossed to the detectives' office. 'Drew, a moment of your time.'

Detective Sergeant Drew hurried across to the DDI's office. 'Sir?'

'Drew, I've just been talking to a villain by the name of Jed Thorn who's got form as long as your arm. He's also Liz Parsons's pimp.'

'Liz Parsons, sir?' Drew's face assumed a perplexed expression. He had not the faintest idea what Hardcastle was talking about.

'God Almighty, Drew, you were with me when we went to the Britannia Hotel. She's the tom who was bedded by Sir Nigel Strang there once a week. D'you remember it now?'

'Yes, sir. Sorry, sir, I wasn't quite following you.'

'Well, Drew, it occurred to me that Strang's fondness for jumping in and out of ladies' beds, including, don't forget, those of Mrs Chandler and Mrs Tait, might not have anything to do with his getting topped.'

'I see, sir,' said Drew, doing his best to follow Hardcastle's somewhat diffuse argument.

'It caused me to wonder if the Germans might just have had a hand in this here topping, and could've greased Thorn's palm with a substantial amount of silver, if you take my drift.'

At last Drew followed the DDI's reasoning. 'D'you think so, sir?'

'No, Drew, I never think things. All I'm saying is that it's a possibility. What I want you to do is to have a word with Mr Quinn, and see what he thinks of the idea. But before you do that, Thorn is downstairs waiting for Wilmot and Catto to take him back to his drum in Lewisham, which they are then going to search. I want you to go with them, because you know what you're looking for. If there's anything there that might indicate that he's a cat's-paw for old Fritz, you'll know what to do. And while you're about it, check all the keys in his possession. On second thoughts, seize them, and we'll have a look at them.'

'Keys, sir?'

'Yes, Drew, keys. If one of them happens to fit the private entrance to Sir Nigel's office, we might be getting somewhere.'

'I see, sir. Yes, certainly.'

'If, on the other hand, all that Wilmot and Catto find is stolen property, which I think is more likely, they'll know what to do. Understood?'

'Yes, sir.'

'Right, off you go.' Hardcastle took off his shoes and spats, and began to massage his feet.

'Are you married?' asked Wilmot, as the three detectives escorted Thorn through his front door.

'Yeah.'

'So where's your missus?'

'Working down the Arsenal,' replied Thorn churlishly. 'Never see the silly cow, and I wouldn't take her out if she was here, not with her face all yellow.'

'What's he talking about, Wilmot?' asked Drew.

'The women who work at Woolwich Arsenal get yellow faces, Sergeant, from the stuff they're handling. The explosives, and that.'

Catto remained with Thorn, mainly to ensure that he did not secrete anything that might be of interest to the police. Drew and Wilmot started the task of searching the house.

'Bit of a tip, isn't it, Sergeant,' observed Wilmot as they reached the front bedroom on the first floor. The bed was unmade, and clothing – male and female – was scattered about. And there was an overpowering odour of unwashed flesh that extended throughout the house, mixing with a smell of boiled cabbage.

Slowly and thoroughly, Drew and Wilmot worked their way through the house, from top to bottom.

'Anything?' asked Catto, when the two detectives joined him in the sitting room.

Wilmot shook his head, but then made for the fireplace. He was an experienced searcher, and knew where criminals tended to keep things that they didn't want the police to find. Kneeling down, he put his hand up the chimney and withdrew a brown paper envelope.

'And what have we here, Thorn?'

'Dunno. It's nothing to do with me. I ain't never seen it before.'

'Must have been something that Father Christmas left, last

time he came down your chimney, then.' Wilmot opened the envelope. 'Well, well,' he exclaimed, as he withdrew a quantity of banknotes. He counted the money, and then looked up. 'Ten pounds exactly, Sergeant,' he said to Drew. 'In nice new Bradburys.'

'I ain't never seen it before,' Thorn repeated, but there was no conviction in his statement.

'In that case, you won't mind if we take it with us, will you, Thorn?' asked Wilmot. 'We might even find who lost it.'

Detective Sergeant Drew took the neat pile of notes, and flicked through it. 'The numbers are in sequence,' he said.

'So it won't be what you get from the team of toms you run in Shepherd Market, will it, Thorn?' said Wilmot. 'Not unless they pay you a tenner at one go, having first gone to the bank to draw it out.'

Jed Thorn remained silent.

'So, where did it come from?' asked Drew.

'I dunno. My missus must've put it there.'

'In that case, we'll have to have a word with her,' said Drew. 'What time does she get in from the Arsenal?'

'About now,' said Thorn miserably, as he glanced at the clock on the mantelpiece.

'We'll wait, then,' said Wilmot. 'It'll be a nice surprise for her, won't it? By the way, where did you nick that clock?'

'I never nicked it,' protested Thorn. 'It was a wedding present.'

It was some ten minutes before the waiting police officers heard a latchkey in the front door. Moments later the sitting room door opened, and a woman of about forty entered the room. Her face was indeed yellow, as Jed Thorn had said, and she had on a cotton print dress, over which was a woollen cardigan. In place of a hat, she wore a scarf wrapped around her hair, and fastened beneath her chin.

'What's all this, then?' demanded the woman.

'This is my missus Edith,' said Thorn.

Edith Thorn's glance fell at once upon the pile of banknotes on the table.

'Yes,' said Wilmot, placing his hand on the notes. 'Interesting, isn't it?'

'And who the hell are you?' said Edith.

'We're police officers,' said Drew.

Edith Thorn turned accusingly to her husband. 'Are you in trouble with the law again, Jed Thorn?'

'No, honest, Edie.'

'Then what are three rozzers doing in my sitting room, eh, Jed Thorn? Answer me that.'

'Your husband suggested that this money was yours, and that you put it up the chimney, Mrs Thorn,' said Drew.

'I bloody wish,' said Edith vehemently. 'If I had ten pounds, I wouldn't stuff it up no chimney. I'd be up West enjoying meself.'

'Who said it was ten pounds?' asked Wilmot.

'Well, it looks like there's ten quid there,' mumbled Edith Thorn unconvincingly.

Drew turned his attention to Thorn once again. 'Well, what have you got to say?'

'Nothing.'

Drew entered into a whispered conversation with Wilmot. He was unsure what they should do next, but Wilmot was in no doubt.

'Jed Thorn, I'm arresting you for the unlawful possession of ten pounds.'

'I tell you, I ain't never seen it before.'

'You can lock him up and throw away the key, as far as I'm concerned,' yelled Edith, as the three police officers escorted Thorn into the street, and placed him in a taxi.

When Drew, Wilmot and Catto arrived at Cannon Row police station, DS Drew had a quiet word with the station officer.

'This man's been brought in for questioning, Skipper. He's been searched, and DC Wilmot here will give you the property found at his dwelling house. Lock him up until the morning, by which time we'll be able to question him further.'

'Right you are.' The station officer rose from his chair, and took a large bunch of keys from a hook on the wall. 'Come along, matey,' he said to Thorn, and seized his arm in a vice-like grip.

Seconds later, Thorn heard the familiar noise of his cell door banging shut. He sat on the bench and wondered how he would explain to the police how ten pounds came to be up his chimney. Ten pounds he had never set eyes on before.

TWELVE

Hardcastle caught his usual tram to Westminster. Sitting in the rear seat on the top deck so that he could enjoy his first pipe of the day, he glanced at his copy of the *Daily Mail*. The headlines were stark: FOLKESTONE RAID – 80 KILLED. There followed an account of a daylight air raid the previous Saturday when sixteen enemy aircraft flew over Folkestone and dropped bombs on Tontine Street. The raid had taken place between five and six in the evening, and the street was crowded. Most of the eighty people killed were women, but twenty-six proved to be children.

'Bloody Germans!' muttered Hardcastle, to the surprise of an old lady three seats in front who turned and stared at him.

Arriving at the police station, Hardcastle followed his usual practice. Sitting down at the station officer's desk, he put on his spectacles, and examined the books. A few petty thieves had been arrested overnight, and two drunks, but it was the name of Thorn that caught his eye.

'Ah! Good. What property did this Thorn have, Sergeant?' asked Hardcastle.

'The usual pocket contents, sir, plus a bunch of keys and ten pounds in banknotes.'

Hardcastle rubbed his hands together. 'Splendid,' he said. The news tended to evaporate the gloom that had descended upon him after reading of the Folkestone air raid. He stood up, and made his way upstairs whistling *It's a Long Way to Tipperary*. Much to the station officer's surprise.

'The DDI seems cheerful about something this morning, Sergeant,' said the duty constable.

'Get on with your bloody work unless you like walking a beat,' growled the station officer.

Hardcastle opened the door to the detectives' office, and ignoring the chants of 'Good morning, sir', beckoned to DS Drew.

'What's the story about Thorn, then, Drew?'

Following Hardcastle into his office, Drew explained, as succinctly as possible, what had taken place at Thorn's house at Farley Road, Lewisham.

'And he says he doesn't know anything about this ten pounds.'

'He denied all knowledge, sir. The numbers were in sequence, so either he's robbed a bank, or it was some sort of bribe.'

'He's the sort of idiot who'd rob a bank and come away with only ten quid,' said Hardcastle. 'Well, we'll have to see if we can't shake the truth out of him, Drew, won't we? I'm told he had some keys, as well.'

'Yes, sir.'

Hardcastle returned to the detectives' office. 'Wood.'

'Sir?' Detective Sergeant Herbert Wood sprang to his feet.

'See the station officer, and collect the bunch of keys that were in Thorn's possession when he was nicked. Take them up to the Ministry of Munitions and speak to a Mr Sinclair Cobb. He's an assistant secretary. Ask his permission to try all of those keys in the lock to the private entrance. Then come back here and tell me the result.'

The unshaven Jed Thorn presented a sorry picture as he shuffled into the interview room. Deprived of his neckerchief and his braces, he was obliged to hold up his trousers. But no station officer who wanted to keep his stripes, never mind his job, would allow a prisoner to keep any item with which he might do himself harm, even to the extent of hanging himself.

'Well, Thorn, my lad, you've got some explaining to do. Ain't he, Marriott?' said Hardcastle, turning to his sergeant. He placed the banknotes on the table between himself and his prisoner.

'Indeed, sir,' said Marriott.

'Are you going to tell me one good reason why I shouldn't put you on the sheet for topping Sir Nigel Strang?'

This turn of events terrified Thorn; he could see nothing to connect the search of his house with Hardcastle's awesome allegation. And his eyes remained fixed on the money.

'I never had nothing to do with that,' protested Thorn, 'and that's the God's honest truth.'

'My officers found ten pounds stuffed up your chimney, Thorn. That ten pounds.' Hardcastle pointed at the notes. 'How did it get there, and who gave it to you?'

'I've never seen it before, guv'nor,' pleaded Thorn. 'I don't know whose it is, or what it was doing up my chimney.'

'How long have you lived at Farley Road, Thorn?' asked Marriott.

'Since nineteen-ten, guv'nor.'

'How old are those banknotes, Marriott?'

'According to the bank, sir, they were issued early this year.' Marriott had no idea when the notes had been issued, and there had been no bank open between the time of Thorn's arrest and now. But Thorn had not the wit to realise that.

'And that means they must have got up the chimney while you were the legal tenant of the property,' said Hardcastle, a satisfied half smile on his face.

'I swear I don't know how it got there.' Thorn was sweating now.

'Then perhaps it wasn't stuffed *up* the chimney,' said Hardcastle. 'Perhaps a Zeppelin dropped it *down* the chimney.'

'It must've been my missus,' said Thorn lamely.

'Yes, I suppose so,' mused Hardcastle. 'Always a good idea to blame the missus. Well, in that case, we'll have her in and ask her a few questions, and I'll tell her you suggested it.'

'Do what you like, but that ain't mine,' said Thorn, gesturing at the ten banknotes that had so interested Hardcastle.

'You don't seem too well dressed for a pimp,' said Hardcastle, disconcerting Thorn by suddenly changing the subject. 'Have these toms been cheating on you?'

'I've give it up,' said Thorn, hoping that that would satisfy this nasty detective.

'Is that a fact?' Hardcastle smiled disarmingly at the man opposite him. He was not worried about Thorn's activities with the Shepherd Market prostitutes, but in the absence of anything else, he would be quite prepared to charge him with living on immoral earnings, or at least arrange for 'Posh Bill' Sullivan to do so. On the other hand, the most likely explanation was that another pimp had taken over Thorn's prostitutes under threat of bodily harm. 'Well, my lad, you're being held here until I get a satisfactory explanation for this here money. And if I was you, I'd think very carefully about it before I come and talk to you again.'

Leaving Marriott to return Thorn to the cells, Hardcastle mounted the stairs and called, once again, for Drew.

'I'm not happy about this money, Drew. Thorn denies knowing anything about it, and reckons it belongs to his wife.'

'She denied knowing anything about it as well, sir, when we interviewed her.'

'Of course she did, Drew. Anyone caught with ten quid stuffed up their chimney's going to deny it if they didn't come by it legally. But one thing's certain: it's not Thorn's rake-off from pimping. He'd never make that in a month of Sundays, and anyway, as you pointed out, the notes are in sequence.'

'It's a mystery, sir,' said Drew.

'Yes, it is. And the job of a detective is to unravel mysteries. Was this woman there when the money was found?'

'No, sir, she wasn't in the house at that time. She arrived after it was found.'

'Where was she, then?'

'At work, sir, at Woolwich Arsenal.'

'Was she indeed?' Hardcastle's eyes narrowed. 'The Arsenal, eh? Now that's very interesting, Drew, but more interesting to you than me, I think.'

'It is, sir?'

'Good God, Drew, put your thinking cap on. The woman works at Woolwich Arsenal, and you find ten quid in new banknotes stuffed up the chimney. And Jed Thorn, despite me threatening to put him on the sheet for murder, reckoned he knew sod all about it. But according to Wilmot, she knew it was ten quid before you told her. I'm not one of you clever Special Branch officers, but I've a passing fancy that she might've been given that money by someone who wants to know what goes on at the Arsenal. And I reckon that that someone might just go by the name of Fritz. So, I suggest you pop across the road to Mr Quinn and see what he thinks about it.'

'Yes indeed, sir,' said Drew.

'And do yourself a favour, Drew. Tell Mr Quinn you thought of it. I won't let on.'

'Thank you, sir,' said Drew with a grin.

'In the meantime, just to hurry things up, I'll send a couple of my officers down to Farley Road to nick Mrs Thorn.'

When DS Wood and DC Catto appeared in Hardcastle's office, he told them to arrest Mrs Thorn.

'What if she's not at home, sir? Do we keep watch?'

'It might come to that, Wood, but if she ain't there, go to the Arsenal and nick her. That should slow down the war effort.'

It was nigh on eleven o'clock by the time that DS Wood and DC Catto returned from Lewisham.

'She's downstairs, sir,' said Wood.

'Was she at home?'

'Yes, sir. She was due to start the late shift at two o'clock this afternoon.'

'Any trouble?'

'Not really, sir. She was screeching like a banshee when we told her we was knocking her off, but we got her here.'

'Right. Ask Sergeant Drew to see me.'

DS Drew joined Hardcastle some moments later. 'I've spoken to Mr Quinn, sir, and he's very interested in this business of the money, combined with the fact that Mrs Thorn works at Woolwich Arsenal.'

'Thought he might be,' said Hardcastle. 'In that case, you can come down with me and have a few words with her.'

Edith Thorn was dressed all in black, with a black straw hat perched on her upswept hair.

'What's the meaning of this?' she demanded, the moment that Hardcastle and Drew entered the interview room. 'I was due on lates at the Arsenal. There'll be trouble about this, you mark my words. I'm engaged on important war work, I am.'

'We know all about you, Mrs Thorn,' said Hardcastle, by

way of beginning the interview. 'Who was this man who gave you ten pounds to share some of the Arsenal's secrets with him?'

Drew was staggered that Hardcastle had made such a bold accusation without a scintilla of evidence to support it. But he said nothing.

Edith Thorn's face blanched. 'I dunno what you're talking about.' Suddenly, the initial hostility vanished.

'This officer is Detective Sergeant Drew, Mrs Thorn,' continued Hardcastle, 'and he's attached to Special Branch. If you didn't know already, it's Special Branch that arrests German spies. And German spies get hanged.'

Edith Thorn's eyes rolled up into her head, and with a slight moan, she slumped sideways in a dead faint.

'That'll be guilty knowledge, Drew,' observed Hardcastle mildly, as he stepped across to the recumbent body of Jed Thorn's wife. 'Get some water, will you.'

By the time that Drew had returned with a mug of water, Edith Thorn had made a partial recovery. 'What happened?' she gasped.

'You fainted when I told you that you was likely to get hanged, Mrs Thorn,' said Hardcastle. 'Of course, if you tell us all about this mysterious man, you might just get away with a prison sentence.'

'I never done nothing wrong, honest.'

'Where did the money come from?'

'This man.'

Hardcastle sighed. 'What man was that, Mrs Thorn?' he asked patiently.

'I was having a drink in the Brockley Jack pub on Brockley Rise, and this bloke come up and bought me a drink.'

'Were you alone?'

'No, I was with a friend of mine called Gladys. She's working on the trams, and we sometimes meet up there for a sherry and lemonade. If we're on the same shifts, like. Anyway, like I said, this man comes up to me, and asks if he can speak to me private like.'

'Did this man introduce himself?' asked Drew, looking up from the copious notes he was making. 'Did he give you a name?'

'No, he never said who he was.'

'Can you describe him, then?'

'He was about your height, I s'pose, with brown hair. That's about all I can tell you.'

'Did he speak with any sort of foreign accent?'

'No, he never had no accent. He just spoke like any Londoner.'

'Get on with it, then,' said Hardcastle.

'He said that he knew as how I worked down the Arsenal, and that I might be able to do meself a bit of good. He said he was working for the government, and was a secret inspector who checked up from time to time on how it was going down there.'

Hardcastle raised his eyes to the ceiling at this stark and totally unbelievable tale.

'Did he say what he wanted to know?' asked Drew.

'He said he'd like to know . . .' Edith Thorn paused in thought. 'Yes, he wanted to know how many six-inch calibre howitzer shells we was turning out every day. I think I've got that right.'

'And did you tell him?'

'No, I couldn't, not straight away, 'cos I didn't know. But I said I'd find out.'

'And that's when he gave you the money, was it?'

'Yes. He handed me an envelope and told me to put it in my bag. Then he said he'd get in touch again to get the answer, and he'd have some more questions.'

'And has he been in touch, Mrs Thorn?' asked Drew.

'No. But when I left him, he said he'd meet me tomorrow night in the same place, and that there'd be some more cash in it for me if I helped him.'

'Who decided on tomorrow night?'

'I did. He said he wanted to see me tonight, but I told him I was on the late shift.'

'Was this man drinking, Mrs Thorn?' asked Hardcastle.

'Yes, brown ale, I think.'

'He wasn't by any chance eating a German sausage while this little tête-à-tête of yours was going on, was he?'

'No, he wasn't eating nothing.' Edith Thorn obviously took Hardcastle's comment seriously.

Hardcastle turned to Drew. 'It looks to me, Drew, as though the rest of this little pantomime is yours.'

'Indeed, sir.'

'Right. You can lock her up, and then come up to my office.'

'Well, Drew, what d'you think? It seems a daft sort of story to me.'

'It's not that daft, sir.'

'But it all seems a bit far fetched to me,' said Hardcastle. 'D'you believe this story about some bloke going up to her in a pub, and asking her to spy for the Germans? Even I can see that this tale about being a government inspector was all my eye and Betty Martin.'

'I'm afraid I do believe it, sir. The German Intelligence Service is not noted for its ingenuity, or its originality. And your question about the German sausage wasn't far from the truth, either. There was a spy – a German national – arrested in Scotland last month who had an attaché case with him. Inside it was a German sausage, and you can't get those for love nor money over here since the war started.'

'God Almighty, give me an honest villain any day of the week,' exclaimed Hardcastle, shaking his head. 'What happens now, given that Mrs Thorn and her ten quid's of no further interest to me?'

'I'll speak to Mr Quinn directly, and we'll set traps for this man in the Brockley Jack tomorrow night. We'll get Mrs Thorn to meet him, and then we'll nick the pair of them.' Drew paused. 'On the other hand, MI5 might just let them run.'

'Run? What d'you mean, you won't arrest them?' Hardcastle's face portrayed his disbelief at such a cavalier approach to espionage.

'It might be in MI5's interest to see if there's anyone else in the chain. This man might just be what they call a pawn. It's possible he has a spymaster somewhere. In that case, we'd like to lay hands on him.'

'I wish all my jobs were as easy as that, Drew. If you happen to hear anything about Sir Nigel Strang's murder, or you find out that Jed Thorn had a hand in all this, let me know, will you?'

'Yes, sir,' said Drew, 'and thank you for your assistance. I'm sure Mr Quinn will be delighted. I must say that I was surprised that she confessed so easily, but I suppose it was the way you suggested that you knew all about it that made her talk.'

'I can see you've got a lot to learn about interrogation, Drew,' said Hardcastle.

'Well, that was a waste of time, Marriott,' said Hardcastle, 'apart from us having given Special Branch a sitter.'

'Wood's back, sir. He tried all the keys that were seized from Jed Thorn. None of them fitted the lock of the private entrance to the ministry.'

'No,' said Hardcastle dolefully, 'I didn't think they would.'

'Chuck him out, then, sir?'

'No, not yet, Marriott. I want another word with him. I can't see how this mystery man just picked Edith Thorn out of the blue, so to speak. He must've found out from someone that she was working at the Arsenal. And I'd put money on it being Jed Thorn who tipped him the wink. Anyhow, I've asked Drew to let me know if anything comes out of it. But it was a wild-goose chase as far as we're concerned, because we're no nearer finding out who topped Sir Nigel.'

'I suppose he could've followed her from the Arsenal when she left work,' suggested Marriott.

'Yes, that could be a strong possibility, and, I suppose, the most likely explanation.'

'Are you going to see Thorn now, sir?'

'Yes,' said Hardcastle, 'but I can't be bothered to get him up from the interview room. We'll talk to him in his cell.'

When the two detectives entered, Thorn was sitting on the wooden board that doubled as a bed.

'D'you know the way to Holloway Prison, Thorn?' asked Hardcastle as his opening gambit. 'Because your missus is in deep trouble, and you'll likely be visiting her there for the next ten years or so.' He repeated the story that Edith Thorn had told him.

'I don't know nothing about that,' said Thorn, picking nervously at the edge of the bed.

'Really? Then how d'you think some smart Alec came to know that she was working at Woolwich Arsenal, eh?'

'I dunno.'

'Well, I'll tell you what I think, Thorn. I think that you made the acquaintance of this man, and you told him where your missus was working.'

Thorn laughed. 'Why would I do that?'

'I think you found him and told him because you could see a few quid coming your way. Like the ten quid that was up your chimney.'

'Not me,' said Thorn.

'Well, I hope you're right, Thorn, because if my friends in Special Branch find out that it was you who made the introductions, so to speak, you'll be hanging on the end of a rope one fine morning.'

'Christ!' exclaimed Thorn, his face losing its colour. 'I never. Honest, I never.'

'We'll see, won't we?' said Hardcastle mildly. 'Because your missus is meeting this man again tomorrow night, and he'll have his collar felt. The next thing you know is that he'll be standing in the dock at the Old Bailey. And your missus will be standing beside him. And if he spills the beans on you, you'll be there too.'

'I don't know nothing about it,' protested Thorn once again.

'Is that so? Well, any thoughts you might have had about tipping him the wink that we're after him ain't going to happen. And just to make sure, you'll stay banged up here until that little performance is all over and done with.'

THIRTEEN

I t was on the following Monday morning – in fact it was just before ten o'clock – that a second murder took place within the boundaries of A Division.

'Excuse me, sir.' The policeman, whose four stripes indicated that he was a station sergeant, hovered deferentially in the doorway to Hardcastle's office.

'What is it, Skip?'

'I've just had a report that a man has been murdered on a number 59 bus, sir.'

'Really?' Hardcastle did not stir from his chair. 'Where was this?'

'At the bus stop in Bridge Street, sir, not more than ten minutes ago.'

'Who reported it?' Hardcastle liked to obtain as many facts as possible before deciding on his course of action.

'PC 133 Clarkson, sir. He was on the Clock Tower post when he was called.'

The Clock Tower post had been instituted following complaints from Members of Parliament entering the House of Commons by the door at the foot of Big Ben. It seemed that the cabs, both motorised and horse-drawn, bringing Members from Waterloo railway station, had experienced difficulty turning in the face of westbound trams crossing Westminster Bridge in the centre of the road. As a result, a policeman had been placed there to facilitate their return to Waterloo.

'And what did this officer report exactly?'

'The conductress called him, sir, and he found that a man had been stabbed to death on the outside.'

'What d'you mean, on the outside?'

'It's what they call the upper deck, sir, on account of it being an open-topped bus.'

'I'd better take a look, I suppose,' said Hardcastle with a sigh. Donning his bowler hat and seizing his umbrella, he opened the door of the detectives' office. 'Marriott, Wood and Catto come with me,' he shouted. 'Immediately.'

'What about me, sir?' asked DC Wilmot, as he scrambled to his feet.

'You stay as reserve, Wilmot,' said Hardcastle before making his way downstairs to the main part of the police station.

'Sir?' Marriott caught up with the DDI as he reached the main door of the police station.

'Someone's got hisself topped on a bus, Marriott.'

'Very good, sir.'

'I'm glad you think so, Marriott,' growled Hardcastle as the pair strode down Cannon Row, the street that gave their police station its name. 'We still haven't discovered who topped Sir Nigel yet, and now we've got another one to sort out. Apart from the spying Thorns and their ten quid.'

A PC drew himself to attention and saluted as Hardcastle and the others approached the bus. 'All correct, sir.'

Hardcastle grunted a response to this pointless, and in this case palpably untrue, form of reporting. He glanced at the divisional number on the policeman's helmet. 'Tell me what you know, Clarkson.'

'I was called from my point at nine fifty-one a.m., sir, by the conductress of this bus.' Clarkson indicated the vehicle with a wave of his hand. 'She told me that there'd been a rumpus on the outside deck. When she went upstairs, she found that a man had been attacked. I went up there, sir, and found a man dead. He appeared to have been stabbed. I called to PC 196 Holroyd, sir, the man on the traffic point at Parliament Street, and told him to inform the station.'

'Where's Holroyd now?'

'Back on his point, sir.'

'And the conductress?'

'She's inside, sitting down, sir. She was took a bit queer at the sight of the blood, but luckily a female passenger had smelling salts with her. Oh, and I also instructed the passengers that none of them were allowed to leave the bus, sir.'

'I should hope so, Clarkson. Is the conductress able to come out here?'

'I don't know whether she's all right now, sir. I'll just find out.' The PC boarded the bus and spoke briefly to a young woman in the uniform of the London General Omnibus Company who was sitting on the seat immediately inside. 'She's still feeling a bit queer, sir,' he said, when he returned. 'Perhaps you could speak to her inside.'

'I'm Divisional Detective Inspector Hardcastle, lass,' began the DDI, when he joined the conductress.

'Oh, I know your Kitty, sir. She's sometimes on this route.'

'I daresay,' muttered Hardcastle impatiently. 'What's your name?'

'Megan Davies, sir.'

'Tell me exactly what happened, Megan.'

'I was downstairs collecting fares, sir, when I heard a lot of shouting and screaming outside.'

'By which you mean the upper deck, do you?' Not only was Hardcastle a stickler for accuracy, he also abhorred jargon. Despite his frequent use of it.

'Yes, sir. So I was about to go up and find out what all the to-do was about, when two men come charging down the stairs and pushed me out of the way. They jumped off the bus and ran away.'

'Which way did they go?'

The conductress pointed towards Westminster Bridge. 'Over the bridge, I think, sir.'

'What did they look like, lass?'

'They was dressed quite rough, sir. They had caps on, and mufflers round their necks, but I never really got a good look at them.'

'What did you do next?'

'I went upstairs and saw this poor man lying back on one of the seats. He had blood all over him, sir. It was quite horrible.'

Hardcastle turned to the policeman. 'Did you see anyone running away, Clarkson?'

'Yes, sir. I did notice a couple of men running over the bridge, but it didn't mean anything to me immediately. By the time I found out what had happened, they'd long gone.'

'Can you give me a better description than Miss Davies did, Clarkson?' asked Marriott, busily taking notes in his pocketbook.

'No, Sergeant. I only caught a glim of 'em. Rough dressed is about all I can say.'

'Where did these two men get on, Megan?' asked Hardcastle.

'I don't know for sure, sir. The last time I collected fares outside – er, up top – was Trafalgar Square, and they weren't there then.'

'When did the man who was attacked get on the bus, then?'

'I think he must've jumped on at the top of Northumberland Avenue. It's not a stop, but we'd been held up by the policeman who was directing the traffic. But there's a proper stop at Horseguards Avenue. We calls that the War Office stop on account of it being near the War Office.'

'Yes, I suppose you would,' commented Hardcastle drily.

'I s'pose it's possible them two men got on at the top of Northumberland Avenue as well, but, like I said, I was downstairs collecting fares. I must've had my back to them. And when we got to the War Office stop, all I did was to look over my shoulder to see that the platform was clear of passengers, then I rang the bell.'

'Well, I don't know,' muttered Hardcastle. 'They get on near the War Office and commit a murder outside Scotland Yard. That's what I call thumbing their noses. Well, they won't be so bloody cocky when they take the eight o'clock walk, and that's a fact.' He sighed. 'I suppose we'd better have a look at our latest victim, Marriott.' The DDI began to mount the stairs of the bus, paused, and turned to Detective Sergeant Wood. 'While we're doing that, Wood, you and Catto take the names and addresses of all the passengers on the lower deck, and see if they can add anything; then they can go. Sergeant Marriott and me'll take care of them what's upstairs.'

There were seven passengers on the top deck, apart from the man who lay slumped in his seat. He looked to be about forty years of age, and the front of his waistcoat was stained a dark crimson. There was also blood dribbling from the corner of his mouth. Hardcastle took hold of the man's wrist and felt for a pulse. There was no sign of life.

'I reckon he's a goner, Marriott. Make sure, will you?'

Marriott felt for a pulse, but he could not find one either. 'Yes, he's gone, sir.'

'Search the body and see if he's got anything on him that might tell us who he is, Marriott.' Hardcastle looked around at the other passengers. 'I'm a police officer,' he announced. 'Who can tell me what happened?'

The passengers all started to speak at once, and Hardcastle held up a hand. 'One at a time,' he said. 'How about you, sir?' he asked, addressing a man at the front of the bus. 'What did you see?'

The man, immaculately dressed in a dark suit, a wing collar and a homburg hat, said, 'I heard shouting, Officer, and turned to see a man leaning over that man there.' He gestured at the dead body. 'I heard him say, quite clearly, "*Liebe Gott. Nein, nein*". Then I saw one of the men stabbing him several times. I jumped up and tried to stop them, but they turned and ran down the stairs. I tried to do what I could for the injured man, but I could see that he was already dead.'

'Take this gentleman's name and address, Marriott,' said Hardcastle, 'and a description of the attackers.' He turned to a young woman, and asked her what she had seen.

But by the time Hardcastle had finished interrogating the remaining passengers, and Marriott had taken their personal details, he had come to the conclusion that none of them had anything useful to contribute to his investigation.

'Get hold of Clarkson, and tell him to arrange removal of the body to St Mary's at Paddington, Marriott.'

'Clarkson's on a fixed point, sir,' said Marriott, a note of caution in his voice; he was aware that officers on such points should not leave their post, and should not do so even when called to a murder.

'Bugger the fixed point,' said Hardcastle. 'The Members of Parliament and their hacks will just have to manage without him for half an hour. Once you've done that, send a message to Dr Spilsbury, tell him we're sending him a dead body, and ask him to do the post mortem.'

'Yes, sir,' said Marriott, trying hard to disguise his irritation at being told, yet again, how to do his job. 'By the way,

the dead man had a British passport on him, sir. Name of
Joseph Hurley, born Dublin sixth of March 1877.'

'Must be an Irishman who speaks German,' muttered
Hardcastle.

A bus inspector appeared on the scene. 'What's going on
here, then?' he demanded.

'A man's been murdered on the top deck of one of your
buses,' said Hardcastle.

'But this bus was due off this stop twenty-five minutes ago.'

'Very likely, but it's not going anywhere right now,' said
Hardcastle, 'so I suggest you take it out of service until my
officers have finished examining it.'

The inspector muttered irritably to himself, and took a
small logbook with wooden covers from his pocket. He made
copious notes before storming off down the road, still
muttering.

Hardcastle returned to his police station in a furious mood.
He now had two murders to solve, one of which was the death
of an important civil servant. And to think that there were
senior officers at Scotland Yard who thought that nothing much
ever happened on A Division, apart from the occasional political demonstration. Fortunately for the overstretched police,
the suffragettes had suspended both their demonstrations and
their campaign of malicious damage for the duration of the
war.

He put his head round the door of the detectives' office.
'Drew, a moment of your time, if you please.'

'Yes, sir.' Detective Sergeant Aubrey Drew donned his
jacket and followed the DDI.

'How did your job at the Brockley Jack on Saturday night
turn out, Drew?'

'We had the place covered, sir. Special Branch and MI5.'

'And did this man turn up?'

'Yes, sir, he did. As I thought, MI5 decided to let him run,
and once the man had had a chat with Mrs Thorn, and they
split up, the MI5 people set about following him.'

'Any of your people take part in this following business?'

'No, sir. Mr Quinn's directions were that we should leave
it to MI5.'

'And was the Thorn woman given any more money?'

'Yes, sir, another ten pounds.'

'But I suppose you'd warned her not to tell him anything.'

Drew smiled. 'She had nothing that she could tell him, sir. She's not too bright, that one.'

Hardcastle spent a few minutes scraping at the bowl of his pipe, and filling it with tobacco. Once he had expended three matches in getting it alight, he leaned back in his chair.

'A funny thing happened this morning, Drew. A man was murdered on a bus, about an hour ago, right outside the Yard. Personally I call that bloody cheeky. However, one of the witnesses claims that he heard the victim cry out—' Hardcastle turned to his sergeant. 'What was it he said, Marriott?'

'According to the witness on the top deck, sir, the victim said *Liebe Gott. Nein, nein.*'

'Yes, that was it. That's German, ain't it, Drew?'

'Yes, sir,' said Drew, a fluent German speaker.

'So, what d'you make of that?'

'The victim was a German, sir,' suggested Drew tentatively.

'I can see why you're a Special Branch officer, Drew,' said Hardcastle sarcastically. 'However, we examined his personal effects, and among other things he had ten pounds and some loose change on him, and a British passport in the name of Joseph Hurley, born in Dublin.' The DDI tossed the document across the desk.

Drew picked up the passport and opened it at the page bearing the victim's photograph. 'Good God!' he exclaimed. 'This is the man who met Mrs Thorn at the Brockley Jack last Saturday.'

'Oh dear!' said Hardcastle mildly. 'It looks as though your friends at MI5 made a bit of a dog's dinner of following him.' He paused. 'Unless it was them what topped him,' he added.

'I'd better speak to Mr Quinn right away, sir,' said Drew.

'Good idea,' said Hardcastle, a smug smile on his face.

But Hardcastle's air of satisfaction at MI5's apparent blunder was dispelled with Drew's return some fifteen minutes later.

'Mr Quinn would like to see you at your convenience, sir. And would you take Hurley's passport with you.'

'A serious business, Mr Hardcastle,' said Quinn. 'Mr Thomson is taking a great interest in the matter.' Basil Thomson was the Assistant Commissioner for Crime, but these days took a greater interest in espionage and the supervision of Special Branch than he did in ordinary crime.

'I imagine so, sir,' said Hardcastle, for want of something else to say. He always found it a trying experience to converse with Quinn.

'Drew tells me that the dead man was the agent who contacted . . .' Quinn paused, and reached for a sheet of paper. 'The Edith Thorn woman.'

'So I understand, sir. Drew identified him from the photograph in the passport that was in the man's possession. The passport gave the name of Joseph Hurley.'

'Let me see it.' Quinn held out his hand.

'Yes, sir.' Hardcastle passed the document across the superintendent's desk.

For a few moments, Quinn examined the passport, carefully going through all its pages. 'I'll give this to MI5, Mr Hardcastle. I suspect it may be a forgery in view of what Drew tells me the man uttered when he was struck. German, I believe.'

'According to a reliable witness, sir.'

'And I think that it would be a good idea, before we go any further, if Drew saw the body. Just to make sure we're talking about the same man.'

'I'll arrange it, sir. Did MI5 have any information to offer?' Hardcastle posed the question more out of devilment than a need to know.

Quinn's face assumed a bleak expression. 'It appears that they succeeded in losing him, Mr Hardcastle. Hurley – although I doubt it's his real name – seems to have been a man skilled in the art of counter-surveillance.'

'Most unfortunate, sir,' murmured Hardcastle. The implication was that had the MI5 officers not failed in their duty, he would not have been saddled with another murder enquiry.

'Yes,' said Quinn tersely.

'Do you think he was a German spy, sir?'

'I think there's little doubt of it, Mr Hardcastle, but what is vexing us at the moment is why he should have been murdered.'

'To keep him quiet, I should think, sir.'

'That's certainly a possibility that we're considering.'

'It's possible, I suppose, sir, that he was being watched by his own side during his conversation with Mrs Thorn,' suggested Hardcastle, warming to his subject, 'and that they also saw that the police were watching Hurley, or whoever he is.'

'You could well be right, Mr Hardcastle.' For a moment or two, Quinn surveyed the DDI sitting opposite him. 'Although they're more likely to have spotted the MI5 watchers. There are times when I—' But he broke off, deciding to keep his criticism to himself.

'I wonder if there's a connection between Hurley's murder, and Sir Nigel Strang's,' mused Hardcastle, and instantly regretted having spoken his thoughts aloud. The last thing he wanted was to be transferred to Special Branch. He much preferred dealing with common criminals; he understood them, and knew that they feared him. But political work was vastly different, and, from what little he had gathered of Special Branch, its officers could not employ the strong-arm tactics so often used to the advantage of the ordinary divisional detective.

'I have to admit that the possibility that Strang was working for the Germans had crossed my mind,' said Quinn.

'Is there anything to support that, sir?' This was a suggestion that went much further than Hardcastle had meant to imply.

Quinn shook his head. 'Not at present, but MI5 are looking into it.'

Hardcastle felt like saying that he hoped their men were more proficient at that aspect of their work than they had been with their surveillance of the man Hurley, but decided that he had said enough already. There was, however, one other point he felt impelled to raise.

'Might it be a good idea to afford Mrs Thorn some protection, sir? If the killers went after Hurley, they might have a

go at Mrs Thorn. She hasn't told us much, and I don't think
she knew much. But Hurley's killers probably don't know
that.'

Quinn appeared to give that matter some consideration. 'I
think perhaps you're right, Mr Hardcastle,' he said eventually. 'No doubt you'll be able to provide officers from your
own resources to guard her.'

'Yes, sir.' Hardcastle stood up, at once regretting putting
forward a suggestion that would result in taking some of his
own men from their ordinary duties. 'I'll continue with my
enquiries, then, sir.'

'Be sure that Drew is kept informed, Mr Hardcastle.'

Back in his own office, Hardcastle sent for Catto and Wilmot.
'I've got a job for you two,' he said. 'You're to provide a
round-the-clock armed guard on Mrs Thorn. Wherever she
goes, you'll go, even to the Arsenal. You know where her
house is, and what it's like, because you searched it last
Thursday. Draw firearms from the station officer. Got that?'

'Yes, sir,' said the two DCs in unison.

'But where do we kip, sir?' asked Catto plaintively.

'Anywhere you can get your head down, lad. On the floor
of her salubrious parlour if necessary, and just remember
you'll still be better off than them poor sods in the trenches.
And I'll have a PC from the local nick posted to the front
door.'

'Yes, sir,' said Catto, who was none too pleased at the
prospect of sleeping on the Thorns' sitting room floor.

'Good, well don't make a Mons of it, and report daily by
telephone. You do know how to use the instrument, I suppose,
Catto?'

'Yes, sir.'

'And you can tell Mrs Thorn exactly why we're taking
care of her. That should put the wind up her, so she'll do
anything you tell her to do.'

'Yes, sir.'

With an expertise born of years of practice, the mortuary
attendant flicked back the sheet covering the face of the man
known to the police as Joseph Hurley.

'That's definitely him, sir,' said Drew, having taken a brief glance at the victim.

Hardcastle turned to his own sergeant. 'Show Drew that list of the numbers of the banknotes found on Hurley, Marriott?'

'Yes, sir.' Marriott handed his pocketbook to Drew.

After studying the list closely, Drew nodded. 'Yes, sir, they're in sequence to the ten pounds Hurley gave to Mrs Thorn the second time they met.'

'Seems to clinch it, then,' said Hardcastle.

But it only confirmed that Hurley, whoever he was, had been the man who had met Edith Thorn in the Brockley Jack, and there was little doubt about that anyway. Hardcastle knew that there would be much more work to put in before he arrested Hurley's killers. And those of Sir Nigel Strang too.

FOURTEEN

I t was two thirty on the Monday afternoon by the time that Catto and Wilmot arrived at the Thorns' house in Lewisham, having first drawn Webley pistols from the station officer at Cannon Row, and attired themselves in suitable clothing.

A uniformed PC from the local police station barred their entrance.

'And what can I do for you?' he demanded, feet apart, and thumbs tucked beneath the flaps of his tunic pockets.

By way of a reply, Catto produced his warrant card. 'We're here to keep an eye on Mrs Thorn,' he said.

'Best of luck, mate,' said the PC with a brief, humourless laugh. 'A right bloody pain in the neck is that one.'

Jed Thorn opened the door. 'What the hell's going on?' he demanded. 'And what's that copper doing on my front door?'

'Where's your missus?' asked Catto, pushing his way in.

'Upstairs, why?'

'We want a word with her.'

'She's resting. She's just come off the early shift at the Arsenal.'

'Fetch her down . . . *now*.' Catto, unhappy at being saddled with what appeared to be the endless task of protecting Edith Thorn, was in no mood to be thwarted.

A few minutes later, Edith Thorn, in a pink woollen dressing gown, appeared on the threshold of the sitting room. 'Oh, not you lot again,' she exclaimed. 'What is it this time? And what's that copper doing on my doorstep?' she asked, echoing what her husband had asked earlier.

'D'you remember the man you met in the Brockley Jack last Saturday night?'

'Course I do. What about him?'

'He's been murdered.' Catto noticed, with some degree of satisfaction, that Edith Thorn's face paled dramatically.

'Murdered?' Edith put a hand to her mouth.

'And the powers-that-be at Scotland Yard think that you

might be next,' continued Catto. 'On account of you having done a bit of business with him.'

'Oh my Gawd!' muttered Edith, and promptly collapsed on the worn settee.

'My bosses think he was topped to shut him up, see.' Catto was beginning to enjoy himself. He pulled back the skirt of his jacket to display the heavy pistol at his belt. 'That's why we're here, Fred Wilmot and me, to make sure you don't get killed an' all.'

'But I've got to go to work tomorrow morning.'

'We know,' put in Wilmot, 'and we'll be going with you.'

'Not that we'll mind if you take a couple of days sick leave,' suggested Catto, who did not particularly want to spend ten hours of every day at Woolwich Arsenal. 'Come to think of it, Edith, you do look a bit sick.'

'Don't you worry about that, copper, I'm not going anywhere.'

'At least that rozzer on the door will scare the rent collector away,' said Jed Thorn. 'Bloody landlord never does anything we ask him. The damn place is falling down.' He waved a hand round the room.

There were damp patches on the ceiling, even now in the height of summer, and Wilmot – something of a handyman – had noticed that the brickwork on the outside of the house badly needed pointing. And as for the wallpaper, that curled down from the ceiling in at least half a dozen places.

'What do you do for a living, Mr Thorn?' asked Wilmot, although Hardcastle had advised him and Catto of Thorn's pimping activities.

Thorn looked shifty. 'Bit of this and a bit of that,' he said archly. 'But I'm between jobs at the moment.'

'I'm surprised you haven't been called up for the army,' said Catto.

'They wouldn't take me, I've got flat feet,' said Thorn, but there was no conviction in his statement.

'So have half the army in Flanders,' said Catto, and made a mental note to inform the authorities that a man apparently eligible for military service lived at Farley Road, Lewisham. 'But I heard you were a pimp.'

'Not me, guv'nor,' said Thorn hastily. 'Someone's been telling you wicked lies.'

'My inspector doesn't usually tell lies,' said Catto mildly, a comment that afforded Thorn little comfort.

It was on the Tuesday morning that Hardcastle received a surprise visitor.

'There's a Mr James Cresswell downstairs, sir,' said the station-duty constable. 'He's asking to see you. He says it's urgent.'

'Show him up, lad.'

Shortly afterwards, the acting permanent secretary at the Ministry of Munitions appeared in the DDI's office.

'I'm sorry to call on you so early, Mr Hardcastle,' said Cresswell, 'but a matter has arisen that I feel you should know about.'

Hardcastle glanced at his watch: it was ten thirty, and far from early by his standards. 'And what might that be, sir?' he asked, briefly winding his hunter, and dropping it back into his waistcoat pocket.

'It concerns Sinclair Cobb.'

'The assistant secretary?'

'Yes. He's gone missing, Inspector.'

'One moment, sir.' Hardcastle rose from his seat and crossed the corridor. 'Marriott, come in here a moment.'

Once Marriott had joined them, Hardcastle asked Cresswell to repeat what he had just said, and bade him continue.

'He didn't come in to work yesterday, that is Monday the fourth of June,' said Cresswell.

'Oh? And why was that?'

'I'm afraid I don't know. It's most out of character for Cobb to take a day off without informing the office.'

'I imagine so,' murmured Hardcastle. 'Has he come to work this morning?'

Cresswell brushed a hand over the knee of his trousers, and looked up. 'I'm afraid he hasn't, Inspector, and we have no idea where he's gone.'

'Don't you think it would have been a good idea to have informed me immediately, Mr Cresswell?'

'I didn't think it was that important.'

'Shortly after Sir Nigel Strang is murdered in his office, a man in possession of a key to the private entrance goes

missing, and you didn't think that that was important? In my
view, you should've notified me yesterday, because I'm
certain that whoever killed Strang entered the building by
that private entrance. And failure to tell me that Cobb was
missing almost amounts to obstructing the police in a murder
enquiry.' Hardcastle leaned back in his chair and surveyed
the civil servant with a frown on his face.

Sitting slightly behind Cresswell, Marriott gasped
inwardly. He thought that the way in which Hardcastle was
speaking to a very senior civil servant was courting a repri-
mand. But he need not have worried.

'Well, I, er . . .' Cresswell dithered. 'Surely you can't for
one moment imagine that Sinclair Cobb had anything to do
with Nigel Strang's death, can you?'

'You tell me,' said Hardcastle, who was rather enjoying
Cresswell's discomfiture.

'Have any enquiries been made at Mr Cobb's address,
Mr Cresswell?' asked Marriott.

Cresswell turned in his chair. 'Yes. I had my private secretary call there yesterday, but his landlady said that he left
the house on Saturday, and she's not seen him since.'

'That would be Saturday the second of June, would it?'

'Yes,' said Cresswell.

'You said "landlady", Mr Cresswell. Does that mean that
Mr Cobb isn't married?' Hardcastle leaned forward to take
his pipe from the ashtray. He spent a few moments filling
it, and lighting it.

'No, he's not married, Inspector.'

'Is he courting?'

'Not that I know of.'

'Perhaps you'd let my sergeant have a note of his address,
sir. It's obvious that we'll have to make some enquiries.'

'Yes, I suppose so.' Cresswell hesitated. 'But I doubt that
you'll find out any more than my secretary discovered.'

'Your secretary's not a detective, Mr Cresswell, but I am,'
said Hardcastle bluntly. 'It seems to me that this whole business has been treated in a rather slapdash manner.'

Cresswell accepted the rebuke with a slight nod of his
head. 'Is there any way of keeping this out of the press,
Inspector? A senior civil servant missing from our ministry

– in particular our ministry – is likely to cause some conster-
nation if it becomes common knowledge.'

'I can't be responsible for what appears in the newspapers,
Mr Cresswell, but you can rest assured that I shan't tell them
anything. Of course, it's quite possible that a member of your
staff has spoken to the newshounds of Fleet Street already.'

'I think that unlikely, Inspector.'

'I'll let you know what we learn, Mr Cresswell.'

'Thank you. I'd be grateful.'

'I've no doubt,' said Hardcastle, but determined that
nothing would be said to anyone in the Ministry of Munitions
until he had resolved this latest mystery.

'I'll bid you good morning, then, Inspector.' A somewhat
chastened James Cresswell left the DDI's office, hoping that
the abrasive Hardcastle would not report his dereliction to
higher authority. Like the minister.

The address for Sinclair Cobb that Cresswell had given
Hardcastle proved to be in Chadwick Street, Westminster. It
was an old house, and had probably been the residence of a
wealthy family in years gone by. But now it comprised a series
of rooms accommodating single professional gentlemen.

An attractive woman of about thirty answered the door.
Her blonde hair was piled high, and although well dressed,
she had the bearing of a woman once better off, but who
had now fallen on hard times.

'Good morning, ma'am,' said Hardcastle, raising his bowler
hat. 'We're police officers. I would like to speak to the lady
who owns this property.' In his opinion, this woman was
much too young to fit the conventional perception of a
rooming-house landlady.

'I'm the owner. I'm Beatrice Cooper.' The woman raised
an eyebrow, wondering what two policemen were doing on
her doorstep.

'That would be *Mrs* Cooper, would it?' Hardcastle
wondered briefly if she had been the owner since the property's more affluent days.

'Yes, it is,' said the woman, an amused twinkle in her eye.

'I'm given to understand that you let rooms to a Mr Sinclair
Cobb, ma'am.'

'Yes, that's correct. Perhaps you'd better come in?'

'Thank you.' The DDI followed Mrs Cooper into a sitting room at the front of the house.

'Would you care for some tea? I've just made some.'

'Thank you, ma'am, that would be most welcome.'

'Do take a seat. I shan't be a moment.'

The two detectives sat down in armchairs in the well-appointed room. The furniture was of good quality, but beginning to show signs of shabbiness, as was the carpet. On a side table there was a collection of photographs – of Beatrice Cooper's family, Hardcastle presumed – but the prominent one was of an army officer in the uniform of a captain in the Machine Gun Corps.

'I see you're admiring my picture gallery,' said Mrs Cooper, as she entered the room with a tray of tea. 'That was my husband. He was killed at the Somme in July last year. He was in the Machine Gun Corps, but he was attached to this new Tank Corps. I'm afraid I have to let out rooms to make ends meet. Mercifully, we didn't have time to have children.' She glanced at Marriott. 'Would you be so kind as to move that table nearer the sofa?'

Marriott leaped up and did as he was asked, and for the next few moments, Mrs Cooper busied herself pouring the tea and handing it round. 'Now, gentlemen, how may I help you?'

Hardcastle introduced himself and Marriott. 'I understand that Mr Cobb left here last Saturday, the second of June, Mrs Cooper.'

'Yes, that's correct. As a matter of fact I had a young man call here yesterday. He was from the ministry where Mr Cobb works. He seemed quite worried that Mr Cobb hadn't arrived for work.'

'It beggars belief,' muttered Hardcastle, but forbore from criticising Cresswell and his people for their lack of urgency in the matter of a missing civil servant. It struck him as nothing short of cavalier to have taken no action until the day after Cobb had disappeared. But Hardcastle's concept of urgency obviously did not accord with that of the civil service.

'Is there something wrong, Inspector?' It was noticeable that Beatrice Cooper's eyes did not meet either Hardcastle's or Marriott's.

'Only that I'm surprised that Mr Cobb should have disappeared without informing his employers, Mrs Cooper.'

'I did think it rather strange,' said Beatrice Cooper. 'I mean anything could've happened to him.' She frowned. 'Oh, goodness! Is that why you're here, Mr Hardcastle? Has something dreadful happened? An accident, or something of the sort?'

'We don't know, ma'am. And that *is* why we're here. Tell me, did Mr Cobb offer any explanation for his departure? Did he say where he was going?'

'No, he just went out on the Saturday morning – I thought to buy a newspaper – but he didn't return.'

'Did he have anything with him, ma'am?' asked Marriott. 'Such as a suitcase.'

'No, nothing.'

'Has he ever done anything like that before?'

'No. He was a man of very predictable habits. Always left for the office at exactly the same time, and nearly always returned at the same time each evening. Unless there was a special meeting of some sort. He never spoke of the work he did. I suppose because it was secret. He never even told me exactly where he worked. Only that it was in Whitehall.'

'Have you heard from him since he left, Mrs Cooper?' asked Hardcastle. 'A telephone call, for instance.'

'No, not a word.'

'And you've no idea where he's gone.' Hardcastle wanted to make absolutely sure of that point.

'No, none at all.' Again Beatrice Cooper avoided Hardcastle's gaze.

'And you say he didn't take anything with him.'

'No, he didn't. In fact, all his things are still here. I've been wondering what to do about it. I can't really afford to have a room empty, and Mr Cobb only paid up to the end of this week.'

Marriott leaned forward to place his empty cup and saucer on the tray. 'Did Mr Cobb mention the murder of Sir Nigel Strang, Mrs Cooper?' he asked.

'Not really. There was a piece in *The Times* about it, and I asked Sinclair – er, Mr Cobb – if he knew the man.' Beatrice Cooper coloured slightly. 'But he said he didn't.'

That interested Hardcastle, but he did not comment on it. 'Well, thank you for your help, Mrs Cooper,' he said, as he stood up. 'It's a real mystery. But perhaps you'd let me know if he does return. I can be reached at Cannon Row police station, just off Whitehall. It's opposite Scotland Yard.'

'Yes, of course.' Beatrice Cooper rose from her chair intent on seeing her callers to the door.

'And thank you for the tea, ma'am,' said Marriott.

'And what did you make of that, Marriott?' asked Hardcastle as they strode towards Great Peter Street.

'I don't think she was telling the truth, sir.'

'I think she was lying, Marriott, and there's a deal of difference between not telling the truth and lying. Did you notice the way she blushed when you mentioned Strang's murder.'

'Perhaps she was telling the truth about that, sir. I suppose it's possible that Cobb hadn't told her where he worked, and to admit to knowing Strang would have given the game away.'

'No, there's more to it than that, Marriott. I'm bloody certain she knows where Cobb's gone. What's more I wouldn't be surprised if she and Cobb weren't a bit closer to each other than landlady and tenant, if you take my drift. She's an attractive young widow, after all, and men of the calibre of Cobb are a bit thin on the ground since we started losing so many over the other side of the Channel.'

'But why has he run, sir?'

'Maybe he topped Sir Nigel, Marriott, and thought we were getting a bit too close to him.'

'But why, sir?'

'I've no idea, Marriott, but I intend to find out.'

But how Hardcastle proposed to do so did not become clear to Marriott until they both returned to the police station.

'What are the names of those two new men who were posted in from Vine Street, Marriott?'

'Carter and Lipton, sir.'

'Good. Fetch 'em in.'

The two detective constables appeared in the doorway of Hardcastle's office within seconds.

'Which of you is the senior?' asked the DDI.

'I am, sir. I'm Carter.'

'Well, don't stand there like a dying duck in a thunder-
storm, come in,' said Hardcastle, as he sat down and began
to fill his pipe. 'Now then, there's a very attractive young
widow what lives in Chadwick Street. Sergeant Marriott will
give you the exact address.'

'Very good, sir,' said Carter.

'I haven't finished yet, so don't interrupt,' barked
Hardcastle. 'I want her watched. I've half a mind that she'll
be going somewhere either this evening or tomorrow morning.
Wherever she goes, you go, the pair of you. Understood?'

'Yes, sir, but what if she goes out of the Metropolitan Police
District, sir?' Carter was mindful of the way in which the DDI
at Vine Street had scrutinised claims for expenses, and had no
reason to believe that Hardcastle was any different. In fact, it
was the consensus among the junior detectives at Cannon Row
that Hardcastle was as careful with the Commissioner's money
as he would be if it were coming out of his own pocket.

'For pity's sake, Carter. Have you got cloth ears or something? Didn't I just say that wherever she goes you go?'

'Yes, sir.'

'Well, I don't care if she goes to Glasgow or Dublin or
Cardiff, or for that matter, America. You follow her. And
don't be seen.'

'Yes, sir.'

'Well, don't stand there, man, get on with it. And keep
me informed.'

Carter and Lipton fled, unhappy that they were saddled
with a task that could easily take all night, if not longer. Just
when they thought it was about time to go home.

'D'you really think Mrs Cooper knows where Cobb is,
sir?' asked Marriott.

'I've no idea, Marriott, but putting Carter and Lipton on
her tail is one way of finding out.'

'Supposing she does go to see Cobb, sir. What then?'

'Then we'll have a few words with him. I just hope to
God he's not another spy. I've had quite enough of getting
embroiled with Special Branch and that MI5 lot to last me
a lifetime.'

FIFTEEN

With three-storied houses on each side of the road, and nowhere to hide, Chadwick Street was not the best of places to keep a discreet observation. In common with most officers carrying out surveillance work, Carter and Lipton each felt that they were sticking out like the proverbial carbuncle on a vicar's nose.

From six thirty onwards the two detectives witnessed the arrival and departure of several men, but Hardcastle had not explained that they were probably boarders in Mrs Cooper's house.

At eleven o'clock, Carter, the senior of the two DCs, made a decision.

'I think we'll knock it off for the night, Harry,' he said to Lipton. 'I doubt that the woman will go anywhere now. We'll pick it up again at eight tomorrow morning.'

'What are you going to do about reporting to the guv'nor, Gordon?' asked Lipton.

'It's no good trying to do so now, Harry,' said Carter, glancing at his watch. 'The DDI will be long gone. Tomorrow morning, I reckon.'

Lipton took up the observation the next morning while Carter went to Cannon Row police station to make his report. He had been placed in the invidious position of having to keep watch in Chadwick Street *and* make a report. It was one of those difficult situations where whatever he did was wrong, and if he did nothing, that was wrong too.

'Good morning, sir.' Carter waited on the threshold of Hardcastle's office.

'What are you doing here, Carter? I thought I'd given you an observation in Chadwick Street.'

'Yes, sir, but you told me to keep you informed.'

'So inform me, Carter.' Hardcastle scraped at the bowl of his pipe and filled it with tobacco.

'We kept observation from six thirty until eleven o'clock, sir.'

'When?' snapped Hardcastle. 'One of the things I won't stand for is sloppy reporting, Carter.'

'Er, last night, sir. We saw several men entering and leaving the premises and, in my opinion, there's no doubt that it *is* a brothel.'

Hardcastle lit his pipe, and gazed in wonderment at his detective. 'What the hell are you talking about, Carter? Have you taken leave of what few senses you've got? Who said anything about Mrs Cooper's address being a knocking shop, eh? I know you spent a few years on C Division, but there are crimes that don't involve prostitutes and bawdy houses.'

'Er, well, I thought . . .' Carter stuttered to a halt.

'Thought?' roared Hardcastle. 'It's obvious to me that thinking is the one thing you're not equipped to do, lad. I told you to keep watch on the house and follow Mrs Cooper wherever she happened to go, did I not?'

'Yes, sir.'

'Well, bugger off, and do what you're told to do, Carter.'

'Yes, sir.'

Carter had joined Lipton less than twenty minutes after his bruising encounter with Hardcastle. Ten minutes after that, the trim figure of Beatrice Cooper emerged from her house.

Attired in a tweed costume, with a fetching tricorn hat, and high boots, Mrs Cooper was a picture of elegance. Carrying a small valise, she walked through to Horseferry Road where she hailed a cab. Fortunately for the two detectives, another cab was right behind it, and Carter and Lipton leaped in, Carter giving the driver that instruction so beloved of fiction writers: 'follow that cab'.

At Victoria railway station, Mrs Cooper alighted and made her way to the bookstall where she purchased a copy of the *Daily Telegraph*. Although the concourse was crowded at that time of the morning, Carter and Lipton managed to keep her in sight. Carter bought a copy of the *Daily Mail* and Lipton bought the *Daily Mirror*. Beatrice Cooper next went to the booking office where the two detectives heard her ask for a third-class return to Brighton. They did the same.

The hour-long journey to Brighton was uneventful, and it was fortunate for Carter and Lipton that Mrs Cooper had not opted to sit in that part of the train reserved for ladies. Although in the same compartment as Mrs Cooper – who, to their surprise, lit a cigarette – the DCs did not sit together, neither did they converse with each other. There was always the possibility that they might have to split up when they arrived at their destination, and it was as well for them not to appear to know each other. Despite Hardcastle's critical opinion of their abilities, each of them was well versed in carrying out a discreet surveillance. It was something they had done many times.

At Brighton railway station, Carter alighted ahead of Mrs Cooper, and spent some time perusing a timetable. Lipton followed the woman out, and bought a penny bar of Nestlé's chocolate from a slot machine as Carter set off in pursuit of their quarry. It was the customary form of tailing a suspect; the police called it 'playing leapfrog'.

Once clear of the station, Beatrice Cooper hailed a taxi. Carter and Lipton took a chance on sharing a cab themselves, and followed for the short journey down Queen's Road to West Street, where Mrs Cooper's cab stopped outside a boarding house. She paid the driver and walked straight in.

'What do we do now, Gordon?' asked Lipton.

'I don't know, Harry.' For a moment or two Carter dithered before making up his mind. 'You hang on here in case she comes out again, and I'll see if I can find a phone and ring the guv'nor.'

'But what if she does come out again? Before you're back, I mean.'

Again Carter gave the matter some thought. 'Wherever you fetch up, Harry, ring the local nick, and if you're not here when I get back, I'll do the same so they can tell me where you are, and I can join you.' And leaving Lipton with that unsatisfactory arrangement, Carter went in search of a telephone.

It was a ten-minute walk before he came across a shop displaying a blue sign proclaiming 'You may telephone from here'. He told the operator the number he wanted, and further advised her that it was an official police call. Minutes later he was talking to the DDI.

'We're in Brighton, sir,' said Carter.

'So tell me what happened,' said Hardcastle impatiently. 'You're not down there just for a breath of sea air, I hope.'

'No, sir.' Carter went on to explain the course of events that had ended at a West Street boarding house.

'Go into the boarding house, Carter, and examine the register. I want to know if Sinclair Cobb's there. In the meantime, Sergeant Marriott and I will catch the next train and join you.'

'If she's moved, sir, and we're not there, I'll have left a message with the local nick so you'll know where we've gone. I hope that's all right, sir.'

'It'll do, I suppose,' muttered Hardcastle gruffly, but secretly he was pleased at the initiative Carter had shown.

It was almost one o'clock by the time that Hardcastle and Marriott arrived at West Street. The DDI was somewhat relieved to discover that his detectives had not moved.

'Well, Carter, what've you learned?'

'I checked the register, sir, and—'

'I know you checked the register, Carter, because I told you to. So don't give me unnecessary information. What did you find out?'

'He's there, sir.'

Hardcastle sighed. '*Who's* there? The King perhaps, or maybe the Sultan of Zanzibar?'

'No, sir, Sinclair Cobb,' said Carter. 'He booked in on Saturday the second of June, and it seems he's been there ever since.'

'And has Mrs Cooper registered?'

'Yes, sir. This morning. Well, I think it was her. The register shows a Mrs Beatrice Cobb of Chadwick Street, Westminster. And she's booked in for the night.'

'Yes, well, it's pretty obvious what's going on here,' commented Hardcastle drily. 'You and Lipton stay here. Come, Marriott, it's time we had a word with Mr Cobb. And for that matter, Mrs Cooper, alias Mrs Cobb.'

There was a table inside the door of the boarding house,

bearing a vase of fresh flowers and a brass bell. Hardcastle struck the bell and waited, but no one responded. He struck the bell again, several times.

The woman who appeared was at least fifty years of age. She wore a long black dress relieved only by a white collar, and her greying hair was dragged back into a tight bun that did little to soften the unwelcoming expression on her lined face.

'You don't have to keep banging that bell, you know. I'm not deaf. And I ain't got any spare rooms. It's the height of the season and we're full up.'

'I'm Divisional Detective Inspector Hardcastle of Scotland Yard, madam.' The DDI saw no harm in inflating his importance with a white lie. 'Are you the owner of this establishment?'

'Yes, I am. Mrs Sexton's my name. And what would the police be wanting with an honest woman like me? Everything here's above board.' The landlady seemed unimpressed by Hardcastle's awesome announcement.

'It's not you I want, madam, it's Mr Sinclair Cobb who is staying at this boarding house.'

'It's a private hotel,' corrected Mrs Sexton with a sniff.

'I don't care what you call it, but I need to see Mr Cobb immediately.'

'Room five, top of the stairs, and turn right.' Mrs Sexton sniffed again, and turned on her heel, vowing to herself that she would give Mr Sinclair Cobb and his floozy their marching orders. It did not do to have the police calling at her respectable establishment. It had never happened before, and she did not want word of it getting around Brighton.

Hardcastle knocked on the door of room five, and entered without waiting for a response.

'What the hell?' Sinclair Cobb and Beatrice Cooper were in bed together, and it did not need a great deal of imagination to work out what they had been doing.

'Good afternoon, Mr Cobb. Mrs Cooper.' Hardcastle nodded in the direction of the woman.

'Inspector, what on earth are you doing here?' asked Cobb, as he recognised Hardcastle. Mrs Cooper clutched the bedclothes and held them to her chin.

'I'm looking for you, Mr Cobb. Apparently you're what might be called absent without leave from the Ministry of Munitions, and Mr James Cresswell is very concerned about you.'

'I've resigned.'

'That's not the information I was given.' Hardcastle turned his attention to Beatrice Cooper. 'You told me that you hadn't seen Mr Cobb after he left your house, and you also said that you didn't know where he was. Now why was that?'

'My liaison with Mr Cobb is none of your business, Inspector,' said Beatrice Cooper spiritedly. 'And now, if you'd kindly leave us, I'd like to get dressed.'

'I'll see you downstairs, Mr Cobb,' muttered Hardcastle, and he and Marriott walked from the room.

'Have you finished?' demanded the landlady, when Hardcastle and Marriott reappeared in the hall.

'Madam, I've only just begun,' snapped Hardcastle testily.

'Well, really, I don't know,' said Mrs Sexton, and tossing her head, flounced through a door at the rear of the hall.

Ten minutes later, Cobb and Beatrice Cooper came down the stairs. Unsurprisingly, Mrs Cooper was dressed in the same clothes that she had worn earlier. Rather daringly, the hem of her skirt was a good ten inches clear of the ground. Had Mrs Hardcastle seen it, she would have told her husband that only a tart would dress like that.

'Sinclair Cobb, I am arresting you on suspicion of having murdered Sir Nigel Strang on or about Tuesday the fifteenth of May this year.' Hardcastle stepped forward and touched Cobb's arm as a token of his detention.

'That's ridiculous,' cried Beatrice Cooper. But she had paled significantly, and placed a hand on the table to support herself. For a moment Hardcastle thought that she was about to faint.

'I don't know what makes you think I had anything to do with Sir Nigel's death, Inspector.' Cobb was nowhere near as taken aback by his arrest as Beatrice Cooper had been.

For his part, Marriott was flabbergasted at Hardcastle's presumption. As far as he could see, there was no evidence that pointed to Cobb as Strang's killer.

'Well, for a start, Mr Cobb,' said Hardcastle, 'you disappeared from your office a matter of days after the murder, and clearly went to some pains to cover your tracks, so to speak. Furthermore, you have a key to the private entrance to the ministry building, and I have reason to believe that the murderer effected an entry by that door.'

'But there are at least nine other people with a key to that door, Inspector.'

'So I understand,' agreed Hardcastle, 'but none of the others ran away without telling anyone where they were going. I shall now take you back to London for questioning.'

'What about me, Sinclair?' asked Mrs Cooper, a plaintive note in her voice.

'I'm sorry, Bea, but there's nothing I can do. Obviously I have to go back to Town with the inspector to sort things out. Then I'll come and see you at Chadwick Street.' Cobb turned to Hardcastle. 'How did you know where to find me?' he asked.

'Your lady friend as good as told us,' said Hardcastle, rather smugly.

'How did I do that?' asked Beatrice, a frown descending on her face.

'I had you followed, Mrs Cooper – or is it Mrs Cobb? – and you obligingly led my officers all the way to Brighton.'

'If you're leaving, I'll need settlement now, Mr Cobb,' said Mrs Sexton, who had silently reappeared in the hall.

Sinclair Cobb opened his wallet and took out a five-pound note. 'That should cover my stay and Mrs Cobb's. And I'll thank you for the change.'

Hardcastle smiled at the pointless pretence that Beatrice Cooper was his wife. He did not believe for a moment that the perceptive Mrs Sexton had been taken in by the couple's deception.

The landlady took the banknote, and examined it carefully. 'Be so good as to write your name and address on the back, Mr Cobb,' she said icily.

Cobb took out a fountain pen, and scribbled his details on the note. Mrs Sexton took a purse, attached by a chain to her belt, from the pocket of her dress, and counted out Cobb's change.

Once that matter was dealt with, Hardcastle, Marriott, Cobb

and Beatrice Cooper descended the steps of the boarding house.

Once in the street, Hardcastle looked around before spying Carter and Lipton on the other side of the road.

'Carter, Lipton, come here.'

'Sir?' said Carter, as he and his colleague hastened across to join the DDI.

'This here is Mr Sinclair Cobb what I've just arrested for the murder of Sir Nigel Strang. Take him back to Cannon Row and lodge him in a cell. I'll speak to him when Sergeant Marriott and me gets back. Understood?'

'Yes, sir.'

During this brief exchange, Beatrice Cooper had been studying the two DCs. '*You!*' she said accusingly, pointing a finger as she suddenly recognised the two men who had shared her compartment on the way from London.

'Good afternoon, ma'am,' said Carter, and raised his straw boater.

It was getting on for six o'clock by the time that Hardcastle and Marriott faced Sinclair Cobb in the interview room at Cannon Row police station.

'Well, Mr Cobb, and what have you to say?' asked Hardcastle.

'Nothing, Inspector, save to say that I had nothing to do with Nigel Strang's murder.'

'Or Daisy Johnson's?'

'I know nothing about that either.'

'In that case, Mr Cobb, why did you run away?'

'I thought you were on to me, Inspector.'

'I was, Mr Cobb, I definitely was, but that doesn't explain your sudden departure.'

'I thought you'd found out about Daisy and me.'

Hardcastle studied the man opposite him. 'What about Daisy and you, eh, Mr Cobb?' he asked, taking a sudden interest.

'I felt certain that you thought I'd murdered her.'

'And why should I have thought that?'

'I thought that Daisy had told you about our assignations.'

'No, she didn't say anything about them, but I think you'd better tell me.'

'I'd been working late at the office, sometime at the end of March. I can't remember the exact date. In fact, I worked all night that particular night. Anyway, about half past five, Daisy came into my office. I'd never seen her before, and I asked her what she wanted. She said she was the cleaner who did the offices.'

'Fascinating,' commented Hardcastle drily. 'Do go on.'

'She was a very presentable girl, and not at all backward in coming forward, if you take my meaning.'

'I don't take your meaning, Mr Cobb, so you'd better explain.'

'Well, I started chatting to her, and she told me about her husband who was in the Grenadier Guards. I mentioned that Sir Nigel's sons were Grenadiers too, and she said something trite, like I wonder if they know each other. Then she went on to say how much she missed her husband. She was quite open about it. She said she missed sleeping with him, and . . . Well, Inspector, one thing led to another and we finished up making love.'

'In your office?' asked Hardcastle.

'Yes. On the desk.'

'Good God!' exclaimed Hardcastle. 'And you thought I knew all about this, did you?'

'I was sure you'd found out. Possibly from Daisy.'

'Was this tumble you had with the willing Daisy the only time?'

Cobb had the good grace to appear shamefaced, and at once mildly offended by Hardcastle's description of his romantic interlude as a 'tumble'. 'No, it became quite regular after that. I would come into the office early, by way of the private entrance, and Daisy would always turn up at about half past five.'

'And when you found out she was pregnant, you murdered her, I suppose.'

'Pregnant!' Cobb's face registered shock. 'I didn't know that, Inspector, I swear it.'

'And did Daisy Johnson provide the same service for Sir Nigel Strang, Mr Cobb?' asked Marriott, looking up from the notes he was taking. 'Or any of the other staff?'

'Good grief!' Cobb stared at Hardcastle's assistant. 'I never thought of that. D'you really think so?'

'I don't know,' said Marriott, 'but we can't ask him now, or Daisy Johnson.'

'It would seem to explain why Sir Nigel was in his office that early in the morning, wouldn't it, Mr Cobb?' suggested Hardcastle. 'Did he work all night, too?'

Cobb shook his head slowly. 'I don't know, but I suppose he did from time to time.'

'When did you have a duplicate key made for the private entrance?' demanded Hardcastle, in such a way as to imply that he knew that to be the case. 'Which you then gave to Daisy.'

'About the middle of April, I suppose.'

'What for? I mean, why did she need a key to the back door?'

'Sometimes I would deliberately work late, and Daisy would come in the private entrance at about midnight. Then she'd go out the same way and come back in by way of the main door at the time she normally arrived for her cleaning job.'

'Taking a hell of a risk, weren't you?' asked Hardcastle.

'Not really. I always locked my door.'

'But didn't Bowles and his colleagues have a pass key?'

'Bowles, Inspector? Who's Bowles?'

'One of the night security guards.'

'Yes, of course. But it made no difference. I always put a "Do Not Disturb" sign on the door. The security people were quite accustomed to people working late. Or even all night.'

'Did you ever give Mrs Johnson any gifts?' Hardcastle had formed the opinion, when first he and Marriott had called at Wild Street, that Daisy was better dressed than her income would seem to have allowed.

'Yes. I sometimes gave her a bottle of scent, and on two or three occasions I gave her some money. She wasn't very well off, you see.'

'So she was a prostitute, as near as dammit,' commented Hardcastle crushingly.

'I think that's a bit harsh, Inspector.' Cobb waved a deprecating hand.

Hardcastle snorted at Cobb's naivety. 'Let's get back to

the present, shall we? How are you going to explain your absence to James Cresswell?'

'I haven't thought about that yet,' said Cobb.

'Have you got that fingerprint report there, Marriott?' asked Hardcastle.

'Yes, sir.' Marriott handed over DI Collins's report of his examination of Sir Nigel Strang's office.

Hardcastle studied it for a moment or two. Although in no doubt, he wanted to confirm to himself that the fingerprints found on the doorplate of Sir Nigel Strang's office did not match those of Sinclair Cobb. DI Collins had taken Cobb's fingerprints for elimination purposes, shortly after Strang's body had been discovered.

Finally Hardcastle set aside the report, and stared at the prisoner. 'Well, Mr Cobb, I'm satisfied with your story for the moment, and I shall release you. However, if you intend leaving Chadwick Street, you must let me know. Is that clear?'

'Yes, of course.' Cobb paused. 'I hope there isn't any need for you to tell Mrs Cooper about Daisy and me, is there, Inspector?'

'There's no reason for me to,' said Hardcastle. 'But, as a matter of interest, how are you going to explain your absence to the acting permanent secretary?'

'I've no idea at all,' said Cobb miserably.

'You'll probably get the sack, and finish up in the trenches,' said Hardcastle. A comment that gave little comfort to the assistant secretary at the Ministry of Munitions.

SIXTEEN

'**W**as it wise to let Cobb go, sir?' asked Marriott, even though he thought Hardcastle's action in racing to Brighton and arresting the errant civil servant had been precipitate. To his mind, there had been nowhere near enough evidence to support a charge of murder against him. But now that Cobb had been released, the DDI's motives were even less clear.

'There's a war on, Marriott,' said Hardcastle mysteriously, as he finished massaging his feet. 'And a senior civil servant in an important ministry who suddenly disappears without trace is of great interest.' He replaced his shoes, and buckled on his spats.

'I suppose so, sir.' Marriott, however, thought that Cobb's absence from his particular place of duty – assuming there were, in fact, sinister undertones – was more a case for Special Branch than for A Division's detectives. 'But do you really think he killed Sir Nigel Strang?'

'Shouldn't think so,' said Hardcastle casually, 'but I don't like being made a monkey of. Sinclair Cobb was having his way with Daisy Johnson in his office, but never saw fit to tell me, nor Mr Metcalfe on E Division, when the girl was murdered.'

'Perhaps he thought that you believed he'd done it, sir.'

'I did, Marriott, but having spoken to him, I've come to the conclusion that he's a rather callow young man who imagined his couplings with Mrs Johnson were the beginnings of some fine romance. Frankly, it worries me when I think that men like him are holding down important jobs, and are in a position to win or lose the bloody war for us. However, I'll have a word with Mr Metcalfe and tell him about Cobb having it up with Daisy. Mr Metcalfe might like to have him in and give him a going over.'

For the next few days, Catto and Wilmot stayed in the house at Farley Road. Edith Thorn had, as she had promised, made no attempt to go to work at the Arsenal. It was obvious that what Catto had told her had scared the wits out of her and she hardly moved from her bedroom.

Either Catto or Wilmot had daily walked the mile to Lewisham police station in Ladywell Road to telephone a report to Hardcastle, and to buy a newspaper on the way back. During the night hours, the two detectives had taken turn and turn about sleeping on the threadbare settee in the Thorns' living room, while the other remained alert. Each wondered how long their boring task was to continue.

During the day, they read the newspapers, and for most of the time played a game of cards – brag mostly – and drank copious cups of tea at the Thorns' expense. But there was little chance of them being fed by Edith Thorn, and most of the time they lived on fish and chips, or meat pies from a shop on the corner of the road.

But it was during the night of Thursday the seventh of June that two events of moment were to occur. The greater one concerned the British Army in Flanders, the other, lesser event, involved Catto and Wilmot at Farley Road, Lewisham.

Captain Guy Strang of the Grenadier Guards was sitting in his 'funk-hole' in the ramparts of Ypres. Despite his comparative youth, the twenty-two-year-old was a seasoned soldier, and had been on the Western Front from almost the day the war had started.

At one o'clock in the morning of Thursday the seventh of June, Strang finally cast aside the returns that he had been completing. They made depressing reading, recording the names of men who had been killed, wounded, or who were missing in action. Rarely a day passed without somebody in his company becoming one of those statistics. At last he turned to his letters. In her inimitable spidery handwriting, his mother had written of her struggles to come to terms with the murder of Strang's father. She went on at some length about how difficult it was to obtain the staple food of everyday life, and listed all the things she had to do without. Her complaint that she was unable to obtain *pâté de foie gras* particularly amused Guy Strang; for the most part he was living on tins of Maconochie's Irish stew. And that was on the good days.

With a sigh brought about by his inability to be of any assistance to his mother, Strang opened another letter. It was from his tailor, and had been forwarded by the Army Postal Service in London. It pointed out that the sum of seven pounds and six shillings was now overdue and the writer looked forward to early settlement. Without a further thought, Strang held the offending letter to a guttering candle. And at last, he turned in, hoping to snatch a few hours sleep before the next inevitable stand-to.

At ten minutes past three, Strang was awoken from his catnap by a series of thunderous explosions, unlike anything – despite his long experience at the Front – that he had heard before. Accompanying this terrifying rumbling the whole earth beneath Strang shook violently as nigh-on one million pounds of explosive rent the Messines Ridge. He rushed to the door of his dugout and pulled aside the sacking curtain.

The eastern sky was alight with flames, and a massive artillery barrage of more than two thousand British guns was pounding the whole area of the ridge.

Strang's company sergeant-major appeared, snapped to attention and saluted.

'What the hell's going on, Sarn't-Major?' asked Strang.

'I reckon they've blown the mines, sir.'

For some months, rumour had been rife about the mines that had been sapped under the Messines Ridge. And now nineteen out of the twenty-two that had been originally set had been detonated from Hill Sixty in the north to Ploegsteert in the south. The cost to the German Army was some ten thousand dead, but sadly, because the one at Spanbroekmolen had exploded minutes late, it killed half a company of the advancing Royal Irish Rifles. Strang was not to know, but the explosion was so intense that in Switzerland, five hundred miles away, it was recorded as an earthquake. And it was heard in London, where it was said it rattled the windows of Ten Downing Street.

'Perhaps it's the beginning of the end, Sarn't-Major.'

'I've heard that before, sir.'

*　　*　　*

One hundred and thirty miles away in Lewisham, moments before that massive explosion, Henry Catto had risen from the Thorns' uncomfortable settee, and made his way to the outside lavatory in the garden of their house in Farley Road.

Just as he reached the wooden door to the privy, he heard the rumble of a tremendous explosion, and the windows of the house rattled.

'Bloody hell,' said Catto to himself. 'What in hell's name was that?' In common with many other Londoners, he thought that a Zeppelin's bombs had finally scored a direct hit on Woolwich Arsenal. If he had been an explosives expert, though, he would have known that, in that case, the explosion would have been much louder.

But then something of greater interest secured Catto's attention. Two men climbed over the fence of the neighbouring garden. Silently, they inched their way to the back door of the house that Catto had left open.

'Police!' yelled Catto, drawing his pistol. 'Hold it right there, you two.'

The men turned and made towards him. One of them was wielding a menacing knife, and looked as though he meant to use it.

'I said stop,' shouted Catto, and somewhat unnerved by the pair's refusal to comply, he raised the unfamiliar pistol. But so nervous was he that he inadvertently fired. The bullet went wide of the two men, and smashed a small window at the side of the back door.

The man with the knife immediately threw it to the ground, and he and his partner raised their hands in surrender. 'Don't shoot, guv'nor. Don't shoot,' one of them cried.

Seconds later, Wilmot, aroused both by the Messines explosions and the discharge of Catto's firearm, came running into the garden.

'What the bloody hell's going on, Henry?'

'I've just caught these two trying to get into the house, Fred,' said Catto, still waving his pistol uncertainly at the pair.

Wilmot ran his hands down each man, ensuring that neither was armed.

'And what were you doing here?' demanded Catto, more confident now that he had support.

'Nothing, guv'nor,' said the man who had been holding the knife.

'Nothing, eh? We'll see about that.' Catto turned to Wilmot. 'Get hold of that PC on the door, Fred, and ask him to run down to the nick and arrange for some transport.' He holstered his pistol and he and Wilmot seized a man each by the arms, and steered them into the house.

'What's all that racket? Can't get a wink of bloody sleep.' Jed Thorn, hair tousled, and wearing long johns and a collarless shirt came running down the stairs. 'And what was that explosion?'

'No idea,' said Catto. 'But I think we've caught the two men who were after your missus.'

At 27 Kennington Road, Alice Hardcastle awoke in some alarm. Pushing at her husband's shoulder, she managed eventually to waken him.

'What is it, Alice?'

'Didn't you hear that explosion, Ernie?' Alice was now sitting up in bed, her hair in the twists of paper she always put in at night to give her hair a good curl. 'It even rattled the windows.'

'Didn't hear a thing,' mumbled Hardcastle, and turned over to go to sleep again.

But at a quarter past four, his night was disturbed once more by a furious hammering on his front door.

'What the bloody hell?' complained Hardcastle.

'Ernest!' Alice used her husband's full name as an indication of her disapproval of his language.

Ignoring his wife's reproof, Hardcastle pushed his feet into slippers and donned a dressing gown. He descended the stairs and opened the front door.

A young policeman from Kennington Road police station stood on the doorstep. 'I'm sorry to disturb you, sir,' he said, saluting, 'but I've a message from Lewisham.'

'Let's have it, then.' Hardcastle held out his hand. Slowly he read through the cryptic message. 'Splendid,' he said. 'Find me a cab while I get dressed.'

'Yes, sir.' The policeman saluted once more, and departed in search of a taxi.

'I've got to go out, Alice.' Hardcastle began to pull on his clothes. 'It looks as though Catto has caught our murderers.'

'You take care of yourself, Ernie,' said Alice, and went to sleep again.

Hardcastle's cab had taken less than twenty minutes to cover the five miles from Kennington to Lewisham police station, and he arrived there at just before five o'clock.

'All correct, sir,' said the station officer, once Hardcastle had proved his identity.

'Where are these two prisoners that Catto and Wilmot brought in, Skipper?'

'In separate cells, sir, and your two officers are in the charge room.'

Hardcastle walked from the front office into the charge room. Catto and Wilmot stood up.

'Well, what have you two been up to, eh?'

Catto explained the series of events that had led to the arrest of the two men. But rather than tell the DDI the truth, he said that one of the men came at him with a knife, and he, Catto, was obliged to discharge a round over their heads to ensure compliance with his orders. He thought it unwise to mention that he had fired his pistol quite by accident as a result of a sudden onset of nervousness. He knew that Hardcastle would have something caustic to say about that.

'Got names, have they, these two villains?' demanded Hardcastle.

'They've refused all particulars so far, sir,' said Wilmot.

'Have they indeed? Well, we'll soon see about that. Get the station officer to bring up the man who wielded the knife. We'll deal with him first. Where is the knife?'

'I've got it here, sir.' Catto handed over the weapon, encased now in a large brown envelope.

Followed by Catto and Wilmot, Hardcastle strode into the interview room.

For a moment or two he stared at the man sitting at the table.

'Name?' said Hardcastle.

'I ain't saying nothing.' The prisoner was about twenty-eight years of age, and was dressed in a seaman's sweater, and a pair of thick flannel trousers.

Hardcastle seized the unfortunate prisoner by the front of his sweater, and slammed him up against the wall. 'Don't bugger about with me, lad, because I'm very much inclined to lose my patience with tuppenny-ha'penny villains who threaten my officers.'

'I want a solicitor,' said the man unconvincingly, but he had been thoroughly cowed by Hardcastle's attack.

'A solicitor?' exclaimed Hardcastle scornfully, pushing the man into a chair. 'Don't be bloody stupid. You couldn't afford one. Now then, are you going to give me your name, or is one of my officers going to take you back to the cells and persuade you to tell him?'

The prisoner glanced at Catto and Wilmot, and capitulated. 'Lomas. Edward Lomas.'

'And what exactly were you and your mate doing in the garden of a house in Farley Road at about a quarter past three in the morning?'

'Looking for a dog.'

'They were looking for a dog, Catto,' scoffed Hardcastle, 'at gone three o'clock in the morning.' He moved closer to Lomas. 'And where did you lose this dog of yours.'

'Oh, it wasn't my dog. It was my mate Bert's.'

'Who we've also got locked up, I suppose. What's his other name?'

'Farmer. Albert Farmer.'

'Well, Lomas, you and Farmer are going to be charged with being found by night with an offensive weapon. And assaulting a police officer. And that's only a start.'

'We never assaulted him,' pleaded Lomas.

Hardcastle groaned and shook his head. 'You threaten one of my officers with a knife, and you tell me you never assaulted him. You offered him violence; that's good enough. You didn't have to touch him. You were put in fear, Catto, weren't you?' he asked, turning to the DC.

'Yes, sir, definitely.' This time Catto spoke the truth.

'There you are, then,' said Hardcastle. 'Well, my lad, I can tell you this without fear of contradiction: you'll be gripping the dock rail at the Old Bailey, sooner rather than later.' He turned to Catto. 'Take him down, and get Farmer up here.'

Albert Farmer was of a similar age to Lomas, and was dressed almost identically.

'What were you doing when my officers arrested you, Farmer?'

Lomas's partner appeared surprised that Hardcastle knew his name, but said nothing.

'You needn't look so surprised, lad. Your mate Lomas has spilled the beans.'

'We wasn't doing no harm, guv'nor,' said Farmer.

'Don't waste my time,' said Hardcastle dismissively. 'You assaulted one of my officers, and you were there with the intention of murdering Edith Thorn.' He raised a hand as Farmer was about to interrupt. 'It's no good denying it. Your mate's just told me all about it.'

'I never knew nothing about no murder, I swear,' said Farmer, now in a state of uncontrollable panic. 'We never meant no harm to anyone. We was just looking the place over in case there was something worth nicking. All right, I'll hold me hands up to a bit of burglary, but murder? No, guv'nor, that's not our line. If that's what Ted Lomas told you, it was more than he told me.'

'Put him down, Catto, and bring Lomas back,' said Hardcastle.

Lomas reappeared in the interview room, the same surly expression on his face.

'Farmer has told me all about your little caper, Lomas. So, you went to Farley Road with the intention of murdering Edith Thorn.'

'The bastard,' exclaimed Lomas. 'I'll swing for him.'

'You probably will anyway,' said Hardcastle mildly. 'Put him down, Catto.'

As Lomas was led away, Hardcastle returned to the front office. 'I'm having those two transferred to Cannon Row, Skipper,' he said to the station officer, 'where I can keep an eye on them. I'll have an escort sent later this morning.'

'It looks like we've got Hurley's two murderers, Marriott,' said Hardcastle. 'And no doubt Mr Quinn will be pleased to hear that, Drew,' he said, addressing the Special Branch officer.

'Have they confessed, sir?' asked Marriott.

'Not yet, Marriott, but they will. Don't vex yourself about that.'

'I'm sure they will, sir,' said Marriott, under no illusion about the outcome of the DDI further interviewing the two prisoners.

'And as they're blaming each other, I'll charge the pair of 'em and let them argue it out in court,' said Hardcastle. 'In the meantime, get this knife across to the scientific chaps and see if they can find Hurley's blood on it. By the look of Lomas and Farmer they won't know the first thing about comparing blood, and they won't have cleaned the knife properly, even if they tried.'

The later editions of Friday's evening newspapers carried graphic accounts of the mining of the Messines Ridge. The article also mentioned that General Sir Herbert Plumer had high hopes that the British assault – it was suggested that eighty thousand infantrymen were taking part – would seize the entire German front line before nightfall. It was a prediction confirmed in Saturday's copy of *The Times* by Colonel Charles Repington, the newspaper's military correspondent.

But on the Friday morning, before any of that had become common knowledge, Hardcastle was seated behind his desk at Cannon Row police station, as usual at half past eight.

At ten o'clock, Marriott entered the office. 'The scientific people have examined the knife that Catto found in Lomas's possession, sir.'

'And?'

'They found traces of blood group O on it, sir, which is the same as the blood group of the man we know as Joseph Hurley.'

'That's it, then,' said Hardcastle triumphantly.

'I'm afraid not, sir,' said Marriott. 'They also told me that group O is the most common blood group, so it doesn't necessarily mean that the weapon was used to kill Hurley.'

'Well, Lomas must've killed someone with it, Marriott, and that's good enough for me. Where's Catto?'

'Across in the office, sir.'

'Good. Fetch him in.'

'You wanted me, sir?' said Catto, as usual wondering what he had done wrong.

'You know where the assistant provost marshal has got his office, Catto, don't you?'

'Yes, sir, Horse Guards Arch.'

'Get yourself down there and find out whether Lomas and Farmer are deserters from the army. In my book they ought to be doing their bit, two strapping young men like that. But don't bother Colonel Frobisher with the enquiry, speak to one of his sergeants.'

'What difference will that make, if they're going to be hanged anyway, sir?' asked Marriott, once Catto had departed to do the DDI's bidding.

'Just another stick to beat them with, Marriott,' said Hardcastle mysteriously. 'If we ain't got enough evidence to pin Hurley's murder on 'em, then perhaps the army'll shoot 'em for being adrift.'

'When are you going to interview them again, sir?'

'Once Catto's come back with what I hope will be good news,' said Hardcastle.

Catto returned forty minutes later.

'Well, what did the military police have to say, Catto?'

'You were right, sir,' Catto began.

'I usually am,' observed Hardcastle mildly.

'Both Lomas and Farmer are deserters. According to the MPs they went on the run round about last Christmas. They were attached to the Sherwood Foresters down near Arras.'

'There you are, Marriott,' said Hardcastle, with a grin. 'Seek, and ye shall find, as it says in the Bible.'

'They wanted to know where the two of them were, sir, so they could go round and feel their collars.'

'And what did you say to that?'

'I told the sergeant he'd have to speak to you, sir.'

'Quite right.'

'The sergeant had a word with the colonel, and the colonel said he'd like to speak to you about it. At your convenience, sir.'

'Good. Thank you, Catto.'

That the DDI had said 'good' was sufficient praise for Catto who rarely received any form of commendation from Hardcastle.

SEVENTEEN

It was only a short walk from Cannon Row to Horse Guards Arch. Mistaking Hardcastle for an officer, the two mounted sentries brought their swords to the salute. Accustomed to such confusion, Hardcastle solemnly raised his bowler hat in return.

'Good morning, Inspector.' Lieutenant-Colonel Ralph Frobisher, the assistant provost marshal for London District, rose from behind his desk and shook hands. 'I understand that you've found a couple of deserters for us.'

'I've got 'em locked up in my police station, Colonel.'

'When can my fellows come and collect them?'

'It's not as easy as that, Colonel. Lomas and Farmer have been arrested on suspicion of murder.'

'Good God! They're Sherwood Foresters, too. My own regiment. What a disgrace. Who did they murder?'

'A man was murdered on a number 59 bus, Colonel, right outside Scotland Yard, and I'm pretty certain they were responsible for it.'

'I heard something about that. Last Monday, wasn't it?'

'Yes,' said Hardcastle. 'They haven't confessed yet, but they will, Colonel, they will.'

Frobisher had had dealings with Hardcastle before, and he knew that this rough diamond of a detective rarely forecast anything that did not come to fruition.

'What was it, a robbery that went wrong?' asked the APM.

'There's a bit more to it than that,' said Hardcastle. 'We think that the man they killed might have been a German spy.'

Frobisher smiled. 'I suppose there's some redeeming feature in that, Inspector.'

'A few days later, they attempted to gain entry to a house in south-east London with the intention of murdering the woman of the house. Fortunately, two of my best officers were there, and effected an arrest, but only after one of them had been threatened with a knife.'

'Good God! It beggars belief.'

'So I doubt we'll ever return them to military custody, Colonel,' said Hardcastle. 'If I have my way they'll have an appointment with the hangman in the near future.' With a macabre grin, he added, 'We might let you have their bodies back, though.'

'It's as broad as it's long, Inspector,' said Frobisher. 'If you returned them to the army, they'd probably be shot at dawn for desertion.'

Hardcastle afforded Frobisher a grim smile. 'We win all round, then, Colonel,' he said.

'It would be of assistance to me if you could find out how they got from Arras to London, Inspector. It might help us to stop a regular escape route.'

'Oh, they'll tell me all right, Colonel,' said Hardcastle. 'Perhaps you'd give me their personal details before I leave.'

'Certainly,' said the APM, and sent for his clerk.

Hardcastle was already seated at the table in the interview room when Marriott brought in Edward Lomas.

'Well, now, *Private* Lomas, you and your mate Farmer are on the run from the Sherwood Foresters in Arras,' he began. 'Fancy spending last Christmas at home, did you?'

'That was a mistake,' said Lomas. 'I was given leave, and I—'

'I've just left the assistant provost marshal, lad, and I know all about you and your mate Farmer deserting. So don't go drawing the longbow in my direction. How did you and your mate get from Arras to London without being caught, eh? I always understood that the military police were on the lookout for deserters.'

'We travelled by night, and kept well away from army units,' said Lomas, 'and when we eventually reached Dunkirk—'

'How far is that?' asked Hardcastle.

But it was Marriott who answered. 'About eighty miles from Arras, sir, give or take a mile or two.'

'Go on, then, Lomas,' said Hardcastle.

'When we got there, we bribed a fisherman to take us across to Dover.'

'And what did you bribe him with, eh?'

'Money, of course,' said Lomas. 'French francs.'

'Where did you get enough money to make it worth while for a fisherman to risk German submarines, just so you could get to Dover?'

Lomas looked away. 'We sort of acquired it along the way,' he muttered.

'You mean you thieved it. Or did you rob some French farmer at knifepoint?'

'Something like that.' It was obvious that Lomas was not to be drawn on his and Farmer's felonious activities on the other side of the Channel.

'Anyway, none of that's of any interest to me, Lomas, because you're facing a sort of Hobson's choice: either you'll be shot for desertion or hanged for murder.'

'Murder? What murder?' Lomas lamely attempted to give the impression that he did not know what Hardcastle was talking about.

'The knife that Detective Constable Catto found in your possession, which was the knife you threatened him with, has been examined by scientists. And, believe it or not, Lomas, Joseph Hurley's blood was on it.'

'Who?'

'Joseph Hurley, the man you murdered on a number 59 bus in Bridge Street last Monday morning, lad.'

'That wasn't me, that was Bert Farmer,' Lomas blurted out.

'Just proves it, don't it, Marriott,' said Hardcastle, turning to his sergeant. 'There's no honour among thieves.'

'Nor murderers, sir,' said Marriott.

'Unfortunately for you, Lomas, you were the one who had the knife that you threatened my officer with. And your fingerprints were on it.' Hardcastle had not had time to have the knife examined by a fingerprint officer, but Lomas was not to know that. 'But what interests me right now is who put you up to this topping.'

Lomas remained thoughtful for some time. 'We was contacted,' he said eventually.

'Oh, you were contacted, eh? Very mysterious. And are you going to tell me who contacted you, or is it a state secret?'

'This bloke come up to us in a boozer—'

'It's quite amazing that these arrangements are always made in a boozer, Marriott,' commented Hardcastle. 'Which boozer?' he asked, turning again to Lomas.

'The Red Lion, down Crown Passage, off of Pall Mall. We was told we might pick up a job there, and we'd put the word in with the landlord to let him know we was looking for work.'

'Go on.'

'Well, one night we was in there when this bloke come up to us and said as how he'd heard we was looking for a job.'

'Who was this man?'

'Dunno his name, 'cos we never asked. Sometimes it's better off you don't know. Anyway, he reckoned he'd heard we was on the run from the Kate Carney, and if we wanted to stay that way, we'd help him out. Otherwise, he'd turn us in.'

'How did he know you were deserters?'

'I dunno. I s'pose the landlord of the pub had worked it out, mainly because one night someone gave a shout that the army coppers were coming down Pall Mall, so we skedaddled a bit *jildi*. And we weren't the only ones, neither.'

'This fairy tale is beginning to stretch my patience, Marriott,' said Hardcastle, and took out his pipe. After a few minutes taken up with filling it with tobacco, and lighting it, he returned his attention to the renegade Sherwood Forester opposite him.

'It's true,' said Lomas, taking Hardcastle's silence as disbelief.

'What was it this strange man asked you to do?'

'He told us where we'd find this man—'

'The man you say Farmer murdered.'

'Yeah, that's right. He wanted us to follow him, and do him in. But he said it had to be some place where you lot wouldn't be able to trace him, the geezer what give us the job, I mean.'

'How did you find the man who was murdered?'

'We was given his address.'

'Which was?'

'Twenty-seven Tarn Street. It's just off of the Elephant and Castle. So we went there, and followed him when he left the house.'

'When was this?' asked Marriott, looking up from the notes he was making.

'Last Monday morning, about half past eight. So we followed him up to Trafalgar Square. He never seemed to be going anywhere particular.'

'Probably going to meet another of his agents,' said Hardcastle to Marriott. He faced Lomas again. 'Yes, go on.'

'Well, all of a sudden he jumped on a bus when it stopped for a copper near the top of Northumberland Avenue. We nearly missed him, and I thought he'd spotted us. But we just managed to get on before the bus moved off. Well, we followed him upstairs, but there was a lot of people there. Any road, we waited till the stop at the War Office, and most of 'em got off. When we got to the next stop, Bert Farmer said it was now or never, so he puts the knife in, and we got off the bus as quick as we could. But I never had nothing to do with it, guv'nor, so help me.'

'It makes no difference who wielded the knife, Lomas,' said Hardcastle. 'You see, as far as the law's concerned, you and Farmer acted in concert, and you'll both hang. But as I told the APM, if you manage to escape the hangman, you'll face a firing squad.'

'But, I never knew Bert was going to top the bloke, guv'nor,' said Lomas desperately, 'or I'd've—'

Hardcastle held up a silencing hand. 'Save it for the Old Bailey, Lomas. But what you haven't told me is how much this mysterious man paid you two to top the man on the bus.'

'A score,' said Lomas.

Hardcastle laughed. 'Twenty quid for a topping, Marriott. These two come cheap, don't they? Any respectable murderer would demand at least fifty.' He stood up. 'Put him down and bring up that other scoundrel.'

It took Marriott less than five minutes to exchange one prisoner for another. But Hardcastle decided there was little point in wasting too much time on Farmer.

'You'll be charged with the murder of one Joseph Hurley on a number 59 bus on Monday last, Farmer.'

'I don't know nothing about no murder, on a bus nor any place else,' protested Farmer.

'Your mate Lomas has told us all about it, Farmer, and he put the finger on you for the topping, so there's no point in denying it.'

Farmer remained silent for a moment or two. 'All right,' he said eventually, 'I was there, but it was Ted Lomas what done for him. I never done him.'

'I don't give a fig which of you did the deed, but I'll tell you what I told Lomas,' said Hardcastle. 'You were both in on it, and it makes no difference who wielded the knife that killed Hurley, you'll both swing for it. And if, by some remote chance, you get away with it, I've been told that the army will shoot you for desertion in the face of the enemy.'

'Deserting, what me? I was never in the army.'

'Then why did you run from the Red Lion in Crown Passage when someone said there was army coppers about?'

Farmer looked down at the table, and said nothing.

Hardcastle referred to the sheet of paper in front of him. 'I have here a report from the military police,' he said. 'Regimental number one-oh-two-hundred Private Albert Farmer of the Sherwood Foresters deserted from his battalion on Friday the twenty-second of December nineteen-sixteen. Also deserting on that day was a certain Private Edward Lomas of the same battalion.'

'It was all a mistake,' cried Farmer in desperation.

'Yes, and you two were the ones making it,' said Hardcastle mildly.

Once Farmer had been returned to his cell, Hardcastle sent for Drew, and related what the two suspects had told him.

'It seems to me, Drew, that there might be some profit in searching this house at twenty-seven Tarn Street. And the sooner the better, although it'll likely be of more value to your lot than to me.'

'I'd better have a word with Mr Quinn, sir.'

Superintendent Quinn had agreed with Hardcastle's suggestion about a search, and directed that he organise it immediately.

'Mr Quinn said I was to accompany you, sir, in case there is anything in the house of interest to Special Branch.'

'If we find anything, I'm sure it will be,' said Hardcastle. 'I certainly don't see it helping me much.'

In addition to DS Aubrey Drew, Hardcastle took with him Detective Sergeant Marriott, and Detective Constables Catto and Wilmot.

It was no surprise that one of the keys that had been found in the late Joseph Hurley's possession fitted the front door.

'Get round the house quickly, Catto, and check if there's anyone here.'

Two minutes later Catto returned to the hall where Hardcastle and the others were waiting. 'There's no one here, sir, and there's no sign of a break-in.'

'We'll get on with it, then.' Hardcastle addressed the two DCs. 'I don't want you roaming all over the place,' he said. 'Sergeant Drew will lead the search on account of he knows what he's looking for, so you'll be directed by him. Marriott, you stay with me.' And with that, the DDI sat down in an armchair in the sitting room, and lit his pipe.

It took over an hour for the detectives to search the house thoroughly, but they found nothing of interest.

'I reckon that whoever paid Lomas and Farmer to murder Hurley, sir,' said Drew, 'came here afterwards and removed anything that might have been incriminating.'

'I think you're probably right, Drew,' said Hardcastle, rising from the armchair. 'Well, that's that, I suppose.'

'Excuse me, sir.' Catto appeared from the direction of the kitchen. 'I found this.' He held out a piece of paper.

'What is it?'

'I don't know, sir, it's foreign writing.'

'Where did you find it?'

'In a tea caddy in the kitchen, sir.'

'Give it to Sergeant Drew.'

Drew took the scrap of paper, and studied it for some time. 'It's in German, sir,' he said, looking up. 'And it has the addresses of Sir Nigel Strang's home and office on it, as well as his club: the Royal Automobile. And there are instructions on how to get to each of them.' The Special Branch sergeant offered the piece of paper to Hardcastle, but he waved it away.

'I don't understand German, Drew, so I'll take your word for it. Did you say that his club was the Royal Automobile?'

'Yes, sir.'

'But Lady Strang told us that he was a member of the Athenaeum.'

'We know he wasn't a member of the Athenaeum, sir,' said Drew. 'I made enquiries there.'

'So you did,' said Hardcastle thoughtfully. 'Now I wonder why he should have told her ladyship that he belonged to a different club.'

'Perhaps he didn't want Lady Strang to track him down when he was visiting one of his lady friends, sir,' suggested Drew.

'Seems the most likely reason,' mused Hardcastle. 'But the question now is whether Hurley murdered Strang, or did some other bugger get there first.' He looked around at the assembled detectives. 'Did anyone find any keys?'

'No, sir,' said Drew. 'There were only those that we found on Hurley's body, but there aren't any in the house.'

'Pity. It's beginning to look like we shall never know who topped Strang.'

'I'll pass this note to Mr Quinn, sir,' said Drew. 'I expect that MI5 might like to take a look at it.'

'What d'you think they'll learn from it that you haven't, Drew?'

'I don't know, sir, but they might have other handwritten notes in their possession to compare it with.'

'Well, I hope they're better at that than they are at following suspects.' Hardcastle was convinced that MI5 was an organisation staffed by inefficient and bungling amateurs.

It was on Friday morning that Hardcastle was sent for, once again, by Superintendent Quinn, head of Special Branch.

'Mr Thomson is very pleased with your swift arrest in the Hurley murder investigation, Mr Hardcastle.'

'Thank you, sir. There's no doubt that Lomas and Farmer were responsible for his murder, although which one of them actually stabbed Hurley is unclear. Naturally enough they're each blaming the other.'

'Makes no difference,' said Quinn. 'They'll both hang.'

'Yes, that's what I told them, sir. It also turns out that they were both deserters from the army.'

Quinn ignored that piece of information; the status of Hardcastle's two prisoners was of no concern to him. 'You might be interested to know that the passport found in Hurley's possession was a forgery,' he said. 'A very skilful forgery, though, and I have no doubt that it was the work of the German Intelligence Service. We have made enquiries of our Special Branch colleagues in Dublin with regard to this man. There is no trace of him in any of their records, including the register of births, and although the passport claimed that he had been born in Dublin, that is not the case. There is no doubt that the man calling himself Hurley was a German espionage agent.'

'What about the notes that were found at Tarn Street, sir?'

'Not much to help us there, I'm afraid. MI5 have nothing on record that bears any similarity to the handwriting.'

'According to Drew's translation, sir, it looks as though they were instructions to Hurley to murder Sir Nigel Strang, but I don't know whether he did, or whether someone else did.'

'Either that, or for Hurley to arrange for someone else to do it,' said Quinn. 'But that's for you to discover, Mr Hardcastle,' he added with a bleak smile.

'I'm still wondering why Hurley was murdered, sir,' said Hardcastle.

'I tend to agree with what you said before. There seems little doubt that someone was keeping watch on Hurley's meetings with Mrs Thorn. It's standard practice with enemy agents, of course, particularly with one who's new to the business.'

'What difference would that have made, sir?' asked Hardcastle, to whom the world of espionage was close to being a complete mystery.

'That's simple, Mr Hardcastle. It's fairly obvious that they realised that Hurley and the Thorn woman were being watched by my officers and MI5, not that any fault can be

attributed to my officers.' Quinn was convinced that Special
Branch officers were skilled in surveillance. 'I suspect they
feared that by bringing himself to the notice of the authorities, Hurley might inadvertently compromise the whole
network, and so they arranged to have him silenced. All of
which was most unfortunate, and I've expressed my views
about that to Colonel Kell. His people can be rather over-
zealous at times, and I fear that their operatives might have
been a little too obvious in keeping watch on Hurley's meeting
with Mrs Thorn. However, it's no use crying over spilt milk,
Mr Hardcastle, so there's no need for you to concern yourself with any of that. I'll let you get on with finding Strang's
killer. I'm withdrawing Drew, but if there is anything that
you come across that might be of interest to Special Branch,
you'll let me know. Is that understood?'

'Very good, sir,' said Hardcastle. 'What d'you want me to
do about the Thorn woman, sir?'

Quinn gazed pensively at the DDI for a moment or two.
'Have her arrested again, Mr Hardcastle. I shall charge her
with offences under the Official Secrets Act.'

'We've wasted a lot of time chasing after spies, Marriott,'
said Hardcastle, when he returned to Cannon Row, 'and now
we've got to set about finding Sir Nigel's killer.'

'Is it possible that Hurley *was* responsible, sir?' asked
Marriott.

'Maybe, but we still have to prove that he did or he didn't.
Although he had a key to his house on his person, no other
keys were found on him or at Tarn Street. I think it's safe
to assume that he wouldn't have been expecting police to
raid his house so, if he did have a key to the private entrance
of the Ministry of Munitions, he wouldn't have thought of
getting rid of it.'

'Even so, he might have got rid of it as a sensible precau-
tion, sir. After all, he'd have no further use for it, and holding
on to it might've incriminated him later on.'

'You're a real Job's comforter, Marriott,' muttered
Hardcastle as he stood up and crossed the narrow corridor.
'Catto.'

'Yes, sir?'

'I want you and Wilmot to go down to Lewisham again, and arrest Mrs Thorn. Bring her to Cannon Row.'

'What for, sir?'

'Offences under the Official Secrets Act. Once you've got her back here, let me know, and Special Branch will take it over after that.' Hardcastle returned to his office. 'Come, Marriott, I think we'll drop into the Red Lion in Crown Passage for a wet,' he said.

Crown Passage was just off A Division. The dividing line between Hardcastle's division and C Division actually ran down the centre of Pall Mall. Not that Hardcastle worried too much about such administrative niceties.

The landlord looked up in surprise. If any CID officers came visiting, it was more likely to be detectives from Vine Street, and on rare occasions, 'Posh Bill' Sullivan himself. That said, he knew the DDI of A Division.

'Evening, Mr Hardcastle. What's your pleasure?'

'Two pints of best,' said Hardcastle.

The landlord drew two glass tankards of beer and placed them on the bar. 'And what brings you here?' he asked.

'A friendly word of warning,' said Hardcastle. 'It's come to my notice that this pub of yours has become a meeting place for army deserters. Now, I don't have to tell you that the licensing justices would likely regard that as unpatriotic, so if I was you, I'd do something about it before the next Brewster Sessions.'

The two detectives finished their beer and walked out into Crown Passage leaving a very worried public house licensee behind them.

'Remind me to have a word with Mr Sullivan at Vine Street tomorrow, Marriott,' said Hardcastle.

EIGHTEEN

'Y ou're looking glum, Ernie,' said Alice Hardcastle when her husband arrived home on Saturday afternoon.

'It seems as though the Russians are going to give up, Alice.' Hardcastle waved the early evening edition of the *Star*. 'According to this they've practically stopped fighting on the Eastern Front. Now that the Tsar's abdicated there doesn't seem to be anyone leading them. It's a bit of a dog's dinner.'

'Is that serious, then, Ernie?' Alice licked her finger and touched the sole of the flat iron she was using to press shirts. Satisfied that it was hot enough, she carried on.

'If that happens, it'll mean that all of Fritz's army, and his chums who are fighting the Russians, will be able to fight us and the French on the Western Front. It doesn't look good, Alice.'

'No, I suppose not. What d'you want for your supper?'

Over the weekend, the DDI had given serious thought to the problem of Sir Nigel Strang's murder. Questions to Hardcastle from his family were met with monosyllabic answers in a way that indicated he had not heard what they had said. So distracted was he, that Alice enquired, somewhat pointedly, if he would rather be at his office.

On Monday morning, Hardcastle called for Marriott and gave voice to those thoughts.

'There were no keys found at Hurley's Tarn Street house, were there, Marriott?' mused Hardcastle. As was his practice, he was going over what they had discovered so far, and what he knew anyway.

'Only his house key, sir, and that was on his person when he was murdered.' There were times when Marriott wondered whether his chief's prodigious memory was beginning to fail him.

'I wonder who owns the property. Find out, will you.'

'Already done, sir. It belongs to a man called Sir Percy Salter. He owns quite a lot of property in the area.'

'Got an address for him, have you?'

'Yes, sir. He lives in Chelsea. In Flood Street.'

'Obviously doesn't like rubbing shoulders with his tenants, then. We'll pay him a visit.'

It was on Monday afternoon that Hardcastle and Marriott arrived at Sir Percy Salter's elegant house in Flood Street.

Following the usual flimflam of the butler telling the two detectives that he would enquire if Sir Percy was at home, they were shown into the drawing room.

Sir Percy Salter was a short, plump man with a rubicund face, and was bald save for a fringe of grey hair that ran from ear to ear around the back of his head. He was standing in front of the empty fireplace, legs apart, index fingers and thumbs stuck in the pockets of his waistcoat, and looked more like a pub landlord than a wealthy property owner.

'And what, pray, brings the police to my door?' Salter removed the fat cigar he had been smoking.

'I'm Divisional Detective Inspector Hardcastle of the Whitehall Division, Sir Percy, and this here is Detective Sergeant Marriott.'

'Sit down, sit down, me dear chaps, and tell me how I can be of assistance.'

'It's rather a long story, sir,' began Hardcastle.

'Better get on with it, then,' said Salter with a throaty chuckle. He sat down in a winged armchair, causing the leather to squeak in protest as he did so.

Hardcastle explained about the murder of Sir Nigel Strang, which Salter acknowledged he had read about, and went on to relate the details of Hurley's murder on a 59 bus in Bridge Street.

'Forgive me for saying so, Inspector, but how does any of this affect me?'

'Hurley, although we now know that that was not his real name, was almost certainly a German spy, and was renting a house at twenty-seven Tarn Street near the Elephant and Castle.'

'I still don't see what any of this has to do with me, Inspector.'

'The Tarn Street house happens to be owned by you, sir.'

'Hell's bells!' exclaimed Salter. 'So how can I help you?' He appeared taken aback by Hardcastle's revelation, and passed a hand over his bald pate.

'I would be interested to know, and so would Special Branch, the circumstances under which Hurley took up occupation of the house.'

'Unfortunately, I know nothing of the day-to-day running of my estate, Inspector. To tell you the truth, I don't really know how many houses I own.' Salter accompanied this admission with a casual wave of his hand. 'Anyway, they're only a part of my business interests. However, I do have an estate manager. He's a chap called John Spencer. He was a chief petty officer in the Royal Navy before the Battle of Jutland deprived him of one of his legs. Very reliable fellow.'

'Where can I find him, Sir Percy?'

'He has an office in Pimlico somewhere. Hold on a moment, and I'll get the exact address for you.' Salter stood up and walked into another room. Moments later, he returned clutching a piece of paper. 'There you are, Inspector. Tell him you've spoken to me, and he's to give you every assistance possible.'

'Thank you, sir, I'm much obliged,' said Hardcastle.

'I hope you catch the fellow who murdered Nigel Strang.'

'Don't you worry about that, Sir Percy, I shall.'

'Yes, I'm sure you will,' admitted Salter pensively. Although the meeting had been brief, he had formed the opinion that Hardcastle was a policeman to be reckoned with.

'We ain't far from Pimlico, Marriott, so we'll see this Spencer fellow now,' said Hardcastle, waving down a cab.

There was a sign on the door that proclaimed the premises to be the offices of Salter Estates Ltd. The door was unlocked, and the two detectives entered.

'Good afternoon, gentlemen,' said a youngish man seated behind a desk.

'Are you John Spencer?'

'That I am, sir.'

'I'm Divisional Detective Inspector Hardcastle of the Whitehall Division, Spencer, and this here is Detective Sergeant Marriott.'

'And what can I do for you, gents?' Spencer stood up, and

aided by a walking stick, limped slowly across the room to
shake hands. 'I'm a bit slow, sir, but I'm still getting used
to my tin leg.'

'I've just been to see Sir Percy Salter, and he assured me
that you might be able to assist me.'

'Ah, Sir Percy, yes, a good man,' said Spencer. 'He was in
the Andrew, too. A rear admiral, he was. I was in the old
Indefatigable at Jutland when she went down. Left me other
leg in her, too.' He laughed, and invited the two police officers to take a seat. 'But that's the Navy for you: always takes
care of its own. But you haven't come here to yarn about an
old salt and his troubles.' He crossed to a side table. Looking
over his shoulder, he said, 'I was just about to make some
tea, gents. Fancy a cup?'

'Very kind,' murmured Hardcastle. As with the two
wounded soldiers that Maud had brought home to Kennington,
he was amazed at the cheerfulness of those members of the
armed forces who had been maimed in the conflict. While
Spencer was brewing the tea, the DDI explained briefly about
the murder of the man known to police as Joseph Hurley, and
that he had rented a house at twenty-seven Tarn Street,
Southwark.

'I remember him, sir,' said Spencer. 'A German spy, you
say. If I'd've known that, I'd've done for him meself. It was
only about a month ago that he come in here and asked about
a house to rent. Well, things were a bit tight, what with them
as have had their houses knocked out by Fritz and his
Zeppelins, but one had just fallen vacant. The one at Tarn
Street.'

'Did he say how long he wanted it for, Spencer?'

'Not exactly, sir, but he did mention something about it
being at least a year. Bit of luck he was topped really, because
I've got a family on me books looking for a place like that.'
Spencer handed mugs of tea to the two policemen, and took
the cap off a bottle of rum. 'I take it you'll be partial to a
drop of pusser's rum, gents.' Without waiting for a reply, he
poured liberal measures into the detectives' tea.

'Did he say why he wanted to rent a house, Mr Spencer?'
asked Marriott.

'He did that, sir. He said he'd just come across from Ireland,

and was looking for a place for his wife and kids while he was working at Woolwich Arsenal. But from what you tell me, that was all my eye and Betty Martin.'

'Did he tell you anything about himself?' asked Hardcastle.

'Apart from saying he was from across the water, no, sir. But I have to say I was a bit suspicious because he never had an Irish accent. But the fact that he'd come across from Ireland didn't necessarily make him Irish, did it?'

'And he wasn't,' rejoined Hardcastle with a chuckle. 'As I said earlier, we're pretty sure he was German.' Drew had mentioned the possibility of Hurley having landed in Ireland from a German submarine, as Roger Casement had done a year earlier. But he saw no need to mention that to Spencer.

'How did he pay the rent, Mr Spencer?' queried Marriott.

'That's the funny thing, sir,' said the ex-sailor. 'He paid three months' rent in advance. Crisp new Bradburys they were. Now that's unusual, I can tell you. Half my work here is taken up with chasing the rent collectors to get the arrears in. Mind you, a lot of the houses are let out to folks whose husbands are in the navy or the army, and they've bairns to bring up. Sir Percy's a generous man, and he's said I'm not to go too hard on them whose menfolk are serving. Apart from anything else, Mrs Barbour's rent strike in Govan brought about the law that said rents was to be held at pre-war rates.'

'Did you ever have occasion to visit the property once Hurley was there?' asked Hardcastle, who remembered the resistance to inflated rents that the women of Govan had mounted, although the name Barbour meant nothing to him.

'No, sir. And the rent collector wouldn't have called there either, seeing as how Hurley had paid three months in advance.'

'It seems fairly obvious that he didn't want anyone calling on him there, Marriott,' said Hardcastle. He turned to the agent. 'Well, thank you for your help, Mr Spencer, and for the tea. Powerful stuff that rum.'

'I hope you catch them as topped Hurley, sir, even though he was a spy.'

'I've caught them already, Spencer,' said Hardcastle, with a satisfied smile. 'Deserters from the army, the pair of 'em.'

'Ah, well, there you are, sir,' said Spencer. 'Funny lot the army. Mind you, we'd have had a job running from the navy.

Not unless you were a good swimmer,' he added with an easy laugh.

'Don't you get any deserters from the navy, then, Mr Spencer?' asked Marriott.

'Chance would be a fine thing, sir. Whenever we were in at Portsmouth, the town was always thick with shore patrols. Be asked for your pass ten times before you got to a pub. Hardly worth going ashore.'

On Tuesday morning, Hardcastle decided to pay a visit to Fred Metcalfe, the DDI of E Division, at his office at Bow Street police station.

'Hello, Ernie. What brings you here?'

'I was wondering if you'd got anywhere with Daisy Johnson's murder, Fred.' Hardcastle settled himself in one of Metcalfe's chairs, took out his pipe and began slowly to fill it.

'Nothing, Ernie. No one saw a blood-soaked man running away from Wild Street, and Mrs Harding, Daisy's mother, couldn't tell us a thing.' Metcalfe sighed. 'How are you getting on with the murder of your civil servant?'

'I'm up against a brick wall, Fred. We got involved with Special Branch because the man who was murdered on a bus in Bridge Street turned out to be a German spy using the name of Hurley. We found some notes in German in his place at Tarn Street that gave details of Sir Nigel Strang's address and his club. But whether he topped him or not is anybody's guess.'

'I wonder if they're tied up,' mused Metcalfe. 'Seems a funny thing that Daisy was topped not long after Strang. D'you reckon she saw something?'

'Are you suggesting she actually witnessed Strang's murder?' asked Hardcastle, pausing with his pipe half way to his mouth.

'I don't know, Ernie. It's your enquiry, but I did wonder.'

'I doubt it,' said Hardcastle. 'We interviewed her not long after the body was found, and she was in a right two-and-eight. I doubt she was good enough an actress to put it on. But there's still the problem of how Strang's murderer got in.'

'We still can't be sure whether someone had a spare key to the back door, sir,' Marriott reminded his DDI.

'Yes, and that's what's worrying me.' Hardcastle sighed and stood up. 'If you come across anything that might be useful, Fred . . .'

'Yes, I'll let you know,' said Metcalfe. 'And perhaps you'll do the same for me.'

'What about Daisy Johnson? Learned anything about her?' asked Hardcastle.

'Only as much as you know, Ernie. A hard-working lass with a couple of kids and a husband who's a sergeant in the Grenadiers. Of course, there was the business of her being pregnant, and I'm wondering whether it was the sergeant's kid. We spoke to the neighbours, but they couldn't help. They all said she was a quiet woman who kept herself to herself. Mind you, they had quite a lot to say about Fanny Harding. Always minding other people's business, and earwigging when she had the chance. A real busybody by all accounts. They reckon she never had a good word to say about anyone, particularly her son-in-law. Daisy tried to keep the peace between them, but without much success. From what I've gathered, Sergeant Johnson was probably better off at the Front.'

It was on the following day that two coincidental events occurred, one of which was to further muddy the waters of Hardcastle's investigation. Ironically, it was the Germans who inadvertently contributed to it.

The air raid started at about half past eleven in the morning. Fourteen Gotha bombers flew unchallenged up the River Thames and dropped some of their deadly loads on Liverpool Street station and the surrounding area. But the most outrageous incident was the callous bombing of a school in Poplar. Some sixteen children died and a further thirty were injured. All in all, resulting from that one raid, over a hundred and fifty people were killed and three times that number injured.

Detective Sergeant Charles Marriott had been to the Army and Navy Club in Pall Mall to investigate a series of petty thefts that had occurred over a period of fourteen days. The miscreant was readily identified as a young maid who had been taken on to the domestic staff a month previously. Almost at once the pilfering began. But two weeks later she had been caught red-handed in the act of stealing another maid's purse.

The housekeeper reported the matter to the secretary who promptly dismissed the girl. However, when the club chairman, a fiery brigadier-general, got to hear of it, he insisted that the police were called.

Marriott took statements from the housekeeper and the club secretary. He also took details of the girl – she lived in Victoria – and assured the chairman that he would arrange for her arrest.

'I should damn' well think so too,' said the chairman.

Rather than taking a cab, Marriott decided to walk across St James's Park to return to the police station.

When he was half way across, the anti-aircraft guns began to open fire. Mingling with the drone of the hostile aircraft were the few British fighters that had been sent up in a vain attempt to intercept the raiders.

People who were walking in the park immediately began to run, seeking the inadequate shelter that they erroneously thought would be afforded by the larger trees. Among those taking flight, Marriott noticed a man dashing towards Wellington Barracks where there was a detachment of the Grenadier Guards. In the event, the route the man took turned out to be a coincidence.

But what was of great interest to Marriott was that the man was none other than Sergeant Gerald Johnson, Daisy Johnson's widower, who had told the police at Bow Street that he was returning to the Front immediately after his late wife's funeral.

Marriott knew something of the army, and knew that it tended to move personnel, even entire divisions, apparently upon a whim. His brother-in-law, a sergeant-major in the Middlesex Regiment, had several times been the victim of such administrative manoeuvres.

However, the strangest aspect of Johnson's appearance was that he was wearing civilian clothing; in wartime soldiers invariably wore uniform. Apart from it being a regulation, it also guarded against well-meaning, but nevertheless vindictive, women who unhesitatingly thrust white feathers upon those they believed to be evading military service.

Marriott thought no more about it, but by the time he reached the police station, he decided that it was worth mentioning to Hardcastle.

'Interesting,' said Hardcastle, and lit his pipe. It was several seconds before he spoke again. 'Might be worth having a word with the military, I suppose. D'you reckon that air raid's over and done with now, Marriott?'

'I think so, sir. I saw a PC cycling down Whitehall with an "All Clear" placard on his chest.'

'I hope he picked up the right placard,' muttered Hardcastle, and seized his bowler hat and umbrella.

The sentry at the gate of Wellington Barracks in Birdcage Walk directed the two detectives to the guardroom. The sergeant of the guard summoned a runner who eventually escorted them to the office of the regimental adjutant.

The runner crashed to attention on the threshold, and saluted. 'Two gentlemen from the police, sir,' he said.

'Geoffrey Hope-Bowen, gentlemen.' The officer, dressed in adjutant's traditional frock coat despite the war, shook hands and invited Hardcastle and Marriott to take a seat. He glanced at his watch. 'A glass of Madeira?' he enquired, raising an eyebrow.

'Thank you, Captain,' murmured Hardcastle. 'Most kind.' He would have preferred a pint of bitter, but doubted that a Guards officer would keep any in his office.

For a moment or two, Hope-Bowen busied himself pouring the wine into crystal glasses, and handing it round.

'Now, gentlemen, how may I assist you?' Hope-Bowen sat down, and indicated, with a flourish of his hand, that the detectives should be seated also.

'I'm Divisional Detective Inspector Hardcastle of the Whitehall Division, Captain, and this here's Detective Sergeant Marriott. We're investigating the murder of Sir Nigel Strang, permanent secretary at the Ministry of Munitions.'

'Yes, I heard about that. Strange business. His two sons are in the regiment, don't you know?' Hope-Bowen stroked his moustache, and took a sip of Madeira. 'But how d'you think I can help you, eh what?'

Hardcastle went on to explain about the subsequent murder of Daisy Johnson. Although that was the concern of DDI Metcalfe of E Division, Hardcastle was still convinced that there was a connection between the two killings.

'This is all very interesting, Inspector, but I don't see how it involves the Grenadier Guards, other than that the dead woman's husband is in the regiment.'

'Ah, but now I come to the point, Captain.' Hardcastle turned to Marriott. 'Tell Captain Hope-Bowen about your sighting this morning.'

Marriott explained to the adjutant how he had seen Sergeant Johnson earlier that day crossing St James's Park towards Wellington Barracks. 'I thought it rather odd that he wasn't wearing uniform, sir.'

'Yes, indeed. Damn' funny, that,' said Hope-Bowen. For a moment or two, he gazed out of the window at a squad drilling under the directions of a colour-sergeant. 'Makes me wonder what a fellah who's supposed to be at the Front is doing roamin' about London in mufti.'

Hardcastle was amazed at this somewhat casual attitude. 'Does that mean he's a deserter, Captain?' he asked.

'Jolly well looks like it.' The adjutant lifted his walking stick from his desk, and rapped loudly on the wall. Moments later, a warrant officer entered the room.

'Sir?'

'This is Orderly-Room Quartermaster Sergeant Phillips, Inspector,' said Hope-Bowen, by way of introduction. 'He's the chief clerk, and he knows everything that goes on in the Grenadiers. Ain't that so, Mr Phillips?'

'We aim to please, sir,' said the ORQMS diplomatically.

'These gentlemen are from the police, Mr Phillips, and they're making enquiries about a Sergeant Gerald Johnson. What can you tell them about him?'

'He's run, sir,' said Phillips stiffly.

'Has he really?' said Hope-Bowen. 'How did you know that without looking it up?'

'It's most unusual for a full sergeant to go adrift, sir,' said Phillips, 'and when one does it tends to stick in the memory.'

'Mmm, yes, I suppose so. Not the sort of thing we're accustomed to in the Brigade. Ain't that so, Mr Phillips?'

'Indeed, sir.'

'Well, there you are, gentlemen.' Hope-Bowen turned to face Hardcastle's assistant. 'And you've seen the fellah skulking about London, eh?'

'Yes, sir,' said Marriott. 'I'm in no doubt that it was Johnson.'

'Well, what do we know about this man, Mr Phillips?' asked the adjutant.

'According to my information, he returned to the United Kingdom from Wipers on Monday the twenty-eighth of May, sir. I'm told he was granted compassionate leave to attend his wife's funeral on the Tuesday. He should have reported back here the day after that in order to be documented for his return to the battalion, sir. But he never showed up. He's been posted as absent without leave.'

'I see. And what's been done about it?'

'Sergeant Johnson's particulars were passed to the military police at Horse Guards, sir.'

'Have you an idea why he should have deserted, Captain?' asked Hardcastle.

By way of reply, Hope-Bowen glanced at the ORQMS. 'Mr Phillips?'

'No idea, sir. The only thing I can think of is that he didn't fancy going back and facing the Hun across the plonk, sir.'

'Yes,' mused Hope-Bowen, and brushed his moustache again. 'Seems the most likely explanation.' He turned to Hardcastle. 'Well, there you are, Inspector.'

'Did you ever set eyes on Sergeant Johnson, Mr Phillips?' asked Hardcastle.

'No, sir. We received a flimsy about him from his battalion.'

'May I ask why you're interested in this man Johnson, Inspector?' asked Hope-Bowen. 'Apart from the fact that he's been posted as absent.'

'I think he might be able to assist us with our enquiries into a matter of murder, Captain.' Hardcastle was being his usual circumspect self, as he tended to be when dealing with the military.

'Ah, yes, I see.' Hope-Bowen expressed no surprise at this revelation.

'Was Johnson a sergeant or a lance-sergeant, sir?' asked Marriott. The fact that he had seen Johnson wearing a sash at his wife's funeral still worried him.

'Mr Phillips?' Again Hope-Bowen turned to the ORQMS for an answer.

'Promoted to full sergeant about three months ago, sir.'

NINETEEN

Hardcastle and Marriott walked the length of Birdcage Walk to return to Cannon Row.

'Seems a bit of a rum business, sir,' said Marriott.

'It's more than that, Marriott. I reckon that Johnson is a likely suspect for the murder of his wife, if not Sir Nigel Strang. Not that I was going to tell Hope-Bowen that.'

'D'you honestly think so, sir?' Marriott was aghast. Once again, Hardcastle had taken a leap into the unknown without a shred of evidence to support his allegation, save that he, Marriott, had seen the Guards sergeant running away in St James's Park. 'But if Johnson was granted compassionate leave the day before his wife's funeral, he can hardly have been responsible for her murder, or Strang's.'

'Nevertheless, it's worth looking into, Marriott, but I must say that Captain Hope-Bowen don't seem too vexed about one of his sergeants going adrift. I think we'll have a word with the APM. See what he's got to say.'

And with that statement of intent, Hardcastle turned left into Horse Guards Road, and crossed the parade ground at a swift pace.

The dismounted sentry in Horse Guards Arch brought his sword to the salute at the sight of the bowler-hatted inspector. Yet again being mistaken for an army officer, Hardcastle solemnly returned the compliment by raising his hat.

'Good afternoon, Mr Hardcastle.' Lieutenant Colonel Ralph Frobisher rose from behind his desk and shook hands. 'Sergeant Marriott,' he murmured, nodding towards Hardcastle's assistant.

'Good afternoon, Colonel.' Hardcastle sat down.

'Are you here to tell me I can have my two deserters back, Inspector?'

'I doubt you'll see them before the hangman does, Colonel,' said Hardcastle bluntly.

'Then what can I do for you?'

'Tell the colonel about Johnson, Marriott.'

Marriott related how he had seen Sergeant Johnson earlier that day, and that he was in plain clothes. He also mentioned that Johnson was running towards Wellington Barracks, but conceded that he might just have been attempting to find shelter from the air raid.

'So I paid a call on a Captain Hope-Bowen at Wellington Barracks, Colonel, and he knew about Johnson,' said Hardcastle, taking up the tale. 'Or at least his chief clerk did. But apart from advising your people, little appears to have been done.'

'We've got enough names of deserters to fill several large books, Inspector, but forgive me for a moment.' Frobisher struck a brass bell on his desk.

A military police sergeant appeared. 'Yes, sir?'

'Do we have a record of a Sergeant Gerald Johnson of the Grenadier Guards being absent from his unit in Ypres, Sergeant Glover?'

'I'll check, sir. Won't be a moment.'

A minute or two later, Glover returned with a file in his hand. 'Yes, sir. He was reported adrift by ORQMS Phillips of the Grenadier Guards at Wellington Barracks on Wednesday the thirtieth of May this year, sir. But that's not all. When we copied that report to his battalion in Wipers, sir, they replied that he'd been granted fourteen days' privilege leave from Sunday the thirteenth of May.'

'Well, where the hell did this business about compassionate leave enter into it?' asked Frobisher, frowning.

'I've no idea, sir, but I can only imagine that there's been some sort of balls-up with the paperwork at the Wipers end. A case of the left hand not knowing what the right hand's doing. I daresay that when Johnson's battalion received notification of the death of his wife, they automatically granted him compassionate leave, not realising he wasn't there. The chief clerk probably stuck the chitty in front of the adjutant and he signed it without knowing that Johnson was already on leave. They might even have thought he'd been killed in action. The paperwork gets a bit sloppy at the Front, sir. It's hardly surprising when you consider what they've got to put up with. Particularly in the Salient.' Glover had served there briefly in 1915, and knew what it was like.

'Do we know where Johnson was born, Sergeant?' asked the APM.

'Catford, sir,' said Glover without hesitation.

'Thank you, Sergeant Glover.' Frobisher turned to Hardcastle. 'Looks like some sort of military blunder, Inspector. I'm sorry to say it's happening all the time. But do you attach some significance to the fact that he went absent the day after his wife's funeral?'

'Johnson's wife was a cleaner at the Ministry of Munitions, Colonel, and was the one who found the body of Sir Nigel Strang. Then, lo and behold, Daisy Johnson is found murdered in her own home a week later. Sergeant Johnson is what you might call the common denominator. And that strikes me as suspicious.'

'I suppose so.' Frobisher smiled, even though he failed to follow Hardcastle's somewhat obscure reasoning. But he had had dealings with the DDI before, and knew him to be tireless in his pursuit of criminals, and rarely wrong in his assumptions. 'I'll alert my patrols to be especially vigilant, Inspector. If he's still in the London area, we know of places that tend to be frequented by deserters.'

'The Red Lion pub in Crown Passage for one, Colonel,' observed Hardcastle.

'Really?' Frobisher raised his eyebrows. 'How did you know that?'

Hardcastle repeated what he had been told by Farmer and Lomas, the two deserters now standing accused of Hurley's murder.

'Thank you for that information, Inspector.' The APM made a few notes on his pad and looked up. 'I'll certainly have my patrols pay attention to those premises. As Sergeant Johnson is a Londoner, I doubt he'll stray very far. Men on the run tend to stick to an area with which they're familiar. Was there anything else?'

'Not at present, Colonel, and, once again, thank you for your assistance.' Hardcastle paused at the door. 'By the way, I've had a word with the licensee of the Red Lion in Crown Passage, and I doubt you'll find any deserters there in future.

Not unless he wants to lose his licence. On the other hand, he might just let you know when there are any there.'

'I sometimes wonder if we'll ever win this bloody war, Marriott,' said Hardcastle, when they were back at Cannon Row. 'Half the damned army doesn't seem to know what the other half's doing.' He took off his spats and shoes, and began to massage his feet.

'No, sir,' said Marriott, as ever, chary about encouraging one of the DDI's diatribes.

'And if we wait for the military police to get themselves organised, the war will be over before they lay hands on Sergeant Johnson.'

'I don't see that there's much we can do about it, sir. If only I'd known he was a deserter when I saw him in St James's Park, I'd've felt his collar there and then.'

Hardcastle nodded sagely. 'We can all be wise after the event, Marriott,' he said, with uncharacteristic candour. 'But I think we'll set about looking for him ourselves. But first of all we'll call on Mr Metcalfe at Bow Street. He'll likely be interested in knowing that Johnson is still in London.'

'Blimey, Ernie, you'll be taking up residence here if you're not careful.'

'I've got a bit of information for you, Fred, and it might just help you out of the corner you're in over the Daisy Johnson topping.' Hardcastle sat down, and began to fill his pipe.

'All help gratefully received, Ernie,' said Metcalfe. He glanced at the clock, and opened the bottom drawer of his desk. 'You won't say no to a drop of Scotch, will you, Ernie?' Without awaiting a reply, he withdrew three tumblers and poured a substantial measure of whisky into each.

Between them, Hardcastle and Marriott told Metcalfe what they had learned.

'Well, that's a turn-up and no mistake, Ernie. I must confess to being a bit puzzled as to what the hell he's up to.'

'I was wondering whether he's shown up at his old address in Wild Street,' mused Hardcastle.

'I shouldn't think he'd be that daft,' said Metcalfe, 'but

there'd be no harm in going round there and having a chat with that harridan Mrs Harding. Are you game?'

'No time like the present, Fred, but is she up to it? I thought she'd had a heart attack.'

Metcalfe scoffed. 'Heart attack my arse. The doctor at Charing Cross Hospital reckoned it was nothing more than a touch of the vapours coupled with shock. Personally, I think she was three sheets to the wind, even at that time of the morning.'

It was obvious that Fanny Harding was making the most of her recent stay in hospital. She opened the door slowly, a pained expression on her face.

'Oh, it's you, Mr Metcalfe. And Mr Hardcastle. You'd better come in.' Mrs Harding's voice was weak to the point of invoking sympathy. She moved away from the door slowly and with the aid of a walking stick.

Metcalfe shot a sideways glance at Hardcastle and grinned. 'See what I mean, Ernie?' he whispered.

'Have a seat, gents.' Fanny Harding made a great pantomime of lowering herself into a worn armchair, her facial expression implying that she was in great pain.

'It's about your son-in-law, Mrs Harding,' began Metcalfe.

'Huh! Don't talk to me about that waster,' screeched Mrs Harding scornfully, the strength of her voice suddenly returning. 'He brought nothing but trouble to my Daisy, God rest her soul.'

'What d'you mean by that?' asked Hardcastle, leaning forward in his chair.

'Always in and out of work, was Gerald Johnson. Getting barely enough money to feed the children, and what he did earn half the time he pissed away down the pub in Bow Street.'

'That'd be the Kemble's Head, I suppose,' said Metcalfe.

'I'd expect you two to know it, being right opposite Bow Street police court,' observed Mrs Harding. 'Any road, getting called up was the first time he'd had a job he kept for more than six weeks.'

'He's given it up,' said Hardcastle drily.

'D'you mean he's been discharged? Or has he been killed?' A brief expression of hope flitted across Fanny Harding's face.

'No, he's deserted,' said Hardcastle.

Johnson's mother-in-law scoffed. 'No more than I'd've expected of him. Nothing but a bloody ne'er-do-well is that Gerald Johnson. I don't know what my poor Daisy ever saw in him, and that's a fact. Always pretending to be jack-the-lad, and half the time not having two pennies to bless hisself with.'

'Has he called here recently, Mrs Harding?' asked Marriott, intent on stopping Mrs Harding's tirade about her son-in-law.

'No, he ain't, and he wouldn't be welcome, neither. There's no way he'll cross the threshold, and that's gospel.'

'If he does, perhaps you'd let me know,' said Metcalfe. He had considered telling Mrs Harding that he now strongly suspected Gerald Johnson of having murdered his wife, but decided that she would panic if Johnson arrived at her door. And if that happened, he would disappear as fast as morning mist in the summer sun. Alternatively, if she blurted out that the police suspected him of murder, he might murder her too, just in case she felt inclined to inform on him. Fred Metcalfe was not too worried about that, except that it would mean another murder on his patch, and he had quite enough to contend with as it was.

But apart from any of that, Metcalfe had no evidence to support the supposition that Johnson was a murderer. All that could be said was that he appeared to have been in London at the time the murder was committed.

'I suppose we ought to get something to eat,' said Hardcastle, leading the way across Bow Street to the Kemble's Head.

'Good idea, sir.' Marriott was only too well aware that they had missed lunch altogether as a result of Hardcastle's desire to get to the bottom of the mystery of Sergeant Johnson. But he was accustomed to the DDI's dedication to duty, and knew that he frequently forgot time in his quest for evidence.

'Hello, Mr Hardcastle.' The landlord was a huge man with grey sideburns, and a bulky figure that stretched the buttons of his red waistcoat to their limit. It was a standing joke among the Covent Garden porters who frequented the pub that Alf had been there so long that one of the Bow Street Runners had presented him with one of their traditional red waistcoats. 'Don't often see you in here these days. Two pints of the best, is it?'

'Thank you, Alf,' said Hardcastle, 'that'll do nicely. And a couple of your hot fourpenny cannons.'

The landlord placed two glass tankards of beer on the bar, and a barmaid produced two steak and kidney pies straight from the oven. 'There you are, guv'nor,' said Alf. 'On the house.'

'Most kind,' murmured Hardcastle, who would have been affronted had he been expected to pay.

'I hear that Mr Metcalfe's got a bit of a juicy one, guv'nor.' Alf adopted a conspiratorial tone as he leaned forward, his muscular arms resting on the bar. 'Gerry Johnson's missus got topped, so I heard. I reckon he must've been cut up about that, what with being at the Front an' all.'

'I suppose you haven't seen him lately, have you, Alf?' asked Marriott.

The landlord laughed. 'Not likely to see him, Mr Marriott, what with him being in Wipers, wherever that is. Belgium, I think. Bit of a stride just to get a pint.'

'He's deserted, Alf,' said Hardcastle, draining his pint and putting the tankard on the bar with an expectant expression on his face.

'Never! Well, I'll be damned. I never thought he'd run. What's that about, then? I suppose his missus being done in must have affected his mind or something. Or is it this shellshock they're all talking about?'

'Whatever the reason, the Redcaps are after him. Do yourself a favour, Alf. If he turns up here, send your potman across to the nick, discreetly mind, and tip Mr Metcalfe the wink. He'll be very grateful.'

'Yeah, I reckon he would,' said Alf, conscious always of the need to keep on the right side of the law. 'But has he been up to something else other than running? I mean to say, Mr Metcalfe ain't that interested in deserters, is he? Not with a murder on his hands.'

'I don't know, Alf,' said Hardcastle, as the landlord put two fresh pints on the bar. 'But last time I spoke to him, he seemed pretty keen to lay hands on Johnson.' Much as DDI Metcalfe had withheld his suspicions from Mrs Harding,

Hardcastle had no intention of telling the landlord the true reason for police interest in the errant Guards sergeant. He knew that if you told a pub landlord anything, you might as well tell the world.

TWENTY

Hardcastle and Marriott spent the first part of Thursday morning discussing, yet again, the murders of Sir Nigel Strang and Daisy Johnson. As was his custom, and much to Marriott's irritation, Hardcastle insisted on going over everything the police knew about the killings. However, their discussion was brought abruptly to an end by the breathless arrival of the station officer. For a moment or two, the elderly sergeant, his wheezing breaking into a distressing cough, leaned against the doorpost of Hardcastle's office.

'You want to be careful, Skipper,' said Hardcastle in matter-of-fact tones. 'You'll give yourself a heart attack, and then you'll find your name cropping up in *Police Orders* as "discharged worn out", and that'd be unfortunate because you must be close to getting your pensionable time in.'

'There's been a shooting, sir, in St James's Park,' said the sergeant, eventually recovering himself.

'Anyone hurt?' Hardcastle was hoping that he was not about to be faced with a third murder on his division.

'Not according to the latest report, sir, but it seems that PC 142 Robinson on five beat challenged a man under Section Sixty-Six. The man ran off, but then stopped long enough to pull out a revolver and take a pot-shot at him. Then he made off towards Buckingham Palace. There's whistles going off all over the manor.'

'I see,' said Hardcastle mildly. 'So what's the patrolling officer done about it?'

'Inspector Joplin's out with the reserves, sir, and I've alerted Rochester Row and Hyde Park nicks, and B and C Divisions.'

Hardcastle seized his bowler hat and umbrella. 'Come on, Marriott,' he cried. 'We'll get a cab to Wellington Arch. It's a pound to a pinch that he'll be legging it up Constitution Hill.' He pushed past the station officer and raced down the stairs with Marriott close behind.

In Whitehall, Hardcastle hailed a cab. 'Wellington Arch, as fast as you can, cabbie. It's police business.'

'Right you are, guv'nor,' said the cab driver, but, despite the urgency, still found time to turn down the flag on his taximeter.

Halfway up The Mall, Hardcastle spotted PC 313 Dobson running towards the Palace, and stopped the cab. 'Get in, lad, as fast as you can,' he yelled. 'What's the latest?'

'Last seen running across Queens Gardens, sir.' The fit young constable seemed barely out of breath as he settled himself on the jump-seat. 'Looks like he's making for Hyde Park Corner. Either that or he'll cut across Green Park to Piccadilly.'

'There you are, Marriott. I told you that's where he'd make for. Up Constitution Hill, cabbie, and I'm authorising you to exceed the speed limit.'

The cab set off again, and had nearly reached Hyde Park Corner when Hardcastle saw Inspector Joplin, the patrolling officer.

'What news, Mr Joplin?' asked Hardcastle, leaning out of the taxi window.

'He's in Green Park, sir, but we don't know whether he's making for Piccadilly, or perhaps going across towards Hyde Park. He could easily get lost in there.'

'The station officer's alerted Hyde Park nick, and C Division, Mr Joplin. In the meantime, I'll make for Piccadilly. You'd better come with us.'

And so Inspector Joplin was added to the passengers in the cab.

'Up to Hyde Park Corner, cabbie, and then round the top into Piccadilly.'

The cab turned into Duke of Wellington Place, and sped past the Cavalry Club. By now, the cab driver had entered into the spirit of the chase, and was sounding his horn loudly at any traffic in his way.

It was when the cab reached the Naval and Military Club – known to cabbies throughout London as the In and Out, on account of the huge signs on the gates – that Hardcastle spotted a running man. The man leaped over the low railings around Green Park, and made towards the bandstand, thus making his way back towards Buckingham Palace.

'There he goes,' cried Hardcastle, and ordered the cab to stop. He jumped out of the taxi, and followed by Marriott, Inspector Joplin and PC Dobson, gave chase, moving remarkably quickly for a man of his bulk.

'What about my fare?' cried the cab driver, distressed that all his passengers had decamped.

'Send the bill to the Commissioner,' shouted Hardcastle over his shoulder.

'Bloody Keystone Kops,' muttered the cabbie.

Realising that the police were close behind him, the man stopped briefly, and discharged his revolver in their direction. Fortunately he missed all four of the policemen who, for safety's sake, had now formed an extended line abreast.

A nanny, wheeling a bassinet, screamed and started pushing the pram towards a group of trees.

'Get out of the way,' shouted Inspector Joplin.

'I think she's doing that already, Mr Joplin,' said Hardcastle.

A group of people had gathered at the railings in Piccadilly, and were gazing at the scene without any regard for their safety. Some had clambered over the railings, and were following the police at a safe distance, determined not to miss any of the action.

PC Dobson, having at some stage in the pursuit lost his helmet, came sprinting past Hardcastle and, with a flying tackle that would have been the envy of any rugby player, brought their quarry down.

The struggle was brief, but Dobson managed to wrest the revolver from the man's grasp, just as he was attempting to fire it again. He clipped the man on the chin with a forearm smash, and then knelt on his chest.

Hardcastle, Marriott and Joplin caught up, and Joplin assisted in securing the prisoner in a crippling hammer-lock-and-bar.

'Well, well, well,' exclaimed Hardcastle, as he surveyed the prisoner, 'if it's not Sergeant Johnson of the Grenadier Guards. You're nicked for attempted murder, my lad.' He paused. 'Oh, and being a deserter from His Majesty's forces.' He turned to PC Dobson. 'Well done, lad,' he said. 'Good bit of work that. Where's your helmet?'

'I'm afraid it got lost somewhere in the chase, sir,' said Dobson.

'Pity,' commented Hardcastle. 'You'll have to pay for a new one, of course.'

Once back at Cannon Row police station, Hardcastle was in no hurry to interview his prisoner.

'Get his fingerprints taken, Marriott, and send them over to DI Collins at Commissioner's Office as quick as you can. See if this man Johnson's been up to any other villainy while he's been on the run. He's got to have survived somehow, and I wouldn't be surprised to find that there's a few robberies or burglaries down to him. And when you've done that, I think we've earned ourselves a pint at the Red Lion.'

It was at about half past two that Hardcastle heard someone racing up the stairs to his office. The next moment, Detective Inspector Charles Stockley Collins, head of the Fingerprint Branch, burst into the DDI's office.

'Hello, Charlie. You look like the cat that's got the cream.'

'I think you'll like this, Ernie,' said Collins, collapsing into one of Hardcastle's chairs. 'I had a hunch, so first of all, I checked Sergeant Johnson's dabs with the prints I found on the doorplate of Strang's office. And guess what, they match.'

'Is that a fact, Charlie?' Hardcastle picked up his pipe and began to fill it with tobacco. 'Well, I suppose it's time I put one or two questions to him.'

As Hardcastle stood up, he and Collins were joined by Marriott. He laid a key on Hardcastle's desk.

'This key was found in Johnson's possession, sir. I took it to the Ministry of Munitions, and it fits the private entrance.'

'There is a God after all, Marriott,' said Hardcastle, somewhat irreverently.

Hardcastle, followed by Marriott, walked into the interview room at the front of Cannon Row police station, and dismissed the two constables who had been guarding Johnson.

Hardcastle laid the key on the table. 'D'you know what that is?' he asked.

'Looks like a key.' Johnson's answer was dismissive and surly.

'It is,' said Hardcastle, 'and it's the key that fits the private entrance to the Ministry of Munitions.'

'So what?'

'It was found in your possession when you were arrested, Johnson. What've you got to say about that, eh?'

'Never seen it before. You must have planted it.'

Hardcastle laughed scornfully. 'You'll have to do better than that.'

'What's this all about, anyway?'

'We'll start at the beginning, shall we? First of all, you're a deserter from the battalion of Grenadier Guards currently serving in the Ypres salient. And don't bother denying it, because I've the word of both your regimental adjutant at Wellington Barracks, and the assistant provost marshal. Secondly, you didn't come home on compassionate leave when you heard your wife had been murdered, because you were already on the run, and had been in this country for some time prior to that.'

Johnson shrugged. 'That was all a mix-up,' he said. 'The army's always making a balls-up of the paperwork.'

'If you're not on the run, Johnson, why did you shoot at the police officer who stopped you in St James's Park.'

'I've got nothing to say.'

'Well, I've got something to say,' said Hardcastle. 'In fact, I've got quite a lot to say. Your fingerprints were found on a doorplate in the office of Sir Nigel Strang, permanent secretary at the Ministry of Munitions, only a short while after he was murdered. And that puts you at the scene of the crime.'

'That was because my Daisy showed me round the offices where she was working one morning. She was very proud of working there.'

'You earlier told Mr Hardcastle that you didn't know she was working there,' observed Marriott mildly, looking up from his notes. 'And she told us that she cleaned that doorplate every morning, except the morning when she discovered Sir Nigel's dead body in his office.'

'That means that your dabs were put on the doorplate that night,' said Hardcastle. 'And that proves you were there the night Strang was topped.'

Johnson let out a deep sigh, and took a packet of Woodbine cigarettes from his pocket. 'All right if I smoke?'

'Yes,' said Hardcastle.

'I had a letter from Daisy in about March, I suppose it was,' began Johnson, waving out the match and dropping it into the tin lid that served as an ashtray, 'and she told me she was expecting another kid. Well, I'd been in Wipers for a year when I got that letter, and so I knew it couldn't've been mine. So I ran. When I got home, I fronted her with it, and she admitted that she'd been having fun and games; that's what the cow called it: fun and games. So I knocked her about a bit till she told me who the father was. Well, first off, she said it was nobody I knew. As if that made any bloody difference. So I hit her again, and emptied out her handbag. And I found that key.' Johnson pointed to the key that still lay on the table between him and Hardcastle.

'Did Daisy tell you how she got that key?' asked Hardcastle.

'Yeah, she said as how some bloke at the ministry where she was charring give it her.'

'Did she tell you his name?'

'No, except to say that it wasn't his kid. So I give her a good shaking, and made her tell me who'd put her up the spout. Then she said it was this bigwig at the ministry. Sir Nigel someone, she said, and that it was his kid she was carrying. Well, that made me see red, I can tell you. Me risking life and limb at the Front, and my trouble-and-strife's spreading her legs for any bloody frockcoat who asked her to. And if that wasn't all, he'd been giving her money and scent, and all that sort of stuff. I told her she might as well make a career of it, and get her pox-ridden body up Piccadilly.'

'So you decided to top Sir Nigel, is that it?' Hardcastle decided against telling Johnson that Sinclair Cobb had also had an affair with Daisy.

'Yeah. See, Daisy'd told me that he would wait in his office for her, and she'd go in early through the back door with that key. Then, when he'd had his way with her, she'd leave by the back door, and go round the front all bright and sparkly, saying she'd just come to work. So I took the key off of her, and told her it was all over.'

'How did you know that Sir Nigel would be there, Johnson?' asked Hardcastle.

'Knocked it out of her, didn't I? She told me when she was next due to turn a trick for him. So that night, I just went in through the back door, up to this Nigel bloke's office and done him. It was as easy as taking sweets off of a kid, because he was waiting there expecting Daisy.' Johnson emitted a coarse laugh. 'That bloody surprised him, I can tell you.'

'Where's the murder weapon, Johnson?' asked Hardcastle.

'I slung it in the river. It was an army bayonet.' Johnson laughed briefly. 'Eighteen inches of cold steel puts the fear of Christ up anyone.'

'And the revolver?'

'Picked it up on the plonk. There's hundreds of weapons lying about out there. Rifles, bayonets, revolvers, bits of Lewis guns.' Johnson laughed again. 'And bits of our mates, and bits of the bloody Hun. It's all right for you blokes back home, in your cushy billets. You've got no idea what it's like.'

'Don't worry, Johnson,' said Hardcastle. 'You won't be going back.'

'Did Daisy guess it was you who'd murdered Strang, Johnson?' asked Marriott.

'Too bloody right she did. We had a right bull and cow about it, and she said she was going to tell you lot I was on the run and I'd done the topping. Well, there was no way out of that, so I done her an' all.'

'You're going to make a statement about all of this, Johnson,' said Hardcastle, his firm tone brooking no refusal. 'You can either write it yourself, or Sergeant Marriott here will write it for you. Either way, you'll sign it.'

'He can write it,' said Johnson, pointing to Marriott, and just shrugged.

'There's one thing that's puzzling me, Johnson,' said Marriott. 'If you were on the run, why did you chance going to Daisy's funeral in uniform?'

'I had to pay me respects and give her a good send-off didn't I?' said Johnson. 'Anyway the army coppers wouldn't have knocked me off at a funeral.'

Hardcastle silently shook his head. The combination of

arrogance and naivety that was implicit in Johnson's statement amazed him.

It took the best part of two hours for Marriott to record
Sergeant Gerald Johnson's confession, and at the end of it,
Hardcastle took him through to the charge room.

'Get your forms out, Sergeant,' he said to the station officer.
'I'm charging Johnson here with two counts of wilful murder.'

'Should we let Mr Metcalfe know, sir?' asked Marriott.

'Yes,' said Hardcastle, a rare broad grin spreading across
his face. 'I'll telephone him and tell him we've cleared up
the topping of Daisy Johnson for him.'

It was three months later that the trial of Sergeant Gerald
Johnson of the Grenadier Guards began at the Central
Criminal Court, Old Bailey. The trees had begun to shed
their leaves, and there was sufficient of a chill in the air to
cause Hardcastle to don his Chesterfield overcoat. And, as
was his wont at this time of year, he began ruing that he had
not joined the Indian Police.

Johnson pleaded Not Guilty, but it was to no avail. The
twelve men of the jury took less than an hour to find him
guilty on both counts. It had been decided not to proceed
with the count of the attempted murder of PC 142A Robinson,
at whom Johnson had fired a revolver in St James's Park.

'I hope you rot in hell, you bastard,' screamed a woman
from the public gallery.

'Remove that woman,' said the judge, and waited while
two burly policemen half carried Mrs Fanny Harding, Daisy
Johnson's mother, screaming and kicking from the court.

The judge donned the black cap and passed sentence of
death, following which the judge's chaplain intoned a few
pointless words beseeching the Lord to have mercy on Gerald
Johnson's soul.

The court rose at half past midday, and Hardcastle led the
way across the road from the court to the Magpie and Stump
public house. Being in the area policed by the City of London
force, Metropolitan officers stood no chance of free beer; it
would be of no benefit to the licensees. But Hardcastle did
not hesitate, and to Marriott's astonishment, bought beer for
him, and for DDI Metcalfe of E Division.

'I always fancied Johnson for Sir Nigel Strang's topping, you know, Marriott,' said Hardcastle, and took a draught of his bitter.

'Yes, sir, I thought you did,' said Marriott.

'I understand you wanted to see me, sir,' said Hardcastle.

'Yes,' said Superintendent Patrick Quinn. 'I thought you would wish to know that Edith Thorn was sentenced to two years penal servitude for attempting to pass information to an enemy power. Mr Thomson asked me to thank you for your part in the enquiry.'

'Thank you, sir.'

Two weeks after the conclusion of Gerald Johnson's trial, Hardcastle and Marriott were back at the Old Bailey to give evidence in the case against Edward Lomas and Albert Farmer, indicted for the wilful murder of Joseph Hurley.

Detective Sergeant Aubrey Drew's evidence about Joseph Hurley's espionage activities was held *in camera*, not that it influenced the outcome, and, in any case, was largely irrelevant to the crime of murder. It certainly held no sway with the jury whose members promptly returned a verdict of guilty.

Three weeks later Lomas and Farmer were hanged at Pentonville prison, two weeks after the execution of Gerald Johnson. The army, abhorring loose ends, had previously demoted him to private, and discharged him, with ignominy, from the army.

'It's bloody ironic when you think about it, Marriott.' Hardcastle looked up from the newspaper containing the report of the executions of Lomas and Farmer.

'What's that, sir?'

'Two soldiers getting topped for murdering a German spy. If they'd done it in Flanders, they'd probably have got a medal.'